WIDDERSHINS

Also by Jordan L. Hawk

Hainted

Whyborne & Griffin
Widdershins
Threshold
Stormhaven

SPECTR series
Hunter of Demons
Master of Ghouls
Reaper of Souls
Eater of Lives
Destroyer of Worlds
Summoner of Storm

WIDDERSHINS

Whyborne & Griffin No. 1

JORDAN L. HAWK

ISBN: 978-1482528152

Edited by Annetta Ribken

CHAPTER 1

I WAS LATE for my appointment with a dead man.

Unfortunately, even though the man in question had died in Egypt some four-thousand years ago, he had living representatives. Namely Dr. Hart, the director of the Nathaniel R. Ladysmith Museum, who would not look kindly on my late arrival to the all-staff meeting.

I ran down Merry Cat Lane to the waiting omnibus, my arms full of books and loose notes. I'd neglected to wind the alarm clock the night before, caught up in my translations of hieroglyphics until I nodded off in my armchair. I was now hurrying to work in a slept-in suit, my cheeks reflecting the hastiest shave, with neither coffee nor breakfast to brace me.

A group of clerks climbed onto the omnibus. I tried to step on after them, but the conductor blocked my path. "Sorry; full up."

"But—"

The driver cracked his whip, and the bus pulled away, flinging half-melted slush out of the road and onto my trousers.

I swallowed a curse and readjusted my grip on my notes and books. Very well. I'd just enjoy a nice, brisk walk across town, carrying thirty pounds of paper. In my now slush-soaked shoes. The perfect start to the workweek.

At the end of the block, I plunged into the crowds along River Street, the main thoroughfare cutting through the heart of Widdershins. A group of rough-looking men dressed for work in the canning factory jostled me; I murmured an apology and ducked around a flock of chattering shop girls. Cabs raced up and down the street, reckless of pedestrians, and the velvety richness of coffee and pastries wafted from a café, competing with the omnipresent stink of fish.

Newsboys bellowed the headlines from every corner: "Police baffled by grave-robbing! Body of Widdershins founder still missing!"

A good number of blocks lay between my apartment and the Ladysmith. By the time I sprinted up the grand stairs of the entrance, I was completely out of breath. Mr. Rockwell, the chief of security, gave me a hard stare as I rushed through the grand foyer without even a glance at the hadrosaur skeleton which greeted visitors.

"Dr. Whyborne," he said, as if he suspected I might be taking refuge in the museum having fled the scene of some particularly heinous crime.

I nodded as I opened the discreet staff door at the back of the gallery, too out of breath to return his greeting. His small eyes stayed on me until I shut the door firmly between us.

Safely away from the public areas—and Rockwell's scrutiny—I hurried through the back hall in the direction of the large meeting room. Maggie Parkhurst, one of the clerical assistants, called to me as I rushed past her desk.

"Dr. Whyborne—your hat and coat?"

"Oh! Er, yes." Bad enough I was late for the meeting; there was no need to draw further attention. I hastily shucked my hat and overcoat into her waiting hands, juggling my burden of papers and books from one arm to the other. "Th-thank you, Miss Parkhurst."

"Of course, but you'd better hurry—they've been in there fifteen minutes already."

Blast it. Perhaps I could slip in quietly, find an empty seat, and escape the director's notice. I eased the door open, slid through the narrow gap, and discovered every eye on me. I froze, like an antelope wandering into a clearing only to realize the lions were waiting.

All the curators were present, as well as the departmental heads, assistants, interns…everyone really, except for the clerical, janitorial, and library staff. Some of them looked bored, others impatient, and still others amused. None seemed particularly friendly.

Not that I would have expected otherwise.

"There you are, Dr. Whyborne! We've been waiting on you," the director said crossly.

Dr. Hart looked rather like a large walrus stuffed into an expensive, though conservative, suit. The effect was partly due to his extravagant mustache, and partly to the roundness of his physique. He stood at the front of the room, next to a man I didn't recognize.

"Y-yes," I stammered. I couldn't imagine why the director would wait a meeting on me, especially one concerning the Egyptian Gala. I was hardly the most critical staff member working on it, after all. "Er, the cl-clock, I mean the alarm, it, ah…" My ears grew uncomfortably warm, and I slunk toward the nearest empty chair.

"Don't sit down just yet, Whyborne," the director ordered, motioning me to the front of the room. "We've a bit of business concerning you before the meeting."

I couldn't possibly imagine what business would concern me. I'd dedicated my entire life to making sure business *didn't* concern me whenever possible. Still, there was nothing for it but to walk past the long tables, the eyes of all my colleagues fixed on me. I hunched my shoulders instinctively, even as I wracked my memory. What had I done to bring anyone's attention, let alone the director's, down on me? Surely not my latest article in the *Journal of Philology;* my conclusions about the origins of the Phoenician language might have been suggestive, but not so far outside the bounds of scholarly opinion as to damage the museum's reputation.

The stranger gave me a friendly smile as I joined them. He was quite handsome, although his chestnut hair was longer than fashion usually allowed. Perhaps he was newly from the West, where Bill Hickock's flowing locks were more in style.

Oh dear lord, had I remembered to comb my hair? Of course, given its regrettable tendency to stick straight up unless tamed by great quantities of macassar oil, it might not really matter. Which wasn't much of a comfort, actually.

"Mr. Griffin Flaherty," the director said, "allow me to introduce Dr. Percival Endicott Whyborne, our comparative philologist."

"A pleasure to meet you, Dr. Whyborne," said Mr. Flaherty, extending a hand. With no other choice, I shifted the mass of paper and books into my left arm, held out my hand—

A book in the middle of the pile started to slide; I fumbled to keep from dropping everything, but a moment later the whole lot tumbled to the floor in a series of loud thumps.

Several of my colleagues let out loud barks of laughter. Dr. Putnam gave a resigned sigh, and the snigger could only be from Mr. Osborne.

The heat spread from my ears to my face as I dropped to my knees and began hurriedly gathering up the mess. Perhaps lightning would strike the museum, or a cataclysm would open up the ground beneath me.

"Let me help you," Mr. Flaherty offered.

"No need, er, I've…"

But he was already on his knees, gathering up loose papers. "Nonsense. It was my thoughtless action which caused the mishap; you must allow me to make amends."

Up close, my first impression of handsomeness was only reinforced. His eyes were green as malachite, shot through with strands of rust and lapis, and crinkled at the corners with his smile. He possessed a straight nose, firm mouth, and lightly-tanned skin with a spray of freckles along his cheekbones. He wore a sober gray suit lightened by a dashing blue vest, and a tie matching the color of his eyes. Not at all like my gawky, ugly self. I hastily averted my face, gathered my books and papers, then accepted the stack he had amassed.

He climbed back to his feet with the assistance of a sturdy cane I hadn't noticed before: ebony, with a heavy silver head. His height was average, the body under the suit well-formed and broad-shouldered. I hunched my shoulders and tried not to loom, although at over six feet, I couldn't really help it.

"If you're finished," Dr. Hart said, as if I'd deliberately made a spectacle of myself, "let's get down to business. Mr. Flaherty is a private detective in the employ of Mr. Rice."

"The trustee?" I asked. What would one of the museum's trustees need with a detective? If someone had been stealing from the Ladysmith, surely Mr. Rockwell would have dealt with the matter.

And what on earth did any of this have to do with me?

"Quite, quite," the director replied. "Mr. Flaherty needs a book translated, so Mr. Rice sent him to us for assistance."

"The book is in cipher," Mr. Flaherty added. "Mr. Rice would have come himself, but was detained by business in Boston. I hope you'll be able to help."

"Of course he will!" Dr. Hart's mustache bristled alarmingly as he spoke, and I resigned myself to the usual lecture. "There are no substandard employees in this institution, sir! The Ladysmith Museum will finally put Widdershins, Massachusetts on the map, both culturally and scientifically, and to that end I hire only the best. *The best!*"

"Percy? The best *what?*" Bradley Osborne wondered aloud, although the director didn't hear him.

"Then I am reassured," Mr. Flaherty said, although he seemed rather startled at Dr. Hart's vehemence. "Perhaps Dr. Whyborne and I should retire somewhere else to discuss the matter?"

"Oh!" I said. "But the meeting…"

Dr. Hart flapped his hand in my direction. "One of the trustees wants your time, Whyborne. You're at Mr. Flaherty's disposal for as long as he needs your assistance."

Although I resented the gala's preparations for interrupting the museum's steady routine, at least my part in the proceedings would result in actual scientific knowledge. And although I quite enjoyed solving ciphers in my spare time, it hardly seemed reasonable to ask me to put aside my real work to play with a book brought by some detective.

"Oh," I said again, but I couldn't think of anything to add. Dr. Hart and the trustees had final say over my fate, so long as I wished to remain employed at the museum.

I tightened my arms around their burden of books and hopelessly-disarranged papers. "Yes. Well. I suppose you had best come with me, Mr. Flaherty."

~ * ~

I led the way to my office without speaking. Mr. Flaherty followed, his cane tapping lightly on the polished wood of the floors. He didn't limp or lean on the walking stick; it must have been purely a fashionable embellishment.

"The place is rather a maze, isn't it?" Flaherty said after we had walked for a few minutes. I started at the unexpectedness of the sound.

"Er, yes." Although the public areas of the museum were designed to give the appearance of a neat and orderly progression through history, the rest of the building exemplified chaos. Storerooms burrowed deep into the earth, while various wings sprawled off in every direction. The library was a literal labyrinth, and shortly after I'd first been hired, I'd found myself obliged to cross the flat roof of one of the wings as the most direct route from one department to another. Even though the museum was less than forty years old, there were rumors of lost storerooms and offices, and I did not doubt the possibility.

"Construction began in 1859," I offered, "and the architect was a bit, er… well. Th-they say he went mad while designing the library. He was committed to an asylum shortly after construction ended."

Mr. Flaherty shivered. "I see," he said, and did not pursue the matter further.

My office was located on the first floor below ground, down a long hallway with exposed pipes running along the walls. Flaherty glanced about uneasily; no doubt he wondered what "the best" comparative philologist was doing tucked away in a windowless room. What could I say? I liked it precisely because of its isolation. Indeed, when Dr. Putnam was in the field, I might go days or even weeks without ever speaking to another soul.

Mr. Flaherty had been kind so far, even though I'd made a fool of myself in front of him once already, but I doubted he would understand my desire to hide. Perhaps he'd even read something sinister into it; he was a detective, after all.

I dug out my keys and unlocked the office. The books in my arms made the procedure awkward, but at least I managed it without dumping the lot on the floor a second time. The office was in its usual deplorable state. I truly meant to get around to straightening up, but there was always something else more urgent, and as long as I could find everything it didn't seem to matter. Mounds of paper, journals, and books buried the surface of the desk, one chair, and a good deal of the floor. A dozen cold cups of coffee lurked here and there, some of them alarmingly old.

I deposited my burden on top of a teetering pile on the desk and cleared the second chair by shifting its contents onto the floor. "P-please, have a seat, Mr. Flaherty."

"Thank you." Amusement flickered around his mouth, and I looked away.

A tentative rap sounded on the half-open door as I went to seat myself, and Miss Parkhurst stuck her head inside.

"I just wanted to see if your guest—and yourself, of course—wanted coffee," she said breathlessly, her gaze locked on Flaherty.

"Yes, thank you," I said, more waspishly than I'd intended. Clearly I wasn't the only one who'd noticed my guest's good looks. She flushed and ducked back out the door.

I busied myself putting my pile of notes in order. What would Flaherty do if I simply pretended he wasn't there at all?

Complain to Dr. Hart, of course. There was no way around this. Better to accede to his request and have it done with quickly.

"If you wish to leave your book here, I'll see about deciphering it," I said, aiming the words in the general vicinity of my desk. "In between my normal duties, of course."

Flaherty stiffened. "And what are those?" he asked, his tone oddly neutral.

"Translation." How much he would understand? I knew little about so-called private detectives, but was under the impression they went about apprehending bank robbers and breaking strikes. "I work on artifacts brought back from museum expeditions, or those mailed to us by private collectors or other museums wishing assistance. At the moment, however, I am meant to be translating papyrus fragments and canopic jars to be displayed at the Egyptian Gala. My time is at a premium, so I hope you understand if your cipher must wait a bit…"

I trailed off, hoping he would get the hint. Instead, he only stiffened further. "Mr. Rice and the director both assured me I would have the cooperation of this museum."

"Y-yes, of course," I said, defeated.

Flaherty drew a small book from his coat pocket. No title marked its fine leather binding, and I noticed the pages looked rather worn, as if from frequent consultation. "You heard about the death of Mr. Rice's son, I presume?"

"Mr. Rice's son?" A hazy recollection came to me from some museum function or other: a well-built, robust man with a ready laugh and sensitive smile. I of course had been lurking against the wall, hoping not to be noticed by anyone. "That is, no, I didn't."

Flaherty stared at me as if I were some alien specimen brought back from the darkest jungles of Borneo. Miss Parkhurst chose that moment to return with the coffee; by the time we were served and Miss Parkhurst gone, his expression had settled into one of bemusement. At least it wasn't contempt.

"The newspapers kept it quiet to avoid scandal. Philip Rice's body was found in an…unsavory part of town, shall we say."

The docks, then, where the gambling dens and brothels congregated along with the sailors and dockworkers they served. I'd even heard whispers there was a bathhouse in the area, although of course I'd never found out for certain.

My eyes went to the book, still clasped in Flaherty's square, strong hands. Was it a diary? There were reasons a man might keep his private journal in cipher, especially if the contents of those pages might lead to ruinous scandal.

"The day before the murder, Philip mailed this book to his father," Flaherty went on. I tore my gaze away from the book and found the detective watching me closely. "A week ago, Mr. Rice senior hired me to take a closer look at his son's death. This book, obviously, is a potential clue, as Philip considered it important enough to send to his father."

"Oh." Surely if the diary contained *that* sort of information, Philip wouldn't have entrusted it to his father. "I'll do what I can."

The smile Flaherty offered me was unexpectedly warm. "Thank you." He held the leather-bound book out. As I accepted it, our fingers brushed together; my skin seemed to burn and tingle from the accidental contact.

"I-I'll start today," I stammered. "As soon as I have anything, I'll send word, Mr. Flaherty."

He nodded and rose to his feet, hand extended. His fingers were rough against my own, though not as callused as a laborer's. Their warmth, and the smile he gave me along with the handshake, sent a flicker of heat through me. I tamped it down ruthlessly.

"Please, as we're to be working together, call me Griffin," he said

"Good day, Mr. Flaherty."

His smile turned rueful, but he didn't press, the way most would have. "Good day, Dr. Whyborne. I look forward to hearing from you again."

CHAPTER 2

AS SOON AS he was gone, I shut the door and collapsed into my chair. The book lay at the edge of the desk where I had put it, silently daring me.

If it was a diary, it would probably be a simple substitution cipher. B instead of A, D instead of C, that sort of thing. If so, I would have it translated in a matter of hours.

And if it turned out to be a record of the sort of thing no one would want to become public? If the names of other men were mentioned, who would be vulnerable to blackmail? What would I do then? Could I conceal them in some way, assuming they had nothing to do with Philip's death? Would there be any way to know?

The door flew open. I jumped violently, knocking my chair back against the wall.

"Whatever is the matter, Whyborne?" Dr. Christine Putnam asked. Although a proponent of rational dress while in the field, as a concession to the museum she wore a severe skirt and sensible shirtwaist, the width of the sleeves far more constrained than fashion dictated. Her dark hair was pinned rather severely back from her face.

"Come in, Christine," I said, even as she strode into my office and deposited herself in the chair Flaherty had vacated.

"I suppose you think you've had a stroke of luck, getting out of work on this damnable gala," she said, eyeing me narrowly.

I straightened the papers on my desk, careful to remove Philip's book and tuck it into a drawer with a lock. "Hardly. There are several papyri I wanted to analyze beforehand. Now I'll have to work extra hours in order to fit it all in."

"Hmph. Now we'll *both* be kept from our work, and for what? Blast the trustees." Christine ground her teeth together, looking even more ferocious than usual.

"Surely the gala must be something of, er, a vindication," I suggested tentatively. The trustees had nearly gone mad when Dr. Hart hired a woman to lead the museum's Egyptian excavations. But, as the director had told Flaherty, he was truly dedicated to hiring "the best," which meant putting up with all sorts of eccentricities. Including, of course, being female.

Some of the trustees were still unhappy, but Christine's stunning find of the tomb of the Black Pharaoh Nephren-ka had commanded headlines across the globe. Unlike every other tomb discovered thus far, Nephren-ka's had remained completely untouched through the millennia. Although the statues of gold and furniture inlaid with precious gemstones had caught the public's attention, it was the many inscriptions and intact papyri which interested me.

Christine glowered. "I suppose it would be—if I gave a fig what society thought of me in the first place. And if I did that, I would have stayed home and married some awful boy like my mother wanted. Really, Whyborne, would *you* want to be stuck playing host at an overblown party, or would you want to get back to work?"

"No, of course not. I see what you mean."

Christine waved a hand. "I understand you were trying to put a good face on it, although why you of all people would bother, I can't imagine. But the field season in Egypt begins shortly after Christmas. Even if I am able to leave the very morning after this idiotic gala, the season will be half done by the time I arrive. I might as well stay here in Widdershins and write papers, for all the good it will do me."

"Did you know Mr. Rice's son was murdered?" I blurted, desperate to change the subject.

She blinked at me. "What the devil? Does this have something to do with the detective?"

"Yes. There's a book, you see. It could be a diary. I don't…if it is in cipher, he must not have wanted…I'm not sure what to do."

For all her bluster, Christine was not entirely insensitive. "Hmm. Have you looked at it yet?"

"I haven't had the chance, have I?"

Christine laughed at my irritation. "No, no, of course not. Never mind me, Whyborne." She rose to her feet. "I'm off to do battle with the curators. No doubt they'll want to exhibit only the most horribly boring pieces of the whole collection. At least they can't get away without showing the mummy, although I'm sure poor Nephren-ka would be less than pleased to have his earthly remains paraded about like this."

"Indeed," I said, glancing at the drawer in which I'd hidden the book. Would Philip have sent the volume to his father, if he knew his secrets were to be paraded about, as Christine put it?

Perhaps. I'd never known him, after all. Never gotten up the courage to speak to him, or to any of the other attractive young men who regularly turned up at museum events. Confident and at ease in their own skins: they might as well have been of a completely different species, like the bright birds I admired through binoculars.

Even if Philip was the sort to frequent bathhouses, I didn't delude myself into thinking he would have had any sympathy for me, had I managed to stammer out an introduction. I was too gawky, too shy, too *strange*. Most likely he would have laughed in my face.

But he was dead, and I was alive. I could afford him some one-sided sympathy.

Squaring my shoulders, I opened the drawer, took out the book, and began to work.

Whatever else it might be, the book wasn't simply a diary. On closer examination, it proved to be quite old. The cover was of curiously fine-grained leather whose origins I could not identify, its binding worn and cracked. The paper was heavy cotton, remarkably well-preserved. More than one hand had written it, although it seemed the second writer had been annotating or correcting the first. A quick perusal showed a number of curious drawings and glyphs, some vaguely familiar and some wholly alien.

As for the cipher, it was no simple substitution. It would help to know what language the book was written in, of course, but I could only hope it would be one I recognized, even if not one I could translate. What possible interest a wealthy young man like Rice could have had in a tome dating from the medieval era, if not earlier, I couldn't even begin to guess.

Still engrossed in possible methods of solving the cipher, I left my office for a late lunch. As I rounded one of the many corridors in the labyrinthine halls, I nearly walked straight into the two men conversing in the hall.

"S-sorry," I stammered as I stepped to one side.

"Percival! My dear boy, it's been far too long."

Startled, I raised my gaze from the floor. The speaker was my godfather, Addison Somerby.

"Uncle Addy?" I asked in bewilderment, using the childish name automatically. It had been some time since I'd seen him last, and I was shocked at how old he looked. His thick hair had gone entirely white, and his shoulders stooped beneath his black coat. He'd dressed only in mourning clothes for over a decade now. Despite his somber attire, a fisherman's net of wrinkles fanned around his blue eyes and enmeshed his smile.

"You know old Percy, then?" asked Bradley, to whom he'd been speaking.

"Oh yes, yes." Addison beamed at me. "His father and I went to university together. I'm godfather to all of Niles's children, but I have to say Percival was always my favorite. Spent half his childhood at my home instead of his own."

I couldn't bring myself to look him in the face. "Wh-what are you doing here?" Although Addison donated generously to the museum, unlike my father, I'd never before seen him in its halls.

"Mr. Somerby had some questions about Widdershins history," Bradley said smugly. "Of course I offered my expertise immediately."

"An old man's fancy," Addison said with a genial smile. "Mr. Osborne was very kind to take time out of his schedule to show me around. I don't suppose you've made a study of the history of Widdershins, Percival?"

Bradley let out a braying laugh. "Not old and dusty enough for Percy, I'd say. He only cares about things if they've been dead a thousand years, isn't that right?"

Acid chewed at my stomach, but I gave him a tight smile. "I suppose."

"We all have our talents in this world," Addison said to me with his usual kindliness. "Since fate has given us this chance, do say you'll dine with me tonight, my boy."

Clammy sweat broke out on my hands, and my throat threatened to close up. "I'm s-sorry. I have a prior engagement."

"Ah, well. Another time, then. Mr. Osborne, if you'd kindly show me the map you mentioned earlier?"

I stood in the hall like a fool after they left, my hunger replaced by nausea. I couldn't imagine sitting through a dinner across from Addison.

What could I possibly say to him? "I'm sorry I killed your only child?"

I walked up the creaking steps to my third-floor apartment late in the evening, still deeply unsettled. The starchy odor of boiling noodles drifted up from the first floor, and the downstairs neighbors argued in their native Czech. I passed another tenant on the landing, a young man I'd once seen working behind the lunch counter at the department store. I didn't know his name, nor had he ever inquired after mine. It wasn't that sort of place; people here came and went, and for the most part minded their own business. Not even the landlady who came to collect on the first of each month ever inquired as to the details of my life.

I'd bought a loaf of bread at the corner bakery, and now balanced it on top of an armful of books while I unlocked the door to my apartment. I'd decided to spend the evening refreshing my memory on various cryptographic methods, and to that end had removed a number of texts from beneath the forbidding gaze of the museum librarians.

Putting the books on the rickety table in my living room, I stepped into the small kitchen and set the stove to heating. The warmth from the radiator didn't reach into the kitchen; I crowded closer to the stove, shivering as I opened a tin of beans.

As I emptied the beans into a pot, the sudden, overwhelming conviction I was being watched swept over me.

I spun around, almost knocking over the pot. But there was nothing, of course: just the empty apartment with its dingy brown walls, the night pressing against the kitchen window.

Just my imagination. I turned back to the stove and set the pot on to heat.

A soft sound came from the direction of the window, as of leather scraping across brick, accompanied by a sort of gelatinous gurgle.

I put my back to the counter and stared fixedly at the window. There was no access to my third floor apartment from the outside. It must be a bat.

Bats weren't active in late November.

An owl, then. The Draakenwood must be full of the creatures. No doubt the light from my window had disoriented the poor thing.

The wet gurgle came again. Prickles ran over my skin, the hair on my neck standing up in ancient, unreasoning fear. That sound had come from no owl.

I slid open the cutlery drawer with shaking hands, removing the largest blade I owned. Clutching the knife to me, I took one step toward the window, then another.

The kitchen was small; a third step carried me to the window. I steeled myself—then quickly flipped the latch and hurled the window violently open.

Cold air flooded in, accompanied by a charnel stench. Keeping my knife at the ready, I cautiously eased my head out and looked about.

The night was silent and still, except for a cab rattling down the street, the horse's hooves echoing against the brick buildings. No owl flew away from a perch outside my window, nor was there any other movement nearby. Even the strange odor lessened by the second, blown away by the winter wind.

Vexed, I shut the window and redid the latch. I was too old to jump at shadows and imagined noises. It had probably been nothing more sinister than someone's wash blowing in the breeze.

Even so, I drew the curtains tight before returning to my pot of beans.

The rest of the evening was uneventful. No more odd noises intruded, and I was able to immerse myself in the puzzle before me. I ate my dinner of bread and beans in my chair, hunched over my books and making notes on a cheap pad of paper.

I did not look in the direction of the window.

When I was too tired to work anymore, I went into my cold bedroom, slipping a hot water bottle between the covers before changing quickly into my nightshirt. I opened the drawer of the nightstand, intending to secure the book there.

The drawer was empty save for a single object. The photograph was as simple as its silver frame: the portrait of a youth on the cusp of manhood, his fair hair neat, his smile confident, his eyes twinkling with vitality. Leander Somerby: Addison's only child and my dearest friend, dead now these last ten years at the tender age of seventeen.

I picked up the photo and ran my fingers over the cold glass covering Leander's face. Addison didn't blame me, hadn't blamed me even when his son's body was pulled from the water. None of the rescuers who had dragged us from the lake, or the doctors who had nursed me through the bout of pneumonia after, or even my father who found fault in my very existence, had blamed me.

They were all wrong. If I had only been better, stronger, I would have found some way to stop Leander from going down to the lake in the first place. I might have roused the entire household if that was what it took, rather than sneak out the servants' door with him. If I had stopped at the boathouse, convinced him it was madness to go out in the middle of the night in a storm, he would yet live.

I hadn't, though, because I didn't want him to think less of me. I'd wanted him to love me as I loved him.

I returned the photo to the drawer and shut it, putting the book on top of the nightstand instead. Addison had no reason to return to the museum any time soon. I'd translate the book; its contents would prove innocuous, discharging my duty and getting the detective out of my life. Even though there was nothing untoward for Flaherty to discover, no matter how closely he looked into my activities, I couldn't help but feel those green eyes had seen more this morning than I intended.

I didn't want to be looked at. I wanted to be left alone, in my little apartment and my lonely bed, which remained cold even after I'd crawled beneath the covers.

CHAPTER 3

AFTER A RESTLESS night, I shut myself in my office at the museum with the hopes of getting some work done. Someone had left a fragment of papyrus on my desk; a single glance told me it would not be part of the gala. A note in Christine's firm hand asked me to check her translation of the hieroglyphs.

I suppressed a sigh; of course she decided her task of first importance would be of a purely scholarly nature, and not something related to the exhibition. I understood her desire to make a point with the director, but rather wished she'd left me out of it.

I set the papyrus carefully to one side, where it would be safe from any accidental coffee spills, and laid out my notes from the night before along with Philip's book. After a moment to nerve myself, I quickly reached out and flipped open the cover.

The door burst inward without a knock. "There you are, Whyborne!" Christine said, as if I'd been hiding from her. "I suppose you haven't heard the news?"

"Mr. Farr and Mr. Durfee knifed one another in the back galleries?" I asked as she dropped into the chair across from me.

"Don't be absurd. They'd only do murder in the grand foyer, where they'd be sure of an audience."

"You're correct, of course. Perhaps Dr. Gerritson has taken to wearing women's underthings outside of his office?"

"Not after Dr. Hart had a word with him about making sure he kept the door locked when he was 'indisposed.'" Christine made a dismissive gesture. "Sadly, the truth is far more prosaic. It seems some items have been removed from the Zoology and Paleontology Departments."

"A theft?" I straightened in alarm. Thank heavens nothing from our side of the museum had been stolen. "As head of security, Mr. Rockwell cannot be pleased."

"To say the least. Dr. Hart has been shouting at him since this morning and doesn't seem likely to run out of words any time soon. All the watchmen, day and night, have been called in, presumably to allow Rockwell to waste time yelling at them."

"What do you mean?"

Christine folded her work-roughened hands around a knee she had propped up in a distinctly unladylike fashion. "The thing is, nothing of any *value* was taken. No spectacular finds or exceptional mounts. Fragments of saber tooth tiger bone, a moldy old fruit bat, a common crocodile skull, that sort of thing. Nothing anyone in his right mind would want."

"Then…why?" I asked, bewildered.

Christine shrugged. "Probably someone has a grudge against Rockwell. Heaven knows the man's an utter swine. Or one of the staff smuggled out bits and pieces which wouldn't be easily missed, hoping to impress his friends at the saloon. Or for his children to play with, for all I know."

"You think the thief was on the staff?"

"Good gad, Whyborne, you don't imagine a criminal broke in, risking jail and a beating at the hands of the watchmen, just to steal a bunch of worthless junk?"

"No. No, I suppose not." Still, it was disappointing to believe anyone on staff, whether janitor or curator, would take specimens. Such objects might have no value to a thief, but there was no knowing what secrets they might have revealed to science as part of our collection.

My door opened—again without the courtesy of a knock—and Bradley Osborne marched inside. "I say, Percy, have you heard about the excitement?"

Why did my colleagues feel the need to invade my office with news? And was there any way to keep them out?

"I was just telling him," Christine said stiffly.

Bradley gave her a condescending smile. "Of course, of course, Miss Putnam."

"Dr. Putnam," I corrected in the direction of the desk. Bradley ignored me.

"Well, the director will soon put things to rights," he said. "Just you wait and—dear lord, what's on your desk?"

I stared stupidly in the direction of his gaze. "Er, a papyrus fragment? It's from the tomb…"

"You can't just leave such vulgar things lying about!" To be fair, one of the fellows on the papyrus *was* in a rather excited state. "How can you subject poor Miss Putnam to such a sight and still call yourself a gentleman?"

"Er, I…well, that is, I…"

"I excavated the damned tomb," Christine snapped, her spine straightening away from the back of the chair.

"But surely you had someone else remove it—such a thing isn't appropriate for a woman's eyes."

Christine let out a bark of laughter, but I recognized it as a sign of anger and shrank back against my chair. "Dear heavens, Bradley, one can hardly set foot in an ancient tomb or temple without male members pointing at one from every direction!"

Heat scalding my face, I snatched up Rice's book and fled. It would have been a new low, even had I not compounded it by plowing straight into Griffin Flaherty.

"Steady on," Flaherty said, catching my shoulder to keep us both from colliding with the wall. "Is everything all right?"

I tried to think of some plausible lie, since *"I've allowed myself to be driven from my own office by two of my colleagues"* seemed far too pathetic to say aloud.

Christine's voice, strengthened from bellowing orders to workers at dig sites, echoed down the hall. "I will not surrender my profession simply because men throughout history have been unduly enamored of their penises!"

I closed my eyes and hoped the museum basement would swallow me. It failed to rescue me, so I opened them again, to see Flaherty shaking with silent laughter. Blue highlights sparkled in his green eyes, and the smile removed lines of care from his face, leaving behind a certain boyish charm.

His hand still clasped my shoulder. I should have pulled away, but my feet refused to move.

"I see why you were in a hurry to escape," Flaherty said. His fingers tightened briefly, then let go. I fancied I could still feel their outline in the lingering warmth on my coat.

"I suppose you came by to ch-check on my progress with the, er, cipher," I stammered. "We could go to the, um, library, perhaps, to talk."

"We could," Flaherty agreed; his smile had shifted from outright amusement to simply charming. "But I have another idea. How would you like to discuss your progress over lunch?"

"L-lunch?"

"Yes. The meal people eat in the middle of the day? Or is lunch not a custom here in Widdershins?"

My ears grew hot, and I stared down at his shoes. He wore sturdy boots today instead of oxfords; perhaps he meant to do a bit of walking on the icy sidewalks.

"It was a joke," he said gently, when I didn't respond. "Or perhaps you're concerned about leaving Dr. Putnam alone with her adversary?"

Christine had hit her stride, but Bradley was now yelling as well. I caught something about "this is what comes of letting women into universities," and winced.

"No," I said. "Christine is clever enough not to leave Bradley's body where anyone will ever find it. That was, er, a joke as well," I added, when he looked momentarily taken aback.

His surprise morphed into laughter. "Touché, Dr. Whyborne. Lunch, then?"

"My duties—"

"Can wait an hour. Come along. I won't take no for answer."

We ended up at Marsh's, a small diner not far from the museum, which catered to office workers and department store clerks. I seldom ate out, both for reasons of economy and because I feared someone might try to speak to me. Flaherty took over the duty of exchanging small talk with our waiter. Unfortunately, he wanted to chat with me as well.

"Have you eaten here often?" he asked, once the waiter had taken our orders.

"No."

He waited a moment longer, before nodding, as if I'd given a satisfactory answer. "I've noticed most of the restaurants here specialize in fish. Natural for a coastal city, I'm sure, but I do miss a good Chicago steak."

"Oh." I had no idea what to make of him. "Er, the cipher, then?"

Flaherty glanced up at me from beneath thick lashes as he stirred sugar into his coffee. "I had hoped to enjoy a pleasant lunch before we delve into business."

"Oh," I repeated, but couldn't think how to continue.

"I haven't met very many people since moving to Widdershins, and as we are working together for a brief time, I thought to get to know you better."

I had no idea how to respond. To my relief, the waiter returned with our fish sandwiches. Grateful for something to occupy my hands, I picked up my fork and knife and began to cut the sandwich into neat squares. "I'm sure I would seem terribly boring to someone like you," I said.

He took a big bite from his sandwich. "Someone like me?" he asked once he had swallowed.

"A detective. Someone used to, er, excitement."

Flaherty arched a brow. "If you're asking after my qualifications, I was formerly employed by the Pinkerton Detective Agency. I was injured in the line of duty and subsequently decided to go into business for myself."

"I-I didn't mean to imply—"

"It's all right, Dr. Whyborne." He touched the back of my hand lightly. "I only meant to tease. Forgive me."

I disliked being teased…but the look on his face was kindly rather than mocking. "May we talk about the cipher now?"

"As you wish." He took another enormous bite of sandwich and watched me attentively as he chewed.

"It's more complicated than I'd expected." I cut my sandwich into smaller bits, buying time while I sorted my thoughts. "I assumed it would be a simple substitution cipher."

He held up his hand. "I'm sorry, a what?"

I hesitated, unsure if he actually wanted to know, or if his words were meant as a signal to stop talking about things of no possible interest to anyone but myself. He seemed genuinely curious, though. "A substitution cipher. Writing B for A, for example, and C for B. Thus F-L-A-H-E-R-T-Y would become G-M-B-I-F-S-U-Z. Easy enough to decode. At least, if the person decoding it knows the language, or at least recognizes it as words and not a jumble of meaningless letters."

"The director assured me you know twelve different languages."

"I speak thirteen, but I can read more. Many of them haven't been commonly used in centuries, if not millennia, though."

"Why do you sound apologetic? I'd imagine anyone else would be proud of such an accomplishment."

The tips of my ears grew hot. "I, er…"

Flaherty grinned at my discomfort, curse him. "You think me impertinent, don't you?"

"Rather, yes."

"Forgive me. So, you expected a simple substitution cipher. Thus far, you've determined it is not such. Do you know what it might be, then?"

"Not yet. I have some ideas, but I haven't had time to test them."

"Because impertinent detectives insist on inviting you to lunch." His smile implied we were sharing a joke.

"Er, quite?" I said, not sure how to react.

Apparently satisfied, he sat back in his chair. "Well, as long as I'm keeping you from your work, would you care to stop by the police station with me?"

"I…what? The police station? Whatever for?"

"I want to speak further with the detective—the official detective—investigating the case. I've heard his story before, but I hoped a set of fresh ears, as it were, might pick up on something I missed."

I truly didn't want to enter the police station, no matter what the circumstances. I wasn't a criminal, precisely, having never acted on my inclinations. But as those were unlikely to change, nothing good could come of the police noticing me. "I can't imagine I'd be of any use."

"I don't see why not."

How was I to answer? "I, er…I take it you think the detective is lying, then?"

"Not lying as much as…ignoring the truth," Flaherty said with a wry twist of his lips. They were very nice lips, I couldn't help but notice: plump and well-formed. "According to the official report, young Mr. Rice was the victim of a robbery. However, when the body was found some hours after his murder, it was still in possession of a valuable ring and pocket watch. When asked why the thieves would have left those behind, Detective Tilton insists the robbers must have been frightened away by someone who neither took advantage of the murder nor raised any sort of alarm."

"There may be no sinister explanation outside of incompetence," I pointed out. "The tomb of the town's founder, Theron Blackbyrne, was broken into last month and his body stolen. According to the papers, the police haven't so much as a single lead."

"Yes." His lips pursed thoughtfully. "For a place with no medical college, there does seem to be a rather thriving resurrectionist trade. Still, the circumstances of Philip's death are odd even for this town."

I raised my eyebrows. "This town? Whatever is wrong with Widdershins?"

"Besides the grave-robbing?" Flaherty grinned. "Have you ever lived anywhere else, Dr. Whyborne?"

No doubt he was a world traveler. At the very least, his accent indicated he'd been farther west than New England. "Of course. I went to university in, er, Arkham."

"Oh, and *that's* such an improvement," he muttered. "Are you truly content to only imagine far-off places through your studies? To only visit Egypt or Greece in your mind?"

I clenched my hands beneath the table. Of course he didn't—couldn't—understand. "It may be all very well and good for Dr. Putnam to go gallivanting all over the world, but I see no reason for me to join her. I'm quite content where I am."

"Are you?" Flaherty murmured.

The man *was* impertinent. "Of course." Perhaps he deserved a bit of impertinence back. "If Widdershins is such a terrible place, why set up shop here instead of Boston or Providence?"

Flaherty's amusement slipped, like a mask which no longer quite fit. "It seemed the sort of place a fellow could start over, live quietly, and not have to put up with anyone prying into his private affairs."

His honesty surprised me. "I see. Well you're certainly correct. Although it does seem like a strange choice for a man whose business is to pry into the private affairs of others."

"It does make my work more interesting," Flaherty agreed, his grin once again in place. He leaned forward, lacing his hands together beneath his chin, and fixed his eyes on me. "Fortunately, I rather enjoy a challenge."

I lowered my gaze and ate a bite of my sandwich. My imagination was running wild. He wasn't flirting with me. The very idea was absurd.

"Well, Dr. Whyborne, will you accompany me to the police station?" he prodded.

"If you wish," I yielded. "I can tell you won't give up until you get your way."

"Indeed," he said, leaning back with a satisfied expression on his face. "As you will soon see, I can be persistent as a bull dog when I find something I want."

Flaherty led the way to the police station. It was a squat, surly building, flanked on either side by tall, gambrel-roofed houses, which had fallen into disrepair. Almost superstitious fear chilled my blood as I stepped through the narrow door behind Mr. Flaherty. He strolled up to the desk at the front of the large room; from the expression on the face of the officer seated there, this was not the first time he'd visited the station. "Is Detective Tilton available? Dr. Whyborne and I have a few questions about his investigation."

The officer shot me a surprised look. "Let me see, sir," he said, and left his post, scurrying past rows of desks and into the back of the building. I cast a questioning glance at Flaherty, but he didn't meet my gaze, instead concentrating on the task of removing his gloves and tucking them into his coat pocket.

The policeman returned within a few minutes. "Detective Tilton will see you in his office," he said, jerking his thumb over his shoulder in the general direction of the back.

Apparently, Flaherty had been there before as well, because he led the way without hesitation. Feeling more and more out of place, I followed.

The office reeked of cigar smoke. A harried-looking man in an ill-fitting suit sat behind the desk. At our entrance, he half rose and indicated the two seats placed in front of him.

"Mr. Flaherty," he said, sounding less than enthused. His murky eyes regarded me warily, as if not quite certain what I was doing in his office. I shared his uncertainty.

"Detective Tilton, may I introduce Dr. Percival Endicott Whyborne."

I hesitantly extended my hand. Detective Tilton shook it just as cautiously.

Flaherty dropped into his chair with perfect ease. I perched on the edge of mine. Tilton continued to watch me rather than my companion, and my nervousness increased. Were the police somehow trained to spot men such as myself?

"Well, then," Flaherty said cheerfully, "we just wanted to go over the details of the murder of Philip Rice with you once more, detective."

"I don't see what there is to go over," Tilton said, finally looking at Flaherty. "I let you read the official report. It was a robbery gone wrong."

"Of course," Flaherty agreed. "But given the bribe Mr. Rice paid for you to investigate, I would have thought you'd at least have pulled in some poor wretch and beaten him until he confessed."

Tilton stiffened. "I dislike your implication, sir."

"Forgive me—perhaps things are different here than in Chicago." Flaherty smiled, but there was no sincerity to it.

Tilton cut his gaze sharply to me; I shrank back involuntarily. "Dr. Whyborne, I must ask…are you here at your father's request?"

The question was outrageous. "Certainly not! I—"

Oh. Of course. This was why Flaherty had asked me to accompany him.

A sense of stupid disappointment swept over me. Flaherty hadn't wanted my opinion, or even my company over lunch. I had been a fool to think otherwise.

"Excuse me," I said, rising to my feet and clutching at my overcoat, as if it could shield me from embarrassment. "I-I have to go."

For the second time in one day, I fled an office in abject humiliation.

CHAPTER 4

THE WALK BACK through the police station was a blur. As soon as my shoes hit the slushy sidewalk outside, I quickened my pace. Cold air stung my face, but failed to soothe the heat burning there.

"Dr. Whyborne! Wait!"

I could run, but would just end up slipping on a bit of ice and sprawling at Flaherty's feet. "I do not appreciate being used, sir," I snapped, aiming the words back over my shoulder.

I slowed to cross a street, and he used the opportunity to catch up to me. "Dr. Whyborne—"

"You'll have your blasted translation," I said firmly, not looking at him as I strode across to the other corner. Despite his shorter legs, he managed to keep up with me. "I'll finish it as soon as humanly possible, at which point, I trust, you will never again darken my doorstep."

His hand landed on my shoulder once again. The warmth and weight of it sent a little shock through me. I shrugged it off.

"I'm sorry," he said. "Please, slow up."

"You knew, didn't you?" I asked. Bitterness rose like stinging bile in my throat, and for once I didn't bother to disguise it. Of course he didn't want my company at the station because he valued my opinion; he wanted it because he hoped my father's name would intimidate Tilton into telling the truth.

I was a fool. An utter, thoroughgoing fool.

"Of course I know who your father is," he said, not bothering to deny it. "And, yes, I will admit, I'd hoped your name would hold sway with Tilton."

"If you had warned me—"

"Would you have gone?"

"You'll never know now, will you?"

He let out a sigh. "No. Forgive me, if you can. It's just…you are as much a cipher to me as that book."

His words surprised me into glancing at him. His gaze was focused straight ahead, the rusty brown strands in his irises darkening the green now, his mouth pursed in a frown.

"I hardly see how I could be a cipher to anyone," I said stiffly. "After all, you clearly have the facts at your disposal."

"Percival Endicott Whyborne, youngest child of railroad tycoon Niles Whyborne. You neither attended your father's alma mater nor went into the family business, a situation which might be explained by the fact your older brother did both. Except your father has never donated to the museum where you are employed, and you live in a modest apartment, apparently on nothing more than the salary the museum pays you."

"As I said."

"Not at all. I know the *what* but not the *why*."

Even worse. "I am but another mystery to you. A challenge, as you said earlier." A specimen, to be viewed and dissected.

His hand curled around my elbow, slowing me as we turned onto Old Mill Street. "I wish you would give me the opportunity to explain."

"I see no need for—"

Flaherty suddenly yanked me into a fetid alleyway. Before I could think to protest, he grabbed both my arms and shoved me backward, into a sort of alcove formed by the chimneys of adjoining buildings. Rough brick scraped my back, and my shoes sank into something best not examined too closely.

"Wh-what are you doing?" I gasped. "I do not appreciate—"

He laid a finger over my lips, and the sheer audacity of the gesture silenced me. His skin was chilled against my mouth; in his haste, he hadn't put his gloves back on. Even though our only contact was through his finger, warmth flooded my entire body.

"Shh," he murmured, his breath ghosting over my cheek. "We're being followed."

"F-followed?" I whispered, acutely aware of the movement of my lips against his finger.

"Followed." His scent enveloped me: warm skin, damp wool, and sandalwood. "Hold still—I wish to see who has such an interest in our doings."

I nodded dumbly, my thoughts ricocheting inside my skull. Satisfied, he dropped his hand and turned his back to me, peering out in the direction of the street. The curve of one buttock pressed lightly against my thigh, palpable even through the cloth of our trousers.

My heart sped, and blood surged downward, stiffening my member. I shut my eyes and ground my fingertips against the rough brick wall behind me, frantic for distraction. Dear heavens, what was wrong with me? I should not—I *could* not—react like this, not to anyone, and certainly not to a man who made his living prying into the secrets of others.

His posture shifted into a ready stance, and I opened my eyes. Even though Flaherty's overlong hair was nearly in my face, I was quite a bit taller, and could see past him to the entrance of the alley.

A figure had paused there, although whether man or woman, it was impossible to tell. A black cloak enveloped its stooped frame, and a long scarf and wide-brimmed hat concealed its features. Its head lifted slightly, and I had the horrible impression it was sniffing for us, like some sort of enormous bloodhound. The same repulsive scent I'd noticed outside my window last night teased my senses.

Flaherty froze, without even the slight stirring of breath to give us away. I did my best to mimic him, even though it seemed my heart was about to smash through my ribs. An instinctive fear and revulsion for the mysterious figure gripped me, something born from the primitive recesses of my brain, which yet remembered the terror of prey for its predator.

"*Widdershins Enquirer Journal*, only two cents," a newsboy called from the street.

The cloaked figure flinched at the sound—then hurried on past the alleyway.

Flaherty remained vigilant for a few more seconds. Then the tension went out of him with a little sigh. "Well. Not one of Detective Tilton's men, for certain."

"No," I agreed. I wanted to ask: *"What was it?"* But that sounded too mad to say aloud. It had just been a man, after all, or perhaps a woman. There was nothing else it could have been.

"Come." Flaherty touched my arm lightly. "Let's get you back to the museum, shall we?"

On the way back to the Ladysmith, I jumped at every sudden sound and eyed every passer-by with suspicion. No one seemed to give us so much as a second glance, however. Our pursuit, if pursuit it had been, seemed to have given up.

As I started up the broad marble steps to the Ladysmith's public entrance, Flaherty said, "Dr. Whyborne?"

I paused and turned back to him. "Yes?"

He stood at the bottom of the stair, looking up at me solemnly. "I did not only invite you along because of your name, you know."

I knew nothing of the kind, yet I found I believed him. Or wanted to believe him, perhaps. "Oh. That's, er, good."

His parting smile was wistful. "Thank you for a pleasant lunch."

I nodded and climbed the stairs to the museum.

Late at night, I relived the scene in the alley as I dreamed.

As in real life, Flaherty pushed me roughly back against the brick wall. His finger rested on my lips, light as a butterfly's kiss.

This time, however, I parted my lips, let my tongue dart just past their barrier, tasting his skin. There was a knowing look in Flaherty's eyes as he slipped his finger into my mouth for me to suck.

"This is what you want, isn't it?" he whispered, pressing me back against the wall, the whole length of his body against mine.

There was no sense of cold or fear of discovery; nothing in the world but the two of us. I moaned a response, sucking frantically on his finger, desperate for more.

He pulled his finger free, replaced it with his mouth, his tongue probing. I gasped and arched against him, writhing, even as his hands shaped my body through the barrier of our clothing. A barrier which melted away even as he touched me, leaving only skin beneath his hands.

We drew apart; his clothing had evaporated as well. The light of sunset poured into the alley, gilding his bare skin, outlining every lean muscle. I longed to caress him, and his slow smile said he was aware of it and relished the fact.

Then we were together again: skin against skin, body against body, sending a cascade of fire through my blood. He wrapped a hand around my member, stroking, and I—

Awoke.

I lay paralyzed for a disoriented moment, gasping amidst tangled sheets, my every nerve sensitized until it seemed a stray breeze might bring me to release. I could think of nothing but continuing, of wrapping my hand around the thick rod of flesh and finding completion.

"No," I whispered to my empty room.

No. No, this was in my control. This *had* to be in my control.

I rolled onto my side, biting the meaty part of my thumb, until the pain brought me back from the edge. I could not succumb.

I loved Leander, and he had died for it. I had taken notice of other men in the years since, men like Philip Rice, but such notice had never overwhelmed me. That could not change now, certainly not for an impertinent ex-Pinkerton like Griffin Flaherty.

If he knew my dreams, he would scorn me. At worst, he would denounce me to the world as a criminal. At best, he would look down on me as the helpless victim of a mental aberration, to be viewed with condescending pity.

If only I had been born in the time of Heracles and Iolas, or Achilles and Patroclus, or Alexander the Great and Hephaestion. Instead, I was cursed to be a stranger in my own homeland, forever cut off from sympathy and affection.

It didn't matter. No amount of inchoate longing would alter my fate. I would simply have to pretend the dream never happened. My pulse had never quickened at Flaherty's proximity in the alleyway. Any attraction was purely venial; my will was more than sufficient to overcome it.

Things would seem different in the cold light of dawn. This insanity of desire would be seen as the passing shadow it was. I would continue on as I always had.

And if the possibility seemed less comforting than I had expected…this too would pass.

It had to.

Eventually, I gave up on sleep and spent the rest of the night hunched over the cipher. Perhaps exhaustion—or desperation—inspired me, for by dawn I had finally succeeded in cracking it.

I took the book and my notes into work with me, only to spend the morning fending off requests from Christine, who seemed to think I ought to be back to work on the translations for the opening exhibits, and the curators, who insisted on asking me questions which should have been directed at Christine instead. Eventually, I locked my door in disgust and refused to answer even the most insistent knocks.

By late afternoon, I had decoded a good portion of the book, translating it as I went. Unfortunately, the more of its secrets I laid bare, the less I understood.

Shortly before five o'clock, there came a discreet rap on my door. "Dr. Whyborne? Do you have a moment?" Flaherty called.

When I opened the door, it was to find him leaning insouciantly against the frame. I had avoided thoughts of the humiliating dream all day, but the sight of his tousled hair and roguish smile brought it back in vivid detail. I turned quickly away.

"Dr. Putnam said you were hiding in here," he said, following me in. The room was suddenly far too small and hot.

The words stung, although there was no reason for them to. "I wasn't hiding. I'm working. On *your* cipher, as it happens."

He settled into the seat across from me, wrapped both hands around the silver head of his cane, and propped his chin on his knuckles. "I'm glad to hear it, but I primarily came by to see if you've yet forgiven me."

How was it he kept catching me off-guard? I could not understand the man. Why would he give a fig for my opinion? "For the incident at the police station?"

He raised a single brow. "Unless there's something else I don't know about."

How about manhandling me in an alley and inspiring shameful dreams? "Er, no."

"Well?"

I eyed him warily. "Do you promise not to do such a thing again?" It was a stupid question—after I finished translating the book, we would most likely never meet again. Certainly he wouldn't be seeking me out for pleasant luncheons.

"Not without your consent, at least," he said with a little smile.

Damn the man; I could think of far too many things I'd happily consent to. "Then, yes. I forgive you."

"Excellent." He leaned back, and it did seem as if his mood had improved. "I believe you said something about the cipher?"

"Yes." The book lay on my desk. "I fear I don't know quite what to make of it."

"What do you mean?"

"To begin with, it's written in a mix of Aklo and bastardized Latin."

"Aklo? I confess I've never heard of it."

"Nor should you. The language's origins are highly speculative; its main use was as a means of secret communication amongst various medieval cults. This makes sense in the context of the age of the book."

Flaherty leaned forward, a small crease appearing between his brows. "And the book? What is it?"

"It's a grimoire. A repository of spells and alchemical treatises. *Liber Arcanorum* is scrawled in a margin, which I take to be its title. The author, whoever he might have been, drew from the works of Paracelsus, Agricola, Al-Hazrad and the like. Its age and obscurity form its main value, as the contents are the sort of rank nonsense which appeals to occultists and spiritualists. I can't imagine why Philip would have mailed such a thing to his father, except as a sort of joke."

"Perhaps," Flaherty murmured, but he only seemed to be half-listening. He stared off at nothing, or rather at something only he could see.

His reaction surprised me. "Er, does this mean something to you?"

He blinked slowly, then looked at me. The full weight of his scrutiny fell upon me: judging, considering. I looked down and away, because any such judgment would inevitably find me lacking.

"Yes." He resumed his earlier position, resting his chin on his hands. "Are you up for an after-hours excursion, Dr. Whyborne?"

My thoughts went instantly to the alley—and the dream. "I, er, th-that is, what did you have in mind?"

"When I agreed to take the case for Mr. Rice senior, he was able to give me two possible lines of inquiry. One was the book, which you have kindly translated for me. The second was access to his son's banking records. It seems Philip had made several rather large purchases of expensive—and unusual—chemicals. Most of these chemicals are not in wide use, and there was nothing in Philip's business or personal life to explain their purchase. Nor had they been delivered to his home. It took some doing, but while you've been hard at work on the cipher, I've been chasing down various suppliers and delivery companies, and have discovered the final destination for the shipments: a warehouse on the docks. Tonight, I plan on breaking in and having a look around."

"Is that legal?"

"Not in the slightest. I don't intend to steal anything, though, unless I stumble across a signed confession to Philip's murder. But if these chemical shipments are related to this book of alchemy, there may be more texts in the warehouse. Normally I work alone, but in this case I could use an expert eye to identify anything potentially useful."

I hesitated. I had done as the director requested and translated the book. My part was done; there was no reason to involve myself further, especially if it meant aiding a crime. The museum tolerated a great deal of eccentricity in its employees, but even the director wouldn't be able to turn a blind eye if I was arrested for burglary.

"Nothing will go wrong," Flaherty cajoled. "We'll be very careful. At the first sign of a watchman or passer-by, we'll scamper off to safety."

I'd been right the day before; he wasn't the sort to give up until he got his way. "Very well, Mr. Flaherty."

Surprise flickered over his features. Then his expression dissolved into the familiar grin. "Surely we can use first names, as we're to be partners in crime."

"I suppose, er, Griffin," I said, and hoped he put my blush down to heat or shyness or anything other than thoughts of the crime I'd prefer to be partners in.

"Thank you, Percy," he answered with a satisfied smirk.

I winced. "Please, just—just Whyborne. I'm not very fond of my first name, you see."

"Of course." Flaherty—Griffin—rose to his feet and picked up his hat. "Well, then, my dear Whyborne, I'll see you tonight. Meet me on the corner of Front and River streets at ten o'clock. Oh, and wear something dark."

He swept out, his overcoat flaring behind him. I sat and stared at the closed door for a long moment.

"Oh," I said aloud. "Oh dear. What *have* I gotten myself into?"

CHAPTER 5

THE SLUSH OF the streets had frozen after sundown, and the thin crust of ice crunched beneath my shoes as I made my way to my appointment. I huddled into my thick, woolen overcoat, wishing my hat did more to protect my ears from the cold.

The great clock above the courthouse chimed ten just as I reached my destination. As I approached the corner, Griffin stepped beneath the nearest streetlight, a carpetbag in one hand.

"Punctual, just as I expected," he said with a smile.

"Skulking in the shadows, just as I expected."

As soon as the words were out of my mouth, I wished to take them back. Griffin only laughed, however. "I am wounded, sir! Wounded to the quick."

"Somehow I doubt it," I muttered.

"Hmm. And you took my advice on dressing, I see?" He reached out and tugged lightly on the thick, purple scarf wrapped around my neck. "Although I must say, you have unexpected depths to you. I assumed all your clothing was some shade of brown or gray."

"It was a Christmas gift, from one of the servants in my parents' house."

Griffin arched a brow. "Oh? A blushing maid, taken with the youngest son?"

"Of course not! Miss Emily served in the household long before I was even born!"

"Not in contact with your father, but exchanging Christmas gifts with the servants. You are quite the enigma, my dear Whyborne."

"I exchange cards with my family," I protested weakly

"But no gifts, unless I mistake your meaning. Surely not one you would select to wear tonight. Was it for the dark color, or for luck, I wonder?"

I bridled at his determination to dissect me. "Wonder all you wish. I am not one of your cases."

"Is it wrong of me to want to know more about a friend? If so, I fear I'll be begging your forgiveness rather often."

Friends? Us? I did not have friends. I had colleagues. Well, Christine might be considered a friend, although we didn't associate outside the museum. I didn't dislike people, exactly, but I'd never quite got the hang of the casual interactions which seemed to come naturally to everyone else.

Perhaps it wouldn't be such a bad thing, to have Griffin as a friend. Especially since he seemed willing to put up with my eccentricities. His good looks and charm had nothing to do with it.

"I, er, yes," I said. "That is, no. I mean, no it isn't wrong of you."

His smile could make a man imagine he stood on a tropical beach, rather than a freezing street. "Good to hear. Now," he hefted the bag in his hand, causing several things to shift and clank within, "shall we go forward with our excursion?"

This was my last chance to back out. To decide, no, I really didn't want to risk ending up in jail tonight. To go back to my apartment, lock the door, and bury myself in a book. To preserve my quiet existence.

But Griffin was my friend now, and he had asked for my help. Just as Leander had asked so many years ago.

No. This was no boyish fancy: Griffin was trying to bring a murderer to justice. I was not accompanying him out of selfish reasons, but because I might be the only one who could decipher any texts we found. Could I sleep at night, knowing I might have brought some measure of peace to Mr. Rice, but turned back out of pure cowardice?

"I'm ready," I said.

Griffin flashed me a grin. "Come then, Whyborne. We have work to do."

The warehouse was two blocks from the waterfront, tucked along a side street occupied by boarded-up buildings and pawnshops selling the curious objects acquired by sailors in far ports. It was not an area of town I had ever before frequented, and my steps grew more cautious as we left the known streets farther and farther behind. The air reeked of fish, and I glimpsed the stacks of the canning factory only a few streets away. The whisper of the ocean was like the deep throb of a giant's pulse.

At this hour, we encountered few on the streets, except for a handful of wretches seeking somewhere quiet to sleep. The bawdy houses and saloons clustered around Queen Street, four blocks to the south. At least we didn't have to pass any leering dockworkers or red-lipped whores.

Gas had never been installed along the streets nearest the warehouse. The area lay in complete darkness, without a single light to brighten the overcast night. As we reached the last of the streetlights, Griffin paused and removed a pair of police lanterns from his bag. The faint smell of burning kerosene tinged the air as he lit one and passed it to me.

"If I tell you to cover it, obey me immediately," he said, indicating the shutter.

I swallowed hard, and hoped he didn't notice the shaking of my hand as I accepted the lantern. "As you say."

"Then cover it for now, and walk close behind me. The fewer lights we show, the less attention we'll attract." The strong beam of his lantern cut through the night as he spoke. "I wish we could have waited for a moonlit night and forgone them altogether, but there's no guarantee of getting one of those until next spring."

"If then." Dismal rains were rather the mainstay April through June.

"Lovely." He came to a sudden halt, putting a hand to my arm. Even through the layers of clothing separating our skin, his touch felt like a jolt of electricity. "There's the warehouse. I'm going to dim the light—stay close to me."

"I will."

He released me and eased the shutter of his lantern closed, letting only a thin sliver of light escape. We remained on the side of the street opposite our goal, until we stood directly across from it, when Griffin shuttered the light completely.

Instantly, we were plunged into complete darkness. His hand clasped my arm again, and he leaned close, his lips all but pressed to my ear as he whispered: "I came by during daylight, disguised as a dock worker, and didn't see any watchmen. But we'll wait a few minutes just to be sure."

I'd never realized my ears were so sensitive, but I was hyper-aware of his breath on my skin, stirring the small hairs. A shiver raced down my neck, and I began to stiffen beneath my worsted trousers.

This was madness. What had happened, that I was suddenly prey to these urges which I had kept ruthlessly suppressed my entire adult life?

At least the concealing night prevented Griffin from seeing the blood rush to my face. Or anywhere else, for that matter. I nodded my assent, and he withdrew, satisfied.

He spent the next few minutes watching the warehouse for any sign of light from within which would betray a night guard on his rounds. I spent them concentrating on the cold, the unpleasant stink of fish, and how we might possibly explain ourselves if a police officer should happen along. Any distraction was welcome, if it kept my thoughts off the man at my side.

After a wait which seemed agonizingly long, although in truth it could not have been more than ten minutes, Griffin cracked the shutter on his lantern and led the way across the street to our destination. He avoided the main door in favor of a smaller entrance on the side, no doubt meant for deliveries from the alley.

"Hold the light steady on the lock," he instructed, passing me his lantern. He rummaged through his carpetbag again and pulled out a bundle of rolled-up cloth. When spread on the icy sidewalk beneath the door, the bundle revealed a number of thin metal slips and picks. Selecting two, he set to work on the door lock.

"Did the Pinkertons teach you this?" I asked in surprise.

He didn't look away from his work. "Actually, yes. Why—are you imagining a sordid past for me?"

"I begin to feel as if nothing about you would shock me."

"My dear Whyborne, I do believe you think me a rogue," he said as the door popped open. Grinning triumphantly, he took the lantern from me.

"I've yet to see evidence to the contrary," I muttered, eyeing the dark room beyond. Once I stepped in, I would well and truly be on the wrong side of the law. Griffin stopped just within and looked at me expectantly. With a sigh, I crossed the threshold.

Griffin eased the door shut behind us, although he didn't close it all the way, no doubt in case we needed a hasty escape. At his signal, I uncovered my lantern and used it to inspect the room. Perhaps it had been intended as some kind of receiving room, but now it was completely bare and slightly dusty.

He led the way to the door on the opposite wall and cautiously cracked it open. After peering through, he opened it further and beckoned me to follow.

Griffin swept his lantern slowly from one end of the cavernous room to the other. Although the beams were powerful, the lanterns revealed only a sliver of the room at a time, leaving everything outside the small circles of light in complete darkness. Pallets of all sorts lay strewn about, many of them containing large crates. Even a quick glance revealed the marks of a dozen different ports from around the globe.

"I'll poke around down here," he murmured; his breath steamed in the cold, forming a cloud floating through the bright beam of his lantern. "The stairs over there lead up to the offices. If there are any relevant books, that's where they'll be kept."

"You, er, want me to look upstairs?"

"Please."

Why was I so reluctant to leave his side? I'd never been one to fear the dark, and I'd never needed another's company to reassure me against imagined terrors. Yet there was something about this warehouse I most emphatically did not like, a sense that something watched me from the darkness.

Except there wasn't anything lurking, any more than there had been in my apartment. It had been foolishness then and was foolishness now. Straightening my spine, I nodded and made my way to the stair Griffin indicated.

The risers creaked beneath my feet. Despite the cold, the air was oddly close. I caught a whiff of putrefaction. A rat had died in the walls, no doubt. Or an army of them.

I swept my light across the landing on the second floor; something scuttled away, just beyond the beam. Most likely another rat—although it sounded terribly large for a rat. Well, we were near the docks; this was probably some king of its species from Sumatra or Shanghai, newly brought to these shores by one of the many ships crowding the port.

As Griffin predicted, there were indeed offices on the second floor. The one to my right had large interior windows and looked out onto the warehouse floor below. No doubt it was meant for an overseer of some sort. The others might belong to…well, I had no idea who else might work in a warehouse. Someone more important than an overseer?

At any rate, if there was anything of a sensitive nature, it would more likely be kept in one of the closed rooms, where no one could just glance through a window. I chose the first room to my left and tried the door.

To my surprise, it was unlocked. Inside was a simple office: a desk, a filing cabinet, and a bookcase. A quick glance at the books showed only ledgers. I started to leave, then returned to look inside the desk. As I bent over it, I heard another scuttling from the shadows in the hall.

I jerked instinctively, shining the beam of my lantern in the direction of the sound. Nothing there.

Just rats. Rats in the walls.

I opened the desk. A leather-bound book lay inside. Burned into the cover was an unfamiliar symbol. A phoenix rose from flames, clutching in its claws an ouroboros: a serpent eating its own tail.

Griffin would want to see it. I took it from the drawer and tucked it into my overcoat; once I'd finished looking around, I'd show it to my companion before returning it to the drawer.

The next room was no office, as I'd supposed. Instead, it appeared to be a storeroom of some kind. Shelves lined the walls, and on the shelves were rows of cylindrical pottery jars, similar in design to those used by the ancient Greeks to store oil, even though they were obviously of modern origin. A small card was pasted to the shelf in front of each, inscribed with a date and a location. *Salem 1683* or *Providence 1791* or *Widdershins 1812*.

My curiosity aroused, I started to take down the nearest one, when the scuttling in the hall returned, louder than ever. This time, it was accompanied by a stench I couldn't name: the foulness of unwashed skin, clotted with pus and mixed with the dry leathery scent of reptiles.

No rat smelled like that.

I left the shelf alone and hastened into the empty hall. Only one more door; I would look inside quickly, then gather Griffin and convince him to leave this place. My every nerve pulled tight, like violin strings about to snap.

I flung open the final door and froze. After a long, breathless moment, I turned and walked unsteadily back to the landing.

"Griffin?" I called. "I think you should see this."

He came immediately, as if he trusted me to know what was important and what not. It might have warmed me, but what I'd glimpsed in the room had left too deep a chill.

I led the way back, even though I wanted to quit the building altogether. "I…I'm not sure what this is about," I said as we reached the door. "But it cannot be good."

Half the room seemed to be a chemical laboratory, reeking of sulfur. Our lantern beams reflected off glass jars, beakers, telescopes, and microscopes. There were coils of copper tubing, brass burners, and a dozen other instruments of whose function I was ignorant. Neatly-labeled bottles containing various compounds filled glass-fronted cabinets and shelves.

The other half of the room was the display of a madman.

The moldering remains of a dozen coffins lay broken and discarded, filling the air with a reek slightly less nauseous than the chemical stench. Foul rags of clothing formed a second pile, all of them of them encrusted with the unnamable filth of the grave.

"Dear God," Griffin murmured.

"I don't know what Philip was involved in, but whoever did this must be mad." My voice trembled shamefully, but I could not help but stare at those coffins, wrenched from the earth with such violence, and wonder what had become of their poor contents. "They must believe their brand of occultism is real."

Griffin wet his lips. "Yes. Mad." His Adam's apple jumped as he swallowed convulsively. "Was there anything else?"

"Just this," I said, drawing the book from my coat and passing it to him.

Its effect was as immediate as it was unexpected. He started violently, and even in the dim light I saw the color drain from his face.

"Run," he said.

"I-I'm sorry?"

"Run." He tore his gaze away from the book in his hands. "Run, damn you, before it's too late!"

I bolted for the door. But there was something already coming in through it.

CHAPTER 6

THE BEAM OF my lantern revealed a thing for which I had no words.

My mind flailed, trying and failing to make sense of what filled the doorway in front of me. It had four limbs, more or less, and a shape which overall suggested some perversion of humanity. But its naked body was horribly misshapen, the limbs of uneven length, the joints distorted. Thick, coarse skin covered it for the most part, but certain protuberances sprouted scales, and something horribly like human teeth jutted out of an elbow.

Its head was worse, however. Thanks to Christine, I'd spent many an hour bent over the art of ancient Egypt and its animal-headed gods. Those gods had a strange nobility and completeness to them. This thing seemed a mockery of the ancient deities. Its misshapen skull retained traces of humanity, but was hideously flattened and distended into an unmistakably crocodilian form.

Beady eyes fixed on me: blue irises punctured by reptilian pupils. Its jaws opened, the gape huge and lined with savage teeth, and it let loose a howl like something from the lowest pit of Tartarus.

I couldn't move, couldn't scream, couldn't do anything but stare. Had I been alone, it would surely have ripped me to shreds.

The roar of a revolver snapped me out of my paralysis. The hybrid thing jerked from the impact of the bullet, and slick, thin blood burst from its flank.

I threw myself to one side, out of the line of fire. Griffin strode past me: his coat flapping against his legs, emptying the chambers of his revolver over and over again into the horror facing him.

The impact of the bullets forced the thing back; it shrieked every time it was struck. The sound alone was enough to freeze my blood. But Griffin kept advancing, his face set, driving it back until the hammer clicked on an empty chamber.

The monster cowered at the end of the hall. A trail of thin blood covered the floor, but it wasn't dead. Perhaps Griffin hadn't hit anything vital or it simply didn't obey the laws of nature and *couldn't* be killed. When the gun did no more than click, it slowly raised its head, its blue eyes shining evilly.

"Damn it," Griffin said, almost conversationally. "Whyborne, my cane, if you please."

I snatched it from the floor where he'd let it fall and tossed it to Griffin, even as the thing surged back to its clawed feet. He caught the cane almost without looking, gripping it in both hands firmly before whipping out the sword concealed within.

"Whyborne! The stair, quickly."

I'd been standing and gaping like a fool. At his words, I dashed for the stair leading down. Perhaps we could outrun it—

Griffin hadn't followed. Instead, he stood blocking the hall, his sword swinging back and forth in a blaze of steel, fending off the creature.

"Griffin!" I shouted.

"Run!" he barked, even as the horror drove him one step at a time back to the stairs. "Damn it, Whyborne, get out of here!"

I cast about wildly. Surely there must be some sort of weapon, something I could use to defend myself and lend aid to Griffin. But I had nothing except for the kerosene lantern clutched in my hand.

The horror barreled into Griffin with bruising force. The blade of his sword sliced deep into its shoulder, bursting several scaly tumors and releasing a nauseating stench. With a roar, it backhanded him, tearing his sword free of its body and sending him sprawling against the rail.

I had to keep it away from Griffin. With a strangled cry, I rushed at it, swinging my lantern wildly in the hope of driving it back.

Instead, its serrated jaws snapped at me. I jerked back instinctively, and instead of closing on my arm, its teeth crushed the lantern in my hand.

Kerosene and fire burst forth. I'd already released the lantern, but the heat still scorched the hairs from the back of my hand. The thing staggered back, screaming in agony. The flames died almost instantly, but shards of glass and metal pierced its mouth, and whatever kerosene it had swallowed surely did it no good. With a final howl, it crashed blindly into the rail—then tumbled over, falling onto the pallets and crates below.

I turned to Griffin, but he'd already recovered his feet. By unspoken agreement, we raced down the stair, across the room, and out the door.

Griffin finally slowed on bridge where Front Street jumped the Cranch. The thick water of the river rolled beneath us, black in the night. He stumbled to a halt, leaning against the railing and peering over, hands shaking visibly. When he looked at me, his face had the haunted expression he'd worn when he'd glimpsed the symbol on the book and told me to run.

"It…it was real, wasn't it?" he asked. His voice was rough, the words cracking beneath some strong emotion. "The creature…it was real? I'm not mad?"

What was wrong with him? Unsure what else to do, I awkwardly patted him on the shoulder. "There, there, old fellow."

I expected him to pull away or shake me off, but he didn't. Instead, my feeble attempt at comfort seemed to have a bracing effect. He blinked slowly and some of the color came back to his face. "It's real," he repeated. "All of it." He lifted a trembling hand to his eyes, then let it fall. "Dear God. I wish I had been mad after all."

"Er, yes," I said. "But, Griffin, do you think you might tell me what the devil is going on?"

He finally met my gaze. "Yes. Let's go to my house. You and I have a great deal to discuss."

"Welcome to my humble abode," Griffin said, unlocking the door.

We had walked to his home in silence. Griffin lived in an older part of town, modest but not run-down. The two-story house was small, set well back from the street with a tall hedge to offer privacy. No doubt some of his clients wished to maintain as much anonymity as possible.

While I scraped the slush and mud of the streets off my shoes, he went inside. A moment later, the soft glow of gaslight spread through the narrow entry hall.

"Please, make yourself comfortable," he said, divesting himself of his overcoat and hat, and placing them on hooks near the door. I followed suit.

A door to my left opened onto a parlor. "Very nice," I said, glancing at the rather formal-looking decor.

Griffin smiled, a bit ruefully. "This room is to impress the clients. Upstairs is my study. It's far more comfortable."

I followed him up the stairs. An extremely large orange cat bounded down as we went up, darting between Griffin's feet and nearly tripping him. "Blast it, Saul, if you break my neck, who will feed you?" he groused good-naturedly.

The cat stopped to inspect my shoes. I bent down and offered a hand to sniff; apparently finding me to his satisfaction, Saul rubbed his big head against my fingers. I scratched him behind the ears and was rewarded with a rumbling purr.

"He likes you," Griffin said from above me. "Saul's an excellent judge of character, you know. If he hisses at a client, I refuse the case."

I wondered if he was serious. "I wish I could have a cat, but the landlady doesn't allow it."

The stairs creaked under Griffin's feet as he continued. Saul saw his master disappearing and dashed after him. Abandoned, I followed them to the second floor.

The study was located directly above the parlor; as Griffin had promised, it had a more informal, welcoming air than the room downstairs. An overstuffed chair sat close to the fireplace, and the mantel was cluttered with framed photographs, small watercolors, and other knickknacks. A large bookcase filled one wall, a couch opposite it. The spice of bergamot mingled with the warmth of leather and smoke.

A sideboard held several bottles and tumblers. Griffin paused long enough to stoke the banked fire to life, then poured a measure of brandy into a glass. "Would you care for a drink?"

"No, thank you."

"Are you a teetotaler, then?" he asked.

"No." I walked to the fireplace and held my hands to the flames, grateful for the warmth after our long walk in the cold. "I simply prefer to keep my wits around me."

He took his glass to the chair and sat down. Saul hopped into his lap and curled up like a fluffy, orange throw rug. "You're quite remarkable, Whyborne. Most men would want something to ease the shock of seeing…that."

I shrugged at the compliment and glanced away. Whatever else I might be, remarkable certainly wasn't it. I couldn't imagine what he meant by such baseless flattery. "I take it you have seen…whatever it was…before?"

He closed his brilliant eyes for a moment; when he opened them, their look was dull, and he kept his gaze trained on the dancing flames instead. "Not exactly. Do you recall I used to belong to the Pinkerton Detective Agency?"

"Of course."

"My last case…went wrong." A bitter bark of laughter escaped him, and he tossed back the rest of his drink in a single swallow. "Which is a damned poor way of describing the hell I witnessed."

He fell silent, his eyes far away. I drew close to his chair, then hesitantly touched the back of his near hand when he didn't seem to notice me.

It worked; Griffin blinked, gave me a look of surprise, then sighed. "Forgive me."

"If this is too difficult—"

"No." He shifted in the chair, and I withdrew quickly to my position near the fire. "We were hired to find a missing girl. To make a long and tedious story short, we tracked her to a rented house in Chicago. My partner and I broke inside. The upper part of the house seemed normal, but we found a trapdoor beneath a rug in the parlor. We went down…down into the earth."

He closed his eyes and took a deep, shuddering breath. "The basements, the vaults…God, some of them were ancient. The Brotherhood must have known the diggings were there and built the house on top of them."

"I'm sorry—the Brotherhood?"

"The Brotherhood of the Immortal Fire. A secret cult made up of very powerful, very wealthy men. Their existence is barely even a rumor. I would never have known of them if not for the last case. Their symbol is a phoenix clutching an ouroboros."

"The mark on the book we found," I said, feeling a stirring of dread. Surely secret societies and the like didn't really exist; such theories of conspiracy were simply the product of paranoid minds. And yet the haunted look on Griffin's face said otherwise.

"Yes." He hefted his empty glass and looked at it, as if some secret lurked in its depths. "We went down into the catacombs, hoping to find the girl. But instead we found *things*, the like of which I can't even begin to describe. If I said they were gelatinous, and floppy, and had pseudopods and things which must have been eyes…but none of that is quite right.

"Two of us went into that basement. I'm the only one who came out. I told everyone what I'd seen, but of course it sounded like the ravings of a madman. The police raided the place, with a force of Pinkertons, but the Brotherhood had closed up shop. There were no monsters, no horrors. Just dank tunnels and brick walls. They said I'd broken under the strain. I was mad."

The injustice of it made my chest ache. "I'm sorry."

"The thing is…a part of me hoped they were right. If I *was* mad…well, surely madness would be the better option, wouldn't it? Because if I'm not mad, if I really did see those things, then it is the world itself which is insane."

"Griffin." Feeling horribly awkward, I knelt before his chair. I wanted to take his hands, but surely the intimacy wouldn't be welcomed. "These monstrosities, whatever they are, operate on principles of science. The world may be many things: purposeless, random, and filled with happenings we don't have the means to comprehend. But the book you gave me to translate is filled with *formulas*. Methods. Repeatable experiments. The outcomes of those experiments may be horrific, especially as there is apparently more to them than superstitious twaddle, but they are still predictable."

He looked at me as if he'd never seen me before. Then he smiled for the first time since the warehouse and let out a genuine laugh. "My dear Whyborne, I don't think I've ever met anyone quite like you."

I rose to my feet. "Forgive me," I mumbled. I'd made myself look the fool as usual.

He rose as well, dislodging Saul, who mewed his displeasure. Griffin's strong hands gripped my upper arms, compelling me to face him. "Don't be ridiculous. With one sentence, you've given me more hope than I've had in the last two years."

The firelight caught the blue and rust hidden in his green eyes and made them all but glow. Although his smile was not cheerful, it was at least hopeful, and the soft curve of his lower lip caught my gaze and held it.

God. If anyone here were mad, it was me.

"I-I only stated the obvious," I mumbled.

"To you, perhaps." He released me. Thankfully, because it put distance between us and removed the edge of dangerous intensity. I felt sorry for the same reasons. "Does the *Arcanorum* speak of things such as we saw at the warehouse?"

"Er, I'm not certain," I said. "I didn't pay as much attention as I might have, not expecting to actually encounter any of the things described within. I'll rectify that tomorrow. The other book might help as well—do you still have it?"

Griffin's expression fell. "No. I dropped it in my haste to draw my revolver."

"Understandable, but unfortunate. No matter." I knelt on the carpet and busied myself petting Saul, who had come to twine around my ankles. "What is our next move, as it were?"

"Our?"

I'd presumed too much. "Never mind. I-I'll just leave it to the, ah, expert, then."

"Whyborne?"

"Yes?"

"Do you *want* to help?"

I looked up and found him watching me with the oddest expression. As if I'd said or done something so unexpected he didn't know how to react.

Instead of answering, I asked, "What happened to the girl? The one you'd gone to save?"

His mouth tightened with remembered grief. "We were too late. There was just enough left for her mother to identify."

"And if it is within my power to prevent such a thing happening again, do you think I would simply stand by?"

He laughed, as he had earlier: soft and half-amused, half-surprised. "I see. But I work alone, remember?"

Since his partner died, at least. Had the man been more than a colleague, or even a friend? "I understand. I will translate the text, or any other you find, of course." I bit my lip, uncertain if I should continue. It was a miracle he hadn't laughed outright at my fumbling offer. If I pressed further, his good humor might easily turn to contempt or patronizing dismissal.

If it were only myself…but I had kept silent once before, and Leander had died for it. More was at stake here than my pride. At least one man had already been murdered; if Griffin were next, and I hadn't at least tried…

"You asked me to come to the warehouse with you, and your reasoning was sound," I said. "I know I'm not a man of action, or courage, or anything really useful. But now that I better understand what it is we face, I can study the *Arcanorum*. The next time we come upon a scene such as the one in the warehouse, maybe I'll at least be able to tell you what they were about."

I expected him to laugh, or even sneer. Instead, he hesitated, uncertainty in his gaze. "You said earlier you need an expert," I cajoled. "You have one. Make use of me."

He swallowed hard, Adam's apple working. "Stand up, please."

I did, even though it put me several inches above him. He held out one hand, and I took it.

"I could use your help," he said, giving my hand a firm shake. "For this case, at least. Welcome aboard, Percival Endicott Whyborne."

CHAPTER 7

AS I DRESSED the next morning in the clear light of day, the events of the previous night seemed like something from a dream. Surely there had to be some sort of rational explanation for what we had seen. Some sort of tragic deformity, perhaps, like that poor Merrick fellow in England.

As a child, I had once seen a "living curiosity," as the traveling show called the wretch. But the drooling face and malformed body had inspired tears instead of terror—and a sharp blow from my father, who had been embarrassed by my "girlish display," as he called it.

The sideshow freak had been tragic, but there had been something profoundly *wrong* about the creature we'd encountered last night. Something which inspired a loathing far beyond the worst nature could devise. And, God, the smell! Why did the thing reek of the graveyard?

It had snowed overnight. Although not unused to such weather, Widdershins seldom received the heavier snowfalls which plagued some of our inland neighbors, and the streets were far less crowded than usual. I stepped carefully along the treacherous sidewalk in my oxfords. The omnibus probably wasn't even running this morning, so I'd have to trudge all the way to the Ladysmith in the snow.

As I passed the newsstand on the corner, a hand gripped my arm. I flinched back, before realizing the hand belonged to Griffin.

"Good morning, Whyborne," he said, as if we met this way every day. His overcoat was buttoned up against the cold, making him look far more somber than usual. "Do you have an urgent appointment at the museum?"

I wanted to pull my arm away. I also wanted for him to continue to touch me. "Er, n-no."

"Excellent. Then you can accompany me to the Kings Hill Cemetery."

Did the man feel a constant need to drag me all over Widdershins? "Kings Hill Cemetery? Why on earth would we go there?"

"After you left last night, I spent some time going over my case notes. Something you said the day we went to the police station has been itching at the back of my mind ever since."

Something I had said? "What?"

"You mentioned the theft of the remains of the town founder." He let go of my arm and took a folded sheet of newspaper from his pocket.

WIDDERSHINS FOUNDER'S GRAVE VIOLATED screamed the headline, dated November 1, 1897. And in slightly smaller print beneath: *Blackbyrne Tomb Opened During the Night.* The attached article rather hysterically speculated as to possible motives, including extorting a ransom from the town for the return of the body.

Above the fold was a large photograph showing the disturbed grave, the earth black against the white snow. A grim-faced policeman stood to one side. In the center loomed the monument, the words THERON BLACKBYRNE, MARCH 11, 1671 - MAY 1, 1723 still deeply cut despite a century and a half of weathering.

I recalled the moldering coffins in the warehouse, the piles of clothing stiff with the filth of the grave. "Do you think the Brotherhood was behind the theft?"

"I think it a possibility, at least enough of one to investigate further. I'd like to take a look at the gravesite. Would you care to accompany me?"

I could hardly refuse, after arguing to be included. "Of course."

His smile made me forget the snowy morning. "Good man."

A cab let us out near the wrought-iron gates of the Kings Hill Cemetery. The cold air stung my face and ears, and the wind slithered icy fingers through every tiny gap in my clothing. I tugged my scarf more securely around my neck.

The snow outside the old burying ground showed the passage of hooves and feet, and I glimpsed a few black-clad figures entering through the iron gates. I detested funerals, and looked away quickly, as if afraid their grief might be infectious.

Inside the low stone walls, the tombstones stretched out in ragged rows, their tops frosted in white. Leafless trees loomed over all, and in the distance I could make out the dark wall of trunks forming the boundary of the cemetery.

"That's the Draakenwood," I offered, pointing in the direction of the forest. "Blackbyrne's grave was near the trees, in the oldest part of the cemetery. I remember seeing it when my grandmother was laid in the family crypt."

"Your family is buried here, then?"

"All of the old families have crypts." The snow crunched under our feet as I led the way past the funeral. The sonorous voice of the priest followed us on the wind.

As we drew closer to the older section of the cemetery, the monuments grew more worn, and the family crypts appeared. Snow obliterated some of the names, but others I could make out, the letters softened by a century of rain: Marsh, Waite, Abbott, Whyborne. I paused outside our crypt. The padlock on the door had rusted badly; the last time it had been opened had been to inter my grandmother. My twin sister lay within as well, having died within hours of our birth; I was told my life had been despaired of as well for some time after.

Beyond the guardian row of crypts lurked the oldest part of the burying ground, on the pinnacle of Kings Hill: not the physical heart of the cemetery, but certainly its metaphorical one. Here lay the earliest settlers of Widdershins, those souls who had joined Theron Blackbyrne, years after he'd fled Salem one step before the witch hunters. Their graves were simple for the most part, in stark contrast to Blackbyrne's grandiose monument. Unlike the orderly rows of the rest of the cemetery, they radiated out from a central point, forming a loose wheel of sorts. And at the hub of the wheel was the grave of Blackbyrne himself.

Undertakers had refilled the grave at some point since the theft, but I detected a decided concavity even beneath the snow, like the socket of a missing tooth. Stepping carefully around the disturbed ground, Griffin approached the monument and began to examine it in detail. "What do you know about Blackbyrne?" he asked, brushing snow away from the ornate carvings.

"Very little," I admitted. Had Griffin asked me here assuming I would know the history of Widdershins? "He fled the witch trials in Salem. And he died in mysterious circumstances. Otherwise…well, I, er, never made a study of American history, you see."

I stared at my shoes, expecting mockery. But Griffin only said, "No one can be a master of everything, my dear Whyborne."

As he examined the monument, I wandered closer to the dark eaves of the Draakenwood. Unlike the wholesome groves of other forests, the trees of the wood seemed to huddle together, their black branches interlacing to form a deliberate tangle. Nothing stirred in the underbrush around the verge, and even in winter the branches blocked enough sunlight to render an impenetrable gloom a mere few yards in. No one took walks in these woods, and to my knowledge it had never been cut. It was the sort of place where boys dared each other to run in under the trees, although never far enough as to lose sight of their friends waiting outside. Occasionally, there would be rumors of someone who entered the wood and vanished without a trace; out-of-towners for the most part, who didn't know any better.

I took a tentative step just under the branches. Thorny underbrush caught at my coat, as if trying to hold me back. I noticed black feathers snagged on the thorns, and I leaned closer, peering at them. Had some poor bird gotten tangled?

"Whyborne! Come see this!"

Startled by the low urgency in Griffin's voice, I hurried back to his side. He stood in front of the now-bare monument, his gloves caked in snow. He stretched out one hand, then seemed to think better of touching the cold marble, and pointed instead. "Look."

Amidst the bewildering profusion of faces, vines, and symbols carved into the monument there nestled a phoenix clutching an ouroboros in its talons. The symbol from the book last night, which had struck such fear into Griffin.

"The Brotherhood?" I said, bewildered.

"He must have been a member." Griffin's hand curled into a fist, then dropped to his side. "Perhaps this town isn't the only thing he founded."

"But why steal his body? That is, if he was one of them…"

Griffin shook his head. "I don't know." He glanced at me, then down at my hand. "What have you got there?"

I uncurled my fingers, revealing the pathetic bundle of feathers and bone I'd pulled from the underbrush. "A dead crow, I think. It was in the bushes, over there."

He frowned and went to the edge of the wood, before bending down. "There's another here. And another. They're scattered all over. A whole flock."

"A murder," I corrected automatically. "It's a murder of crows." All of them dead, as if the entire group had simply dropped straight down from the trees in which they'd roosted. "Some people believe they carry souls to the afterlife."

"From the state of them, they've been here a while," Griffin said. "A month, perhaps?"

From the shadows beneath the trees came the unmistakable sound of a twig snapping.

Griffin jumped to his feet, the metal of his revolver gleaming in the dull sunlight. I peered anxiously into the wood: surely it had only been a deer, or a squirrel, or—

Something large and dark moved suddenly among the trees, its two-legged gait carrying it swiftly away.

"Someone was spying on us," Griffin exclaimed, and a moment later charged into the woods after the fleeing figure.

I balked, every story and ghost-tale of the Draakenwood I'd ever heard flooding into my mind. But Griffin wouldn't know the stories of travelers who vanished forever under the dark branches.

"Blast him," I muttered, and gave chase.

The trees closed around me in a dense tangle; only a few yards in, and I could barely make out anything beyond the verge. Thorn-covered vines gone brown with winter snagged on my clothes and knocked off my hat. A branch dumped snow on my bare head, and I stopped to wipe it from my eyes. When I looked around again, there was no sign of Griffin.

Some of the snow had gone down my collar, and I told myself that was the reason for my shiver. Selecting the direction I thought he had dashed, I pressed further into the woods.

I'd never been one for exploring the countryside, even as a boy. Within a few minutes, I came to a stop and looked around, disoriented. I couldn't have gone far…but which way would take me back to the graveyard? Was I going in circles? Heading farther in?

The trees gave me no answer, their thick, gray trunks looming on every side. Every direction looked the same now: trees and snow. Even the sunlight was diffused by the heavy clouds, so I was unable to tell exactly where it stood in the sky.

The wind came up, shaking the branches and sifting snow onto my head and shoulders. A low moan echoed from somewhere near at hand.

Branches. Not a moan. Just branches rubbing against one another.

Something moved deeper in the wood, just on the edge of sight, but I couldn't make out what it might be through the trees. I opened my mouth, intending to call out in the hopes it might be Griffin, but my voice seemed lodged in my throat. The way the form moved didn't seem entirely human.

Enough. I was getting out of this damnable wood. Surely even I could retrace the tracks I'd left behind me in the snow. I turned, intending to do just that, and froze.

A man stood watching me.

The trees and shadows half-obscured him, and he wore a dark, hooded cloak. All I could make out was the shape of his jaw, the curve of his lips. Eyes glittered from under his hood, and, realizing I'd seen him, he smiled a cold, cruel smile.

A hand came down on my shoulder.

I jumped, letting out an undignified shriek. "Steady on, Whyborne!" Griffin said.

My heart pounded so hard from my scare I could barely speak. "Griffin—look—there—"

"Where?"

The man was gone. I looked frantically about, half-expecting to see him sliding closer through the shadowy trees, but it was as if he had vanished into thin air. "There was someone watching me. And before, something else was moving in the trees."

Griffin's hand tightened on my shoulder. "I lost the one I chased, assuming it wasn't the same man. I don't think there's anything to gain from staying here longer."

I locked the door to my apartment behind me that night. I could not shake the memory of the watcher in the woods. Bad enough he had vanished with such unnatural swiftness, but that was not what troubled me. Rather, I had the growing conviction those unseen eyes had looked not just at me but *into* me, as if the secrets of my soul were nothing more than words on a page, to be revealed to anyone who knew how to read them. It was a foolish fancy, but I felt slightly safer once the bolt was thrown between my apartment and the world.

Then I remembered the sense of observation I'd had the other night, and the strange sounds from outside my window, and hurried to close the curtains as well.

After our morning adventure, I'd retired to the museum and spent much of the day carefully re-reading the opening chapters of the *Arcanorum*. Many of the mystic formulas contained within required esoteric ingredients far beyond my meager means. Not to mention even the most disinterested of neighbors would object to alchemical experiments carried out in their midst. The stenches alone would drive them to complain to the landlady.

I discovered a few rituals needing only minimal preparation, however, and it was one of these I settled on as an experiment. A "novice's" spell, the text said derisively, something practiced only by rank amateurs. Which certainly described me.

According to the *Arcanorum*, I needed only a combustible material, a certain chant, and a focused will. The book implied the latter was the rare quality, which made a convenient excuse if the whole thing was indeed a hoax perpetrated on the gullible, as I'd originally assumed. *The spell didn't work? Oh, you must not have the strength of will. Try harder next time!*

Having seen what I had seen, I was no longer entirely sure what a failure would prove, if anything. But a success…

I lowered the gaslight, until only a faint glow remained. I sat at my rickety table and placed a single candle before me. Feeling rather ridiculous, I tried to focus on the candle's wick and clear my mind of other distractions.

It wasn't going to work. Why was I even trying? This was nonsense, like believing the sun descended beneath the earth every night and battled monsters, or a rabbit lived on the moon, or a dragon encircled the world and only the chants of priests could keep it at bay.

I cleared my throat and self-consciously spoke aloud the Aklo phrase the book pompously referred to as the "true name of fire."

Nothing happened, of course. But to be fair, I wasn't exactly focused.

I repeated the phrase.

Who had the man been in the forest? Just an innocent nature-lover out for a stroll? But no one went into the Draakenwood just to take a walk.

Blast it. I needed to focus.

I repeated the phrase again. And again.

I went on until the words became meaningless. I focused on the sounds and the wick, and slowly other thoughts dropped away.

The candle burst into flame.

CHAPTER 8

THE NEXT MORNING, nothing seemed quite real. The newspaper boys shouting the latest headlines, the steam rising from the flanks of horses, the early morning light slanting cold and gray over the ocean: they were nothing more than a painted backdrop in a play, meant to distract the eye from the true nature of the theater.

I had lit the candle again this morning. And my stove. As I'd told Griffin after the fiasco at the warehouse, the experiment was repeatable.

Repeatable…but not understandable. I was no physicist, no astronomer, no mathematician. I studied languages, the more dead the better. How could I hope to make sense of any of it?

The spell worked. Although the *Arcanorum* couched everything in terms of gods, demons, and angels, I was not yet prepared to accept such explanations. I might abandon all reason before I reached the final page, but I would not take such a step in these early stages.

I spent the morning at my desk, combing through the book, checking and re-checking my translation. If I was to accept even a portion of the formulae within as genuine, then the Brotherhood had great power at its disposal.

My first priority was determining the nature of the monster we'd confronted at the warehouse. I had my guesses, but wished to have all the facts before I made my report to Griffin. I scribbled copious notes from the *Arcanorum*, then retired to the museum library for further reference and study.

The design of the library had been one of the more eccentric decisions on the part of the Ladysmith's mad architect. The entry was on the first floor, and certain records and journals were kept there. The main part, however, was laid out in a labyrinthine design below ground, yet not accessible by any of the other lower storerooms or halls.

The result was nightmarish; the librarians did constant battle with mold and damp, employing every trick known or imagined to preserve the papers. Random shafts let light in at odd intervals, meaning anyone seeking a particular item had to rely on the dim gaslight from sometimes distant walls, a sunny day and luck, or a lantern. Additionally, sounds had an odd way of echoing, making far-off voices seem near at hand, and distorting ordinary noises until they were menacing and strange.

As a result, most of us disliked the library intensely. Christine and Bradley had spent endless hours in my office complaining about it, and I couldn't count how many departmental meetings were sidetracked into a long session of mutual hate for the library, often combined with suspicion the librarians were hiding critical items for no apparent reason. Perhaps the architecture had driven them mad as well.

I spent hours immersed one of the small rooms near the very back, where certain texts were kept, their remoteness meant to discourage casual perusal. I'd always thought it ridiculous to keep the Pnakotic Manuscripts, *Al Azif*, and other tomes under lock and key. After my experiences of the last few days, I was no longer certain.

Entombed in the depths of the library as I was, none of the usual noises associated with the museum's closing reached me, and when I glanced at my pocket watch, the late hour surprised me. I was probably the only one left in the building.

The shadows of the labyrinth-library seemed suddenly deeper. I hurriedly gathered up my things and left the room. The interconnected chambers and oddly-angled halls were lit only by moonlight streaming from the irregular shafts set into the ceiling. My footsteps echoed strangely, almost as if someone followed behind me. I quickened my pace, which only made it worse.

By the time I reached the entrance to the library complex, my heart thumped hard enough to make me light-headed, and it was everything I could do not to break into a run. Glad beyond words to be quit of the place, I shut the door behind me, turned, and tripped over the body of the night watchman.

I fell heavily; my books and notes went flying, and my palms left skin on the wooden floor. I rolled onto my back, scuttling away from the body like a crab, even as I searched the darkened hallway for the horrors surely lurking there.

The night outside was cloudless; moonlight fell through the windows lining one side of the hall, revealing only the wooden floor, the storage cabinets along the opposite wall, the body, and my scattered things. The air reeked of blood and less pleasant substances. The watchman's glassy eyes bulged from their sockets and his mouth hung open in a silent scream, as if his last sight had been one of terror. Blood pooled stickily around him, and his uniform was shredded, as if from the claws of some frenzied beast.

There was another smell beneath the blood, nauseatingly familiar from the warehouse. My hands began to shake. The *Arcanorum* called them *Custodes*—Guardians.

Panic would get me nowhere. I had no weapons. My only recourse was to try to sneak out of the museum without being seen. Then I would summon the police.

Abandoning my books and notes, I rose to my feet and made my way along the hall as stealthily as I could. Every creak of wood, every scuff of my sole against the floor, even the ragged sound of my breath seemed destined to give me away. At least I knew the layout of the museum by heart; surely the Guardian would be at a disadvantage in the twisting maze of halls and storerooms.

But what was it doing here at all? Surely it couldn't be looking for me, could it? How would anyone even know Griffin and I had been at the warehouse? Or had the man in the woods followed us unseen all the way back to the museum?

I turned into a narrower side-hall, not far from the offices of the Department of Antiquities. There was a small staff door nearby which let out onto an alley behind the museum. I should be able to use it to slip out.

I quickened my step, even though it was a risk. I hadn't smelled the Guardian again, or seen evidence of anyone else in the museum. Just a little farther, and I'd be out on the street, where at least my cries might be heard.

Turning a corner, I collided with someone.

My heart stuttered, and my hands curled instinctively into fists—I wouldn't go down without a fight, even one I was destined to lose—

"Blast it, Whyborne, look where you're going!" Christine snapped. "And what's wrong with you? You're pale as a sheet."

I slumped against the nearest wall, feeling as though I might collapse from relief. "What are you doing here?" I asked.

"What do you think I'm doing? Working on the exhibit, of course. The director wants me on hand for the gala, but I mean to be on a ship bound for Egypt the very next day."

I winced at her strident tones. "Shh. Christine, listen to me, please. Someone's broken into the museum. Th-they've killed the night watchman. We need to get out of here."

Christine paled for an instant. Then, squaring her shoulders, she strode in the direction of her office.

I ran after her; my longer legs allowed me to catch hold of her arm before she reached her office door. "What are you doing?" I whispered. "We have to escape!"

"Let go of me," she ordered. I did, and she continued to her office, marching in and going directly to her desk. "I don't suppose you thought to take the gun off of poor Mr. Dillard?"

"Who? Oh, the watchman? No. I-I'm not sure I'd know what to do with one."

She let out a sigh and shook her head. "Honestly, Whyborne, you're utterly hopeless." Taking her purse out of her desk, she drew out a petite revolver. "This blasted thing is all we've got, then. I wish I had my rifle."

"Surely you can't mean to confront the, er, thieves!"

"Of course I do! Do you know how much collectors would pay for certain items from Nephren-ka's tomb? I'm not letting anyone make off with *my* artifacts, and I'm shocked you would!"

My mind flailed: what I could possibly say, which she might believe? "I think they, er, have some kind of attack dog with them. The guard—Mr. Dillard—was savaged. We need to get out of here and summon a police officer."

Christine pushed past me. Her back was straight, her expression grim. "You go to the police," she called over her shoulder. "I'm going to protect my artifacts."

"Blast it," I muttered under my breath, and hurried to catch up with her.

A small smile curled her mouth, despite the circumstances. "Good man."

"I can hardly let you go by yourself, now can I?" I said. "But let's at least be sensible about this. We should attempt to ambush them, or…something." If we could only get a glimpse of the Guardian without it seeing us, the horror of it would surely convince even Christine to retreat.

"Excellent idea," Christine said cheerfully. I didn't say anything further, fearing to attract the attention of the creature. Christine moved quickly, but far more quietly than I could manage. She cast one or two irritated glances over her shoulder when my shoe scuffed too loudly for her liking.

We made our way toward the front of the museum. The mummy and his tomb-loot occupied the grand exhibit hall on the south side of the main hall. If the Guardian didn't find us before then, we'd discover the exhibit undisturbed. Perhaps then I could talk Christine into fleeing out the front door with me.

But as we drew near, I heard a thump and the muffled sound of a very human curse. Had I been wrong? Had I only imagined the familiar smell outside the library? But no, Mr. Dillard had been ripped apart; no mundane thieves could have done such a thing.

We entered the main hall, clinging to the shadows along the wall. Moonlight poured through the enormous glass ceiling, spilling over the hadrosaur skeleton, which formed the centerpiece of the grand entry. Its empty eye sockets seemed to watch us with sinister intent as we crept past.

The sound of boots on the wooden floor came from the exhibit hall. A great black drape stretched across the entry, to keep the curious public from catching a glimpse of the exhibit before its unveiling. The rope barricade placed in front of the curtain had been torn aside, and the drape hung askew.

Christine's mouth tightened with fury. Holding her revolver at the ready, she eased along the wall, her skirts barely rustling as she moved. When she reached the crack where the drape met the wall, she put her eye to it. After a long moment, her expression transformed to a grim smile.

Then, before I could prevent it, she flung aside the drape and aimed her gun. "Stop right where you are, or I'll shoot you down, sir," she said with remarkable calm.

Skylights let the moonlight into the exhibit hall, competing with the warm glow of the thief's lantern. He bent over a crate, a crowbar in one hand. "Back away, and put down your tools," Christine ordered.

As I stepped up behind her, I caught a whiff of putrescence, like an unwashed body left unburied for too long. All the hairs on my arms and neck tried to stand up. "Christine!" I said urgently.

The ruffian let his crowbar fall. Did the clatter cover another sound, of claws scraping wood?

"Christine!" I repeated.

"Not now, Whyborne! Can't you see I'm busy?"

It emerged from where it had hidden amidst the crates and boxes. Moonlight revealed its awful form, and my gorge rose.

If the Guardian in the warehouse had been some unholy mixture of human and crocodile, then this one bore the traits of man and hyena. Wet fur covered large patches of its body, leaving other parts horribly pink and exposed. A crest of stiff hairs ran from the back of its head down its spine. Its head was a nightmarish thing, one eye and part of the face of a man, lips twisting into the maw of a predator and filled with wicked teeth.

"Run!" I shouted.

Several things happened at once.

Christine caught sight of the Guardian, and her eyes went wide. Swinging her gun around, she fired, and was rewarded by a howl of rage. At the same moment, the thief reached into his jacket and drew out a revolver of his own. It was much larger than Christine's.

"Run!" I yelled again, wondering if I was going to have to drag Christine bodily out of the museum.

She fired two quick shots at the thief, causing him to duck, before turning and fleeing. I ran close on her heels.

We raced across the main hall, dodging around the bones of prehistoric animals as we headed for the main door. A bullet smacked into the marble directly in front of my feet; Christine pivoted smartly and dragged me with her to the door leading deeper into the museum.

The thief fired again, and the bullet blew chips of fossilized bone from the skull of some toothy reptile. I risked a look over my shoulder, and my heart almost stopped at the sight.

The Guardian raced across the hall toward us, running on all fours in a horrible, loping gait neither human nor animal. Its claws scrabbled for purchase on the slick marble tiles of the main hall, which was the only reason it hadn't yet caught up with us.

Behind it, the thief aimed his gun at Christine.

"Christine! Duck!"

She turned on her heel instead, and their guns discharged at the same instant.

I would have sworn his shot actually stirred Christine's hair. She didn't flinch however, and it was the thief who fell backward in a spray of blood.

We didn't stop to find out if the bullet had put an end to him. Instead, we ran through the door, slamming it shut and locking it an instant before the Guardian's heavy body impacted it from the other side.

I backed away, staring at the door, which shook in its frame from repeated blows. Christine swayed and grabbed the wall. Her face was deathly white, her eyes wide with fear.

"What is it?" she asked, and her voice quivered slightly. Perhaps the shock was catching up with her.

"It's called a Guardian."

"You know what it is?"

"Unfortunately. It has something to do with the case Griffin is working on."

The fear drained out of her expression, to be replaced by anger. "And you didn't tell me?"

"Well, I hardly expected one to turn up at the museum, did I?"

With an ominous crack, the wood of the door began to split.

Christine eyed the door in alarm. "It's going to break through."

"Perhaps we can lose it in the storerooms," I suggested, backing away.

We hurried down the hall, made a sharp turn to the right, then one to the left. I paused at the top of a steep flight of stairs leading to the below-ground storerooms. At the moment, it looked like nothing but a black well.

From the distance came the sound of shattering wood.

I took a box of matches out of my pocket and lit one. It wouldn't provide much in the way of illumination, but at least we wouldn't break our necks in a fall.

We crept down as quietly as possible. My heart thudded and my ears strained for the smallest sound. As a consequence, I let the match burn down too far, and dropped it when the flame blistered my fingers.

We were plunged into darkness. "Honestly, Whyborne," Christine muttered, a tremor in her voice. After a moment of fumbling, I managed to light a second match.

We passed silently through the interconnected storerooms, hoping to lose the Guardian in the maze. Or at least, such was my plan, but Christine abruptly seized my arm and nodded to one of the rooms. I frowned at her and shook my head; it was a dead end, and we would be trapped if the Guardian followed us.

She scowled back at me, then stood on tiptoe, putting her mouth as close to my ear as possible. It reminded me irresistibly of the day in the alley with Griffin, although thank heavens Christine's proximity didn't affect me in the slightest.

"Can these things be killed?" she whispered.

"Yes," I whispered back.

Behind us in the darkness, the stairs creaked.

CHAPTER 9

We exchanged a look, and Christine dragged me into the storeroom. Some of the vaults were given over to a single type of item: a room of nothing but antelope horns, or beetles, or shark teeth. Others were stuffed full of artifacts without regard to department: medieval manuscripts filed alongside shrunken heads.

This one seemed at least to be ordered according to provenance, although I couldn't have said what people created the items within. There was a painted canoe made of bark, stacks of woven baskets, armbands decorated with feathers and beads, hundreds of stone arrowheads, blowpipes, bows...and a single long spear with a truly wicked-looking stone point strapped to the end.

Christine grabbed the spear just as the match burned down. I started to light another, then paused.

Would it—could it—work?

I placed the matchbox on the floor a few feet inside the door and fixed the location in my mind. Then I carefully groped my way into the room until I encountered Christine. I put my hands on the spear next to hers to help brace it. Even if my plan worked, this would take both of us.

We stood in absolute darkness for what seemed half the night. Both of us trembled, like a pair of rabbits hiding in a burrow while a weasel scratched at the entrance. At least holding onto the spear relieved me of the awkward decision of whether or not I should offer Christine comfort. My upbringing insisted I should, but knowing Christine, I would likely get punched in the face if I tried.

I strained my ears for any sound. The cloth of Christine's shirt vibrated almost imperceptibly with her breath. Water dripped somewhere nearby, perhaps from a steam pipe. Inside the wall, a mouse began to chew on wood.

Was that the scratch of claws on tile?

No. Yes.

I locked my knees to keep them from shaking. Slowly, slowly the scratching drew closer, accompanied by the sound of snuffling.

It could smell us.

Christine drew in a sharp breath as she came to the same realization. Leaning close, I risked whispering: "Squint your eyes—and when the time comes, do as I do."

It sounded insane, but she nodded, perhaps trusting I knew something she didn't. God, I hoped she was right; if my plan didn't work, we would both very likely die here.

And it wouldn't work. It *couldn't.* I wasn't adept at anything except hiding in my office and reading dead languages. How could I possibly come up with a plan to save us?

It had been Christine's idea to get the spear, though. I drew comfort from that; she'd faced threats to her life a dozen times in her travels. Perhaps we did have a chance.

God, please let us have a chance.

The Guardian drew nearer and nearer, its wet fur reeking of pus and foulness. I swallowed down my revulsion and concentrated only on listening.

It was at the door.

A loud snuffle, and the hinges creaked as the door swung wide. Claws on the tiles.

It was in the room with us.

Squinting my eyes, I focused on the matchbox and spoke the secret name of fire.

The box burst into flames, the light blindingly bright even through my lashes after such utter darkness. The Guardian fell back with a howl of pain, which contained just enough of humanity to make it a thousand times worse than the shriek of a monster.

"Now!" I yelled, and surged toward its cringing figure.

Christine moved with me, both of us lunging forward with all the strength in us. The point of the spear slammed into its hairy chest, grated against bone, then slipped between ribs and sank deep. The Guardian let out another ear-splitting scream, its body bowing as it tried to wrench away from the spear.

Then it began to *crumble.* Patches of its flesh turned bluish-grey, before sloughing away, until the whole of the creature suddenly collapsed into a relatively small pile of extremely fine dust.

In the dying light of the flaming matchbox, Christine and I stared at one another. She took a deep, shaky breath. "What the devil is going on here, Whyborne?"

"I'll explain later," I said. "But please, let's leave while there's still some light. I don't want to end up wandering around down here, lost in the dark."

She paled. "Yes. Yes, I quite agree. Let's get out of here and fetch the police."

I got no sleep at all that night. Indeed, it was just as well my neighbors took no note of my comings and goings, because I didn't even make it back to my apartment.

We found a police officer on patrol almost at once, which was a stroke of luck. I babbled out a story about a dead watchman and thieves, leaving out the fantastic aspects. Something about our wild appearance must have convinced him of the truth; he summoned other officers immediately, most of whom headed for the museum. Two remained with us; they wasted most of the time insisting Christine allow one of them to escort her home, to spare her any further shocks.

The policemen found poor Dillard's body, and the body of the thief Christine had shot. Before the hour was out, Dr. Hart, Mr. Rockwell, and even the museum President, Mr. Mathison, joined us on the Ladysmith's front steps. Rockwell marched inside and left the rest of us shivering in the cold, while he and the police made certain no more ruffians lurked within. None of them noticed the inexplicable pile of blue-gray dust in one of the remote storerooms.

By the time they were done, it was almost dawn. Christine finally gave up and left for home. My notes and books lay where I had dropped them; I gathered them hastily, trying not to look at the pool of sticky blood which awaited the arrival of the janitorial staff. After, I went to my office and straightened my clothing as best I could. Bradley kept a shaving kit in his office; I shamelessly stole the key, trusting Rockwell had better things to worry about at the moment. I suppose I might have waited until Bradley arrived and simply asked, but I was in no mood to endure his vulgar insinuations as to why Christine and I might have been in the museum alone together at such a late hour.

I took a few moments to scribble a hasty note to Griffin, letting him know his case had reached into the museum and suggesting we meet in the evening. I usually spent all of Saturday at work, rather than the half-day required of us, and I had the feeling I'd need the extra hours to finish my researches.

Dr. Hart called an all-staff meeting; as it happened, a garbled account of events had already made the rounds. No doubt the afternoon edition of the *Widdershins Enquirer Journal* would bear a lurid headline such as "MURDER AT THE MUSEUM!" or "THE MUMMY'S CURSE!" or some such rubbish.

Christine returned, looking a bit more refreshed. She volunteered to give an account of our adventure to the meeting, and delivered it with verve. I tried to sink into my chair and look inconspicuous whenever she mentioned my name.

"Ha!" Bradley said, when she arrived at our confrontation with the "thieves" in the exhibition hall. "Whyborne screamed like a woman, didn't he? Come now, you can tell us."

There came a smattering of chuckles. I stared resolutely at the pad of paper in front of me and forced a half-hearted little smile onto my lips. But my fingers clenched until my nails drew blood from my palms. The director hurriedly asked Christine a question, diverting her attention from Bradley before she could make any response; their fights were legendary among the staff.

Eventually, the meeting came to an end. As soon as the director declared it adjourned, I darted for the exit and was gone before anyone could speak to me.

I gathered my books and notes from my office. Some of the papers were edged in blood, where they'd settled too close to Dillard's body. I stared at them for a long time, until I realized I was simply in a daze. There was no time for wit-wandering; I felt exhausted, yes, but the events of the night before had proved the urgency of the case. I could not afford to relax.

I hastily drank down a too-hot cup of coffee poured by Miss Parkhurst, then headed back to the library. Mr. Quinn, the head librarian, eyed me when I entered. With his black clothing and pale, somber coloring, he looked more like a funeral director than a librarian.

"Dr. Whyborne," he said, gliding over to me. His voice matched his aspect: deep and hollow as a grave. "I understand you were the one to find the…body."

"Er, yes, th-that's right."

He nodded slowly, but his pale, bulging eyes never left my face. "I see. Do you think he…suffered?"

"I, er, I couldn't possibly say. I'm sorry, but I have w-work to do." I gestured feebly with my armload of books.

"Hmm." He eyed my burden. "None of those with bloodstains belong to this library, do they?"

What would he do if I answered in the affirmative? Thank goodness I didn't have to lie. "N-no. These are from my, er, personal collection."

He didn't say anything further. I backed away a few steps, then fled his presence. I only breathed again when I was sure he hadn't followed me.

I spent the next few hours ensconced in my nook in the back of the library, amid the moldering tomes. The manner of the Guardian's final dissolution confirmed my theories as to its nature, but I wanted to make absolutely certain before I presented my findings to Griffin.

It was difficult to concentrate on the crumbling pages and cryptic words. Every creak, every hiss of air through a ventilation grate, every distant footstep caused me to start. I'd sat oblivious in this very chair last night, while a man was torn to shreds only a short distance away. What if something came upon me while I worked? Would anyone else hear the sounds of my demise, or would they find my mangled body tonight, when Mr. Quinn appeared to lock up?

Surely the Brotherhood wouldn't try anything in the middle of the day, would they?

The tap of approaching footsteps sent me scrambling to my feet, nearly knocking my chair to the floor. Thanks to the strange architecture, voices carried oddly clear into this room. I started when I recognized Griffin's accents.

"Thank you for escorting me. I don't think I would have been able to find my way alone—the place is something of a maze, isn't it?"

My heart settled to back to something near its usual pace. I was about call out and let him know where I was, when Bradley spoke. "No trouble, no trouble at all. Tell me, did you stop bank robbers, when you were a Pinkerton?"

"Mostly train robberies, actually. I was stationed out west for most of my time with the agency. I also tracked a band of kidnappers over the border into Mexico, and one time—but you probably don't want to hear about any of this."

"Don't be absurd! Your life sounds like something out of a dime novel and quite exciting. You must come to my Christmas party."

"Most kind of you, Mr. Osborne."

"Please, call me Bradley."

Of course Bradley would find Griffin fascinating. Who wouldn't? And surely Bradley, with his parties, would seem far more interesting a friend than me.

"Widdershins must seem terribly boring to you," Bradley rambled on. "After all your adventures out west, that is."

"Not at all. I find it a welcome change of pace."

"Yes, but having to work with old 'Why-were-you-born'...you have my condolences."

I bit my lip until I tasted blood. It was nothing I hadn't head a hundred times before. It didn't matter. Griffin would join him in a hearty laugh, and it. Did. Not. Matter.

The footsteps halted. "Excuse me?" Griffin asked.

"Oh, you know, old Percy." Bradley laughed. "Bit of a useless fairy, isn't he?"

"I believe I can find my way from here, Mr. Osborne," Griffin said, his voice hard and cold as a glacier.

"Oh, come now, Mr. Flaherty, it was only a joke."

"Whyborne is my friend and a good man. I do not appreciate hearing him made the butt of jokes better suited to a boy still in primary school than a grown man."

Bradley let out an angry huff. "Well. Good day to you, sir."

His footsteps faded. A few moments later, Griffin's resumed, accompanied by the tap of his cane. I tried to compose myself hurriedly, but my expression must have given me away, because he paused when he entered the room.

"Er, good day," I said. My ears and cheeks burned, but at the same time, an unfamiliar warmth fluttered in my stomach. "Didn't you get my note?"

Maybe he hadn't. Or maybe he didn't want me coming over to his house after work. Or maybe—

"Yes." He leaned against the doorway, his hands shoved in his pockets. His tie was the color of rust, and brought out the shade in his eyes. "But after seeing the newspaper, I wished to come by and make certain you were all right."

"I…oh. Y-yes. I'm fine." A fine, babbling idiot.

"Have you eaten lunch yet?"

I hadn't even had breakfast; my stomach growled in response. Had he heard? "No."

"Then let me take you out; you can tell me what happened."

"Of course. I suppose Christine should come with us," I added, a bit reluctantly. She needed to be involved, of course, but it would have been nice to have an hour alone with Griffin when we weren't in danger of our lives.

God, I had to stop thinking such things.

"Certainly." Griffin gestured out the door. "Lead the way."

"All right, Whyborne," Christine said as we settled into a booth at Marsh's, "Out with it. What has this detective involved you in?"

I sat beside her, while Griffin took the bench across from us. He leaned over the table and folded his hands in front of him. "What do you know already, Dr. Putnam?" he asked.

She eyed him distrustfully. "I know I was attacked by a creature—a Guardian, I believe Whyborne called it?—which should not exist by any natural laws. I also know Whyborne can apparently set fires merely by speaking a few words."

Griffin gave me a startled look. "Then you know more than I."

The waiter slid in a plate of poached fish in front of me, giving me an excuse not to meet their eyes. "I, er, decided to experiment a bit."

"Repeatability?"

I risked a glance up. Griffin smiled. "Repeatability," I agreed.

Christine glared at me. "Whyborne…"

"Allow me," Griffin said. While we ate, he laid out the facts of the case, including our encounter in the warehouse. I took up the narrative from there, detailing my experiment in summoning a flame. Christine contributed from then on, and together we told Griffin about our adventure in the museum.

When I explained how we had defeated the Guardian, Griffin arched a brow. "That was rather clever. Or devious."

"It seemed obvious," I said, my cheeks warming from his praise. Hopefully neither he nor—heaven forbid—Christine noticed.

"It saved our lives," Christine said matter-of-factly. "I must say, gentlemen, this all sounds rather unbelievable. If I hadn't seen what I did…but I have." She shook her head and scowled down at her plate. "You still haven't said what these Guardians are, however. Or why the one we killed turn into dust."

"Not dust," I corrected. "Salt."

Griffin folded his napkin and set it aside. "Tell us, then."

"I could be wrong, of course, but based on what I've read in the *Arcanorum*, the creatures we saw in the warehouse, and the lists in the book I've found, I think they're…well, they're made from the remains of humans and-and other dead things."

"Do make some sense, Whyborne," Christine said.

"In my readings, there is a great deal of talk concerning alchemical experiments which could *reconstitute* a person—or creature—from its essential salts. As for the, er, non-human bits…one seemed to be part crocodile, and the one last night had hyena in it."

Christine's eyes widened. "The thefts from the museum!"

"I'm afraid so. Once the…parts…were gathered, the salts would have to be properly prepared, again by alchemical means, from the mortal remains."

"That's not possible," Christine interrupted.

"Neither is conjuring up fire with words and willpower."

"Touché," she muttered.

"The Guardians aren't attempts to *resurrect* anyone, per se, merely to use the salts of humans and other creatures to create slaves." The poached fish swam uneasily in my stomach. "Horrors unrelated to the bodies from which they were created." At least I hoped such was the case.

Griffin sat back and stared fixedly at his half-empty plate, although I doubt he saw anything beyond his own thoughts. "Blackbyrne, though. He was one of the Brotherhood, judging by the symbol on his tomb. Would they try to truly resurrect him?"

It was surreal to sit in the normalcy of the diner and discuss such things. "I don't know. It would require a complicated ritual to bring his essence back into true being. As to why they would—and why now, after two-hundred years—I can't guess."

"Could he be the one behind the creations of these Guardians?"

"It's possible, but again, we have no way of knowing."

"Hmm." Griffin rubbed absently at his clean-shaven chin, staring off into nothing. "Putting the matter of Blackbyrne aside, why would the Brotherhood be interested in an exhibit at the museum?"

"Why wouldn't they?" Christine demanded, sounding rather offended.

Griffin unsuccessfully tried to hide a smile behind his napkin. "As fascinating as your studies are, Doctor, I think it would take more than the lure of knowledge to inspire them to create monstrosities."

"Or would it?" They both looked at me, and I hunched my shoulders under their scrutiny. "What if the Brotherhood's motives are no different than ours? What if they wish to regain some bit of lost knowledge? If they stole Blackbyrne's body to resurrect him with some abominable ritual, perhaps they mean to do the same with Nephren-ka."

Christine's eyes widened. "My mummy! Those bastards are after my mummy!"

Griffin frowned slightly at us; no doubt he believed we were jumping to conclusions. “Is there anything special about Nephren-ka?”

Christine and I exchanged a look. “Nyarlathotep?” she asked.

“Nyarlathotep,” I agreed.

CHAPTER 10

"I HAVE NO idea what you mean," Griffin said, looking bemused. "Care to share?"

"Nephren-ka was erased from history," Christine said. She sat on the edge of the seat, her hands clasped eagerly before her, her eyes alight at the chance to expound on her favorite subject. "His name was chiseled off monuments of the era, painted over on papyrus scrolls, even scratched off potsherds. I've never seen such a complete attempt to destroy even the memory of an individual. It took years of searching, but just enough clues remained for me to locate his tomb."

"Which, if the papers were to be believed, was a spectacular find."

"The papers—bah! They go on and on about gold and gems, and ignore the true wealth of the tomb. The entrance wasn't just hidden—it was literally buried beneath tons of rubble. Between the rubble and his effacement from history, no looters got to it. We were the first to step inside after the last mourners left him over four millennia ago."

"I see. And what has this to do with the Brotherhood?"

"In the few references to him which survived, Nephren-ka was called the Black Pharaoh due to his reputation for dark sorcery. Some scholars argue he was mad, and certainly he did a great many odd things, including ordering the construction of an utterly lightless temple to house an object referred to as the Shining Trapezohedron. He was also a heretic and worshipped a being known as Nyarlathotep.

"At any rate, Nephren-ka's enemies feared his wrath enough to bury him in splendor when he at last met his fate, although they did raze the lightless temple to the ground and grind the very masonry into dust. The tomb was typical for its era, aside from one curious thing. Rather than being designed with traps to keep looters out, it seemed more designed to keep its occupant *in*."

A shudder crawled up my spine, and Griffin's mouth tightened. "I see," he said.

"The name Nyarlathotep appears occasionally after," I said, "although much has been lost to history."

"Or to the follies of my so-called colleagues," Christine muttered.

Knowing she could go on for hours about the incompetence of other archaeologists, I hastily said, "Interestingly enough, the name reappears in the Middle Ages, several thousand years after Nephren-ka lived. Again, the references are fragmentary, but they are always associated with alchemy, sorcery, and occultism of various kinds. One of Nyarlathotep's aliases, 'the Man in the Woods,' appears in testimony regarding Theron Blackbyrne, when he was accused of witchcraft in Salem."

I trailed off, remembering again the hooded figure in the Draakenwood. But, uncanny as the apparition had been, I couldn't believe it to be anything more than a creature of flesh-and-blood. Not if I wanted to retain my sanity, at any rate.

Griffin's eyes darkened, and I suspected he was thinking along the same lines. "You mean to say there is a connection."

"I'm afraid so," I said. "However, the question as to *why* remains. What does the Brotherhood want?"

"They want what these sort of men always want." Griffin steepled his fingers in front of his chin and watched us thoughtfully. "Power. Whether such power takes the form of money, knowledge, or something else is probably immaterial to them. If they believe Nephren-ka has something they need, then they will stop at nothing to get it. Tell me, what sort of precautions is the museum taking after last night?"

"The director is practically hiring an army," Christine said. This was news to me, since I'd not paid as much attention as I should have during the meeting. "With the full cooperation of the trustees and the president. There will be no less than twenty guards on the premises, day and night, with four stationed in the exhibit hall itself. The press are going mad, so add in a second army of reporters crawling around the place, snapping pictures, and poking their noses where they don't belong."

"The Brotherhood might raise an army of their own, but not without drawing attention," Griffin murmured thoughtfully. He tapped his fingers against his lips. I clasped my hands in my lap to keep from reaching across and smoothing away the lock of hair tumbled across his furrowed brow.

"Then this is a good thing?" I suggested.

He glanced up at me, and a smile replaced his frown. "Indeed. You and Dr. Putnam have dealt them a serious blow."

I stared down at my hands awkwardly. Christine only snorted. "You had best believe I'll be better armed the next time. Things would have gone far worse if Whyborne hadn't been there. Which is not something I admit lightly; I rather prefer to think I can take care of myself."

"You can," I protested. "Had we been attacked by a charging hippopotamus, I would have left it to you."

"A what?" Griffin asked, bemused.

"A hippo," Christine said. "The most dangerous animal in Africa. One decided to charge my excavation team while we unloaded equipment from the boat. They move quite quickly when they are motivated, so I was forced to shoot the poor thing. And I must say, Mr. Flaherty, you seem very blasé about all of my adventures. Most of the time, I have to put up with men telling me to stop talking, get married, and stay at home. Except for Whyborne, of course."

Griffin chuckled. "Have you ever heard of Kate Warne? If Timothy Webster was Allen Pinkerton's right hand man, she was his left. She formed and headed up the division of Lady Pinkertons. I have worked with determined women before."

"Good. Then you won't object to my assisting you and Whyborne in your investigation."

Griffin arched a brow. "That depends. Can you be of assistance?"

"With all due respect to Whyborne, no one knows Nephren-ka better than me."

"It's true," I said. "Perhaps if we knew what exactly they want from him, we could find some way of preventing them from getting it. After all, the museum can't keep on an army of guards indefinitely."

"True. Although I doubt the Brotherhood will wait very long." Griffin said thoughtfully. "Between the newspapers and the hired guards, they'll probably strike at a time when a large group of people coming into the hall won't seem out of place."

"The gala," I blurted.

Griffin nodded. "Exactly what I was thinking. There will be caterers, guests, all sorts of people wandering about. The guards will no doubt be pulled back to avoid upsetting the wealthy donors, some of whom may well belong to the Brotherhood. It would be the perfect moment to make their move."

"I told the director the blasted gala was a bad idea," Christine said with a sigh.

"How are we to stop them?" I asked. A sour feeling grew in the pit of my stomach. "We can't just walk into the director's office and tell him a secret society is plotting to steal the mummy, because they mean to raise him from the dead to gain his secret knowledge. He'd have us locked up in a madhouse!"

Griffin went pale; had I not been watching him at the moment, I'd never have noticed it. Then he seemed to remember himself, and his expression shifted back to something approaching normal. "Quite right," he said. "Believe me, I face the same difficulties with my client."

"We could show him your-your spell, Whyborne," Christine said.

Griffin gave her a wry smile. "You can barely accept it yourself, Dr. Putnam. Tell me, if you hadn't seen it under the circumstances in which you did, but rather in a well-lit office in the middle of the day, wouldn't you have thought it some sort of cheap trick? A magic act—elaborate, but still an act?"

Her mulish expression suggested she wanted to deny it, but after a moment, she shook her head. "You're right. I've seen plenty of similar tricks on the streets of Cairo, performed in exchange for a few coins."

"Well, then," I said, setting down my fork beside my largely-uneaten meal. "I suppose it's up to us."

Even though totally exhausted, I couldn't sleep that night.

It wasn't simply the enormous task which lay before us, although how a private detective, an archaeologist, and a comparative philologist were to thwart the plans of a powerful secret society, I had no idea.

The *Arcanorum* haunted me; or, rather, some of the rituals within its pages did. I couldn't stop thinking about the lists of chemicals, the methods of preparing the bodies, the salts, the chants.

I sat in bed, the covers pulled up securely to my chest, and held the old photograph of Leander in my hands. It had been such a long time. Whole days passed now when I didn't think of him at all.

If I had been stronger and less selfish, he'd still be alive. If I had been better, if I had deserved him, how many nights might we have sat across from one another over dinner, or in front of a fire? How brilliant a life might he have had; what gifts would he have brought to the world with his wonderful mind?

What if I could fix my old mistake? What if I could use the *Arcanorum* to bring him back?

I put down the picture and took the *Arcanorum* from my nightstand. Turning to one of the pages I'd marked, I read the passage again: "*Yog-Sothoth* opens the gate. *Yog-Sothoth* is the gate."

I didn't know what sort of entity *Yog-Sothoth* might be, but there were many cryptic references to "other spheres" and "those from Outside." Whatever these beings might be, they were clearly not of this earth.

If I brought back Leander, would it *really* be my old friend? Or something else, something unspeakable and terrible?

Wasn't it a chance worth taking, though? How could I let my cowardice condemn him a second time?

Could I talk to Griffin about this? But it would mean confessing my part in Leander's death, and I didn't want him to think badly of me. Quite the contrary.

Perhaps I'd gain some answers as we went further into our investigations. If we were correct, if the Brotherhood had brought Blackbyrne back to life and not simply some horror wearing his likeness, then I would go to Addison. I would lay everything out before him; I would show him my little trick with the fire. He was Leander's father; the decision rightfully belonged to him.

And if he refused?

I put the photo back in its drawer, along with the *Arcanorum*. I'd find no answers tonight. After blowing out the candle, I pulled the covers up around my shoulders and tried not to think.

Sunday afternoon, I was surprised by a knock on my apartment door.

No one ever visited me. Someone must have mistaken my door for another. I ignored the knock, until it was repeated even more insistently. "Whyborne? Are you home?" Griffin called.

I sprang up, annoyed by the way my heart suddenly sped. Why would Griffin call on me at home? A dozen fantasies instantly came to mind, each more unlikely than the last. I wiped my sweating palms on my trousers, tried to compose myself, and opened the door.

Griffin leaned against the wall, dressed like a laborer in a frayed scarf, battered cap, heavy knit sweater, and scuffed boots.

"I, er," I said stupidly. "That is…will you come in?"

His green eyes flashed mirthfully from beneath the brim of his cap. "Thank 'ee, sir, I believe I will," he said in a lilting Irish accent, as if he'd stepped off the boat yesterday. "If yer neighbors willna be thinking it odd."

"This is Widdershins—we keep to ourselves," I reminded him, as I stepped out of the way. "And, forgive me, but why on earth are you talking like an Irishman?"

"I am an Irishman."

"From Kansas."

"It's something I learned from my time in the Pinkertons," he said, dropping the accent and strolling further into the room. "People are quicker to trust those who look and sound like themselves. I intend to pay a little visit to the district near the docks this evening, to speak with one of my informants. I thought you might wish to accompany me."

"I don't think I could pass myself off very convincingly," I said, shutting the door. I glanced around the barren confines of my apartment. How must its drab brown walls and threadbare carpets look to him?

Griffin stood in front of the bookcase and studied the titles. "I don't know; you'd make a convincing clerk."

"Why?" But wasn't I the one who had insisted on being a part of his investigations? What had I been thinking? "I'm willing to accompany you, of course, but I don't see what I have to offer."

He turned from the books and gave me an enigmatic smile. "I suspect you have a great deal to offer, my dear Whyborne."

My ears grew hot—and my trousers uncomfortably tight, even though he surely meant nothing untoward by the remark.

"Well?" he asked. "Will you come with me?"

"Y-yes. Yes. Just let me get my coat and hat." I donned my overcoat hastily, buttoning it closed to hide my erection. What was it about Griffin which strained my control like no one else I'd ever met? His flashing eyes, no doubt, combined with his tousled hair and wicked grin.

Nothing to do with the way he'd helped pick up my things the first day we'd met, or how he'd stood up for me against Bradley, or the way he'd hurried over to the museum to see for himself I was all right.

Blast it.

The icy air outside quelled my unruly member quickly enough. Griffin led the way at a brisk walk, his hands in his pockets and his shoulders hunched against the wind. The air smelled of sea and snow, and I guessed there would be another few inches added to the slush already on the ground by morning.

We made our way to the southern part of the dock district, where brothels, gambling dens, and saloons mixed with cheap boarding houses and rather questionable groceries. The streets were narrow and crooked, and the alleys choked with garbage and sleeping men.

Those we passed on the street eyed us warily. Many of them were unshaven, with faces seamed by the sun. Some were missing hands, arms, or legs, the victims of whaling accidents or shifting cargo. They were a rough-dressed lot, and I was glad I'd taken Griffin's advice and left my pocket watch at home.

"I rather feel as if I stand out here," I confessed in a low voice. It was an uncomfortable sensation; normally my clothing allowed me to blend in and go unnoticed. Even my ties were brown or gray, with no splash of color to catch the eye. Here, though, the quality of my suit set me apart even if the drabness didn't.

"With any luck, we'll be able to turn it to our advantage," Griffin murmured. "If they think you're some innocent clerk come slumming, they may be less cautious of what they say in front of you. Speaking of which, as far as the people we're about to meet know, I'm a day laborer by the name of Greg Flannery. You can be…hmm, how about Weatherby? You're a clerk at the Second Bank of Widdershins."

"What if they bank there? They're sure to know I'm an imposter."

Griffin patted my arm. "My dear Whyborne, banks have this strange habit of requiring people to actually have money in order to do business with them. I assure you, there's only one person in the establishment likely to have ever set foot in a bank, and you won't be speaking with her."

The building we halted in front of was two stories, with solid brick walls and weathered cornices. Nothing from the outside gave any particular clue as to what its nature might be. Griffin looked at it for a moment, and when he turned to me, he was grinning.

"Well, Mr. Weatherby, will ye come along, then?" he asked, before opening the door and ushering me inside.

I entered despite my misgivings. A rather large man stood just within, eyeing me in a most unfriendly fashion.

Griffin slipped around me and gave the man a nod. "Evenin'," he said easily. "Figured I'd bring me new friend Mr. Weatherby around for a spot of fun, eh?"

The man only nodded. Griffin took my arm and pulled me after him.

The end of the hall was covered in a beaded curtain, which let us out into a very large room. Along one wall ran a bar, well-stocked with bottles and kegs. Directly across from the entrance was a sort of low stage: two women wearing very little clothing danced to the tune of an upright piano. A good number of men sat at their ease around tables between bar and stage: drinking, gambling, catcalling, or lavishing attention on the scandalously-clad women sitting in their laps. A stair led up to a long second-floor balcony, lined with doors, and men and women made their way up and down the steps in pairs. The air smelled of spilled beer and floral perfume.

I grabbed Griffin's arm. "Dear heavens, man! You've brought me to a house of ill-repute!"

CHAPTER 11

"DON'T BE ABSURD," he murmured back. "It's also a saloon and gambling den."

"B-But I…that is, we—"

"Sometimes an investigation means we have to go to unsavory places. Don't worry—it's quite reputable, as these things go. No one's been murdered here in at least a week."

I started to point out that the law didn't allow saloons to open on Sundays, before realizing the absurdity of my comment given the circumstances. Griffin was apparently known here already; a man called out to him, and he laughed and waved back.

Draping an arm around my shoulders, he pulled me through the crowd. "These fellows are hard workers, decent enough sorts in their own way, but they have been known to skirt the law. They aren't murderers, but digging up bodies and selling them wouldn't be outside the realm of their experience."

"Oh!" That made sense, at least. "You think they were involved in stealing Blackbyrne's body? Or some of the others?"

"If not them, then one of their close associates. The Brotherhood is made up of wealthy men, most of whom haven't done a day's honest labor in their lives. Other people use shovels and haul caskets, not them, which is why I think these gentlemen may know something. Your task is simply to sit and listen to them talk while you play poker."

"Poker?"

"Don't worry." He tucked something into my pocket. "Use this money. It's part of my expenses, paid by my client. Don't be afraid to lose it. Just sit and keep your ears tuned for anything interesting, all right?"

Before I could respond, we were at the table. Griffin greeted the men seated there enthusiastically. When he'd done calling them each by name, he tightened the friendly arm around my shoulders and grinned. "This 'ere is me new mate, Weatherby. Wanted to see the sights of Widdershins, 'e did, if ye know what I mean."

I didn't, but the others must have, because they all guffawed.

"Er, hello," I said faintly.

"Siddown, then, Weatherby," one of them said; I couldn't recall his name. "Let us deal you in. You, too, Greg."

"Sure thing." Griffin took the seat by me, and a few seconds later I had been dealt a hand.

"Me friend might need the rules explained to 'im," Griffin added, with a quick wink.

Before I could say anything, a tide of cheap perfume swept over me. A young woman slid in between us, one arm slipping around my shoulders and her ample cleavage practically in my face. "Hello, handsome," she said. "I ain't seen you around here before. I know, 'cause I'd sure remember a face as pretty as yours."

I directed my eyes away from her, feeling my cheeks burn. I silently prayed she didn't turn her gaze to my lap and notice a lack of arousal, which surely must be uncharacteristic in this place. Would it have been better or worse if Griffin had taken us to a bathhouse?

Oh God, why did I have to imagine that? At least there would be something to see now if she directed her attention downward.

"Leave me friend be, Nelly," Griffin said. He slid an arm around her waist and pulled her onto his knee. "'Is wife'll skin 'im alive if 'e comes home smelling of perfume. I barely talked 'im into the whiskey and cards as 'twas."

The other men immediately offered sympathy for my imaginary troubles. Not knowing what to say, I clutched feebly at the shot of whiskey another woman placed in front of me. The glass was filthy, and I wasn't sure if I could actually bring myself to drink it.

"Madam saw you come in and said to send you right up," Nelly said, tossing her arms around Griffin's neck. "I'm jealous—why don't you ever come to see me?"

Surely I had misunderstood. Griffin wouldn't have dragged me here with him if he intended to indulge himself with some prostitute.

"I would, me girl, but I dinna want to get ye in trouble with the lady o' the house," Griffin said amiably. She left in a swish of skirts, and he rose to his feet, tipping his hat. "Well, boys, take good care of Mr. Weatherby while I'm gone, won't ye?"

He strutted away and up the stairs to a chorus of catcalls, but it all seemed very far away and unreal. How could he do this? Yes, most men turned to hired companionship at some point or another in their lives. God knew my brother had boasted of the women he'd conquered with money when we were youths.

But to watch Griffin pay to have some doxy, when he could have someone else, someone who cared for him, with the snap of his finger…

He disgusted me. Worse: I disgusted myself. What was wrong with me, burning with jealousy over a man who would never feel the same about me?

If only I'd never met him in the first place.

The dealer cleared his throat. Belatedly, I turned my attention back to the table, to the ring of faces which seemed suddenly alien, as if they belonged to some other species altogether.

"Well, Weatherby," the dealer said with a gap-toothed grin, "shall we explain the rules o' poker to ya?"

The others snickered and exchanged glances. Clearly, Griffin had meant me to play the rube. Well, if such had been his wish, then he should have remained. He had no right to expect me to continue his investigation while he went off and-and rutted with some woman.

Did she have him undressed even now? Was she touching his skin, his erection? Had he thrown her back on the bed and kissed her, the way I wanted him to kiss me?

I snatched up the whiskey and downed it in a single swallow. To hell with the filthy glass; I'd drink anything to stop the images in my head. The stuff was beyond foul, burning down my gullet like industrial solvent instead of liquor, but it did the trick.

Devil take Griffin Flaherty. I'd misjudged him, badly.

And he had misjudged me. "No," I said, picking up my hand. "There'll be no need, gentlemen. I presume five-card stud, nothing wild, and no limit is acceptable?"

"What the bloody 'ell?" one of my companions asked in confusion.

And well he might. I'd spent the money that lout Griffin had given me on rounds for the table. We were *all* confused by now.

Even the alleged whiskey hadn't been enough to douse the coals burning a hole in my gut. The longer Griffin was absent, the less I cared to ever set eyes on him again.

To the devil with this. None of these men had said anything remotely useful. Not so far as I'd noticed, anyway, not having paid a speck of attention to anything beyond the cards and the closed door through which Griffin had disappeared.

Well, no more. I scraped my substantial pile of winnings off the table and stuffed them randomly into my pockets. "I'm taking my leave of you, gentlemen," I said, or tried to; my tongue had trouble shaping the words. "I doubt I will be visiting this fine establishment again, so…er…goodnight."

I made it to my feet without falling, which was actually something of an accomplishment. Ignoring the flabbergasted stares of the would-be cardsharps, I stumbled away from the table, located the door with some effort, and made my way to it.

No one bothered me as I exited the building. I stopped and leaned my back against the brick, hoping its solidity would keep the world from spinning.

The cold air helped a bit, but not much. I'd over-indulged before, but never to this extent, and never with liquor of this awful quality. I'd be sorry in the morning. I was sorry now.

Mostly, I was sorry I'd come there at all. Peeling myself away from the building, I staggered in what I hoped was the right direction.

The rickety tenements loomed over me, blotting out the sky with their overhanging eaves. The sidewalk hadn't been swept for a long time; years of refuse and mud obscured any sign of the stones. My shoes squished unpleasantly in the sucking mud, as did the boots of whoever was behind me…

I was being followed.

Heart pounding, I spun—and fell heavily against the nearest wall, my balance spinning out of control along with everything else in my life.

"Hey, now," said a silky voice. "Don't want you to hurt yourself now, do we?"

"What?" I asked, like an idiot. Two shapes emerged into the light of the nearest streetlamp. Neither of them were cloaked, and both were human, thank heavens. I'd been certain I would see the man from the woods, or something far worse. "Oh. You aren't monsters. That's good. Very good."

They glanced at each other; wolfish grins appeared on their faces, and suddenly I wasn't sure after all.

"That's right," the talker said. I wished the other would speak. But what if he did, and his voice wasn't human? "Give us your wallet and your watch, and we'll be on our way. Nice and quick."

"I-I haven't got a watch," I said. I tried to step back, but I was already pressed against the side of a tenement. The rough brick dug into my shoulders. Would anyone inside come to my aid if I called for help? "Here's my wallet."

I dug it out and flung it at them. The talker bent down and picked it up, but the other kept coming. There was something unsettling about the way his bulging eyes stared without blinking. I had the sudden, absolute conviction he wanted something from me, and mere money would not dissuade him.

"Get back," I gasped, my heart thudding madly. "Please, stop!"

"Oh no," said the first one. In the streetlight, his narrow face took on a sly cast. "You're holding out on us, aren't you? Think I don't see the bills sticking out of your pocket, then?"

Belatedly, I remembered I hadn't bothered to actually put my winnings in my wallet. "Oh, I…"

The blade of his knife gleamed, competing for my attention with the awful, staring eyes of his companion. "I think we're going to have to take you somewhere nice and quiet," he said, and God, the way he spoke, the way his eyes grew glazed as with some fiendish kind of lust. "Yes. Somewhere we'll have plenty of time to play."

The loud crack of a revolver made all three of us jump, and a cry escaped me. Griffin stepped out of the darkness into the pool of light cast by the streetlamp. His expression grim, he aimed his revolver directly at the silent one's head.

"Not tonight, I think," he said.

Both men held up their hands. "Sorry, sorry," said the talker, sidling away from me. Thankfully, his companion followed suit.

"Drop the wallet."

It hit the ground with a wet slap. "Just having a bit of fun, that's all."

"I know the sort of fun you prefer, Billy Waite," Griffin said coldly. "The next time I see you or your cousin around here, I won't fire a warning shot. Am I clear?"

"Clear as glass, sir!"

"Get out of here."

They both ran. Griffin watched until they were gone, then turned to me. "Are you all right?"

"No," I said miserably. And then I threw up on his shoes.

"Whatever am I to do with you, Whyborne?" Griffin asked. He finished wiping the last specks of vomit off of his boots with his threadbare scarf, which he then tossed deep into the alley.

I huddled into my overcoat, relying on the wall to hold me up, since the world was still hurtling about like a merry-go-round. My stomach felt tight and my head throbbed, but least the nausea had subsided.

"I'm sorry," I said, for the fourth time. Or was it the fifth? Sixth?

Thank heavens, Griffin seemed bemused rather than angry. "It's all right. I probably should have warned you against the whiskey. Let's hail a cab; we'll never get you home otherwise."

By the time we found a cab, it had started to sleet, the sting of ice on my skin adding to my misery. The only comfort came from Griffin's arm around my shoulder to hold me steady, but the gesture came with its own measure of pain.

We climbed into the cab, and the driver urged the horses forward. The movement made me dizzy, so I closed my eyes and leaned against Griffin's shoulder.

"Did the gentlemen you were playing cards with happen to say anything interesting?" he asked after a few minutes.

"No. I don't know. Maybe. I won." I took some of the money from my pocket to show him.

A laugh escaped him. "You are truly something, Whyborne. I had no idea you could even play poker, let alone clean out a table of hardened gamblers."

His shoulder was rather comfortable. I closed my eyes and relaxed just a little. "My mother taught me. We'd play for hours. All kinds of card games. She's sick, you know. Has been for a long time."

"I'm sorry to hear it. But, as I recall, your job was to sit and listen, not take their weekly wages and then your leave."

I opened my eyes. Was he mad at me? How dare he criticize me, given his own behavior? "And your job wasn't to-to go have sex with some-some harlot."

Griffin sighed deeply; his shoulder shifted under my cheek with the force of it. "Madam Rosa is one of my best informants. You wouldn't believe the sorts of things men will brag about to a prostitute, when they wouldn't think to tell their own wives. We maintain the fiction I'm one of her regulars, which allows us to meet in private without raising suspicions."

I frowned. This sounded important, but it took a few minutes of intense concentration to comprehend what he was saying. "Wait, wait. *You* pay her for *information*."

"Yes, Whyborne."

"And not for carnal pleasures."

His shoulder vibrated under my cheek; he was laughing at me, damn him. "I assure you, all of my transactions with Madam Rosa have been of a strictly professional nature. And I mean my profession, not hers."

"Oh." I was an idiot. A foolish, jealous, crazed idiot. What must he think of me?

"I should have said something before we went in," he added. "I've gotten out of the habit of confiding my plans to anyone else, I suppose."

"Oh," I repeated stupidly.

Griffin lapsed into silence, and the only sound was the roll of the wheels, the tap of the sleet on the windows, and the clop of the horse's hooves. I still slumped against my companion; his warmth soaked into my skin even through the layers of our clothing.

I opened my eyes. His face was bare inches from mine, and he looked down at me, studying me thoughtfully with those eyes as green as a field of springtime grass. The light of street lamps came in through the windows, slid across his face, revealing his sculpted mouth and strong cheekbones, then vanished to plunge us back into shadow. The aroma of damp wool, leather, and sandalwood rose from his skin, entrancing my senses. My limbs felt boneless, my blood hot with alcohol and need.

His lips parted very slightly. Was he going to kiss me? God, I wanted him to kiss me.

I didn't say that aloud, did I?

He drew in a deep breath. Then he closed his eyes, and his mouth firmed abruptly. He turned to face the window, and although he didn't push me away, the tension in his shoulder stole some of my contentment. Of course he wasn't going to kiss me. People like me weren't kissed.

I closed my eyes and hunched into him, because it was the only comfort I could have. After, things became very hazy indeed. The next thing I knew, he dragged me up the stairs to my apartment, my arm thrown over his shoulders and my feet stumbling. He must have gotten the keys from my pocket, because he opened the door and pulled me in.

Then my bed was in front of me, and I collapsed into it, fully dressed. Someone pulled a blanket up around my shoulders, and a hand lingered in my hair, trailing through the ridiculous, spiky locks, which never would lay flat. But I was on the edge of oblivion, and it might have been nothing but a dream.

CHAPTER 12

I SPENT MONDAY in such utter misery I was forced to send a note round to the museum rather than go in to work.

Of course I was wretchedly ill. The aromas of breakfast from the other apartments sent me running to the water closet, where I spent a good portion of the morning retching up what little remained in my tender stomach. My head pounded mercilessly, and my mouth tasted as if I'd tried to clean Front Street with my tongue.

But far worse was the memory of my foolish behavior. Because of my ridiculous jealousy, I'd bungled the opportunity to do anything useful. Griffin no doubt believed me a complete imbecile. And as for the cab ride home...I hadn't said anything too humiliating, had I? Bad enough I had thrown up on his shoes: what if I'd begged him to kiss me? Or something even more intimate?

I cradled my head in my hands as I sat at my kitchen table, sipping sparingly from a cup of tea, which was the only thing I could keep down. Even if I had said something, Griffin wouldn't report me to the police for soliciting unnatural acts. If he were disgusted enough to wish me jailed, or at least harassed by the police, he wouldn't have seen me safely up to my bed. But he might not wish to continue our friendship. As for wanting my further help in his investigation...I had certainly proved myself utterly incompetent on that score.

Perhaps I hadn't said anything, or if I had, he would assume I'd been too drunk to know what I was saying. Perhaps he only thought me stupid, not perverted.

How could I ever meet his eyes again?

Tuesday was better, if only because the physical effects of my bout of drunkenness had subsided, and I returned to work. I received no word from Griffin either day: no note, no unexpected meetings over lunch. Nothing.

He hated me; I was certain of it.

On Wednesday, Christine stopped in the middle of a rant about the director and stared at me. She sat in her usual chair in my office; I'd been desultorily going through the *Arcanorum* yet again when she'd barged in.

"I say, Whyborne, what the devil is wrong with you?" she demanded.

"What?" I asked distractedly. "The director. Yes. Do go on."

She set her purse on my desk; it clanked rather loudly, and I assumed she was now armed with a much heavier caliber of gun. "You haven't heard a word I've said," she pointed out crossly. "You've barely even spoken all week."

"No less than usual."

"Well, not to anyone else, perhaps, but you normally talk to me, if only because I force you to."

"It's nothing." But my chest ached, like a bad wound full of pus. Maybe if I lanced it a bit, it would start to heal. "I was assisting Griffin on Sunday, and I, er, drank too much and acted rather foolishly. And he hasn't contacted me since, and I thought we were friends, but I…I don't know how to fix this," I finished lamely.

Christine eyed me for a long moment, then shook her head with a sigh. "Oh, Whyborne."

Pity, from Christine? I'd expected impatience, or annoyance, or even quasi-helpful advice, but not pity. "What?"

"You aren't the only person to ever act like a fool in front of a handsome man, you know. You're not even the only person in this room."

Christine knew about me? How could she? Surely I'd mistaken her. "Wh-what do you mean?"

She shrugged uncomfortably. "Hard to believe, I know, but I was young at the time."

"Not that," I said impatiently, although under any other circumstances I would indeed have been shocked. "The other. I mean, why would you think I, er…"

She let out a most inelegant snort. "Honestly, Whyborne, how long have we been friends?"

"Four years, I think, but I don't see—"

"And how many dreadful museum affairs have we been forced to attend together? While we're in the back of the room, having an intellectual *conversation* unlike the rest of the fritter-heads, I've had ample opportunities to observe your behavior. Your eyes glance over the ladies easily enough, but you do have a tendency to linger over some of the gents."

I sank back in my chair, feeling as though she had punched me in the stomach. I'd always tried to be careful, and yet I clearly hadn't been careful enough. Who else might have noticed? Would I lose my position at the museum? "I…I see."

"Oh, do stop fretting. No one else would possibly notice. You're generally quite discreet, I assure you."

"I hope you're right. It would spell my ruin."

"To be fair the museum would probably look the other way for anything short of a public scandal."

"Perhaps. But I would hate to lose, er, anyone's regard because of it." I badly wished to ask if she thought me a pervert, or was secretly revolted by my longing for Griffin, but I feared her answer too much to ask.

Fortunately, she didn't require it of me. "Don't be ridiculous, Whyborne. As I said to Bradley, one cannot go into a tomb or temple without viewing depictions of all manner of, er, acts. I am quite accustomed to the thought of such things, and would hate to lose a friend over something so trivial."

A relieved laugh escaped me. "Thank you, Christine."

"I am simply being practical." She sat forward. "Now, on to the matter at hand. Does Griffin share your inclinations?"

I rubbed at the bridge of my nose. "I can't believe I'm having this conversation with you."

"Stop being dramatic and answer my question."

"I have no idea."

"So it isn't true you just *know* somehow, when you come across another —"

"Christine! Please, don't be absurd!" My face felt hot enough to boil tea.

"Well, I did think it sounded silly, but I wanted to verify," she said placidly. "What did you say to him? Please tell me you didn't confess your undying love."

"Of course not." Christine clearly wasn't going to give up, and perhaps it would bring some relief to unburden myself. The whole sordid affair tumbled out in a rush.

When I was done, she shook her head. "You're right. You did behave like a fool."

"Thank you," I said, annoyed. "I'd already reached that conclusion on my own."

"But you it doesn't sound like you did anything inexcusable. If he wasn't upset about you vomiting on his shoes, he probably wasn't terribly upset about the rest of it, either."

"It isn't the same. Throwing up on someone's shoes isn't criminal behavior."

"If Griffin put you to bed instead of just dumping you on the sidewalk, I suspect he couldn't be too angry."

"Then why hasn't he contacted me?"

"I have no idea. Why haven't you contacted him?"

"I can't." What would I say? What if he responded with contempt?

"Listen here, Whyborne." She rose to her feet and hefted her purse. "If Griffin is truly your friend, he'll forgive your behavior. And if he doesn't, then he didn't deserve you in the first place."

I barely swallowed back a bitter laugh. *Deserve* me? Of course he didn't—he deserved someone a thousand times better. Someone who wasn't gawky and awkward and *strange*. Who could hold a normal conversation without stuttering, who didn't constantly weigh every action, paralyzed by fear until it was too late to do anything.

"It isn't that," I said instead. "I never…I don't have any hopes for, er, anything."

"I know," she said with a sad smile. Then she shook herself and resumed her usual impatient expression. "Don't fret. Things will work out, or they won't. Worrying won't make any difference."

"I know." She started to leave, and I roused myself to say, "Christine? Thank you. For, er…well. For not letting any of this affect your opinion of me."

She paused, and although she didn't turn to face me, what I could make out of her expression from her profile startled me with its fragility. "I know what it is to desire something which all of society says is wrong. At least it wasn't actually illegal for me to attend university, even though I'm sure there are many who would wish otherwise. Do you know when I knew we'd be friends?"

I'd never seen her vulnerable before. "No. I don't."

"It was the first day we met. You addressed me as 'Dr. Putnam' without having to be prompted. And when Bradley insisted on referring to me as 'Miss Putnam,' you…well, you corrected Bradley's shoes, but I appreciated the gesture."

"It was only good manners," I objected.

She glanced over her shoulder, her demeanor once again confident. "Exactly. I'll see you later, Whyborne."

"Good day, Christine."

The door shut behind her. I sat and stared at it for a long while, feeling better than I had all week. True, my circumstances hadn't changed a wit, but I had at least one friend in this world. A friend who might reach her limit with the museum and jump a tramp steamer bound for Egypt at any moment, yes, but I would take what I could get.

With a sense of renewed purpose, I turned back to the *Arcanorum*. Perhaps I couldn't salvage my reputation with Griffin, but I could at least repair some of the damage and prove I was not entirely useless after all.

It was nearly closing time that evening when a brisk knock sounded on my office door. Not Bradley or Christine, then; they would have simply barged in. I closed the *Arcanorum* and tucked it into my pocket before calling: "Come in."

To my utter shock, it was Griffin who entered instead of one of the museum staff. Unlike the last time I'd seen him, he was neatly dressed in a proper suit and hat, with his silver-headed sword cane in hand. Did he wear a disguise when he came here, just as when he went to the docks?

"I…oh," I said. After my talk with Christine, I'd decided to send an apology, but had not yet had the chance to compose it. Having him actually here before me left me floundering. "That is, I mean, would you sit?"

God, I was such a babbling imbecile.

He gave me a curious look, but took the proffered chair. "Thank you."

"Can I, er, offer you anything? Tea? Coffee?" I'd have to run all the way to the upper floor for any refreshments. Perhaps it would give me the opportunity to compose myself.

"No, thank you," he said. Leaning back in the chair, he stretched his legs out in front of him. "I take it you survived waking up Monday morning?"

Lowering my gaze to the notes on my desk, I shuffled them randomly, just to give my hands something to do. "Y-yes. Griffin, about Sunday…I cannot apologize enough. My behavior was inexcusable…what I remember of it," I added with a wince.

"My dear Whyborne, you're hardly the first man I've seen drunk."

It surprised me into looking at him. There was no censure in his expression, no mockery, only a gentle amusement. "And as for my shoes, well, I'm sure you paid for it in full the next day."

"But…I…" Had it all been in my mind? Had he really read nothing more into my antics than a simple bout of drunken excess?

"Did nothing I've not done myself," he said with a grin.

I doubted it, but if he didn't realize what motivated me, then perhaps our friendship wasn't as damaged as I had feared. "Still, I should have remained focused on the case. I know I let you down, but I swear to you, it will not happen again."

His expression shifted, from comradely to concerned. "As I told you Sunday, I should have taken you into my confidence. It was my mistake not to tell you of my part in our little charade, and my mistake to assume you would know to lose at cards."

"I dare say you assumed I didn't know how to play at all," I said resignedly. My ridiculous infatuation had led me to overlook just how different we were.

"The more fool I." He propped his elbow on my desk and rested his chin in his hand, studying me intently. "I already knew there is far more to you than meets the eye, Percival Endicott Whyborne. It's my fault if I didn't remember the lesson."

I straightened the papers I had just disarranged; it gave me an excuse not to look at him. "Don't be ridiculous." I was exactly what I appeared to be: awkward, inept, and boring.

"If I'd known it was weighing on your mind, I would have come by earlier," Griffin said. "Truly."

Why did he have to be kind? If only he'd mocked me, or sneered at me, or merely tolerated me, then I would have known how to deal with him. But he insisted on being kind, on pretending I had some worth. How was I to defend myself against that?

"Don't concern yourself," I said at last. "Have there been any new developments in the case?" At least this was safe ground to tread.

He sat back in his chair. "Yes. I've spent the last few days chasing down clues. I'm not sure if you remember, but Madam Rosa is an informant…?"

"I remember."

"She had some interesting information for me. Unfortunately, it took time to find out whether it pertained to our case. Plus, I had to apologize to the men you cleaned out at poker. They thought I was delivering a rube to them, and were not at all pleased to discover otherwise."

"Forgive me," I began, then stopped. He was grinning at me.

"Perhaps I shall, if you split your winnings with me."

"Absolutely not," I said primly. "Although, if you feel lucky, you may try to win them from me later."

He laughed, and I relaxed. I'd said the right thing for once.

"I'll take you up on the offer." He set his cane before him and used it to rise. "As I said, I've been following a clue here and a clue there, and I think I've identified a house where the Brotherhood has been carrying out some of their experiments. I intend to pay it a visit tonight. Will you accompany me?"

"Of course." He not only forgave me, but wanted me to continue to assist him? It seemed too good to be happening to me. But… "Should we ask Christine to accompany us?"

"Probably, since I still hope to learn what the Brotherhood wants with our friend Nephren-ka."

"I believe she's in the exhibit hall." I rose to my feet and put on my second-best hat, having lost the first in the Draakenwood. "Follow me, if you will."

We found Christine surveying the workmen as they moved an immense statue of Nephren-ka into place. The thing was twelve feet of solid sandstone and weighed several tons.

She arched one brow when she saw Griffin with me, but thankfully said nothing untoward. Griffin explained the situation to her; to my shock, she shook her head.

"If you cannot dispense with me, then I'll come," she said. "Otherwise, I should remain and make sure this lot doesn't destroy all of my hard work."

"Are you certain?" I asked in surprise.

She gave me a quelling look. "Didn't I just say it? The two of you go ahead. If you find anything interesting, I'll look it over later."

Dear lord. She actually thought she was doing me a favor by giving me time alone with Griffin. I shot her a glare, which she ignored.

We hailed a cab in front of the museum. I was careful not to sit too close to Griffin, lest he realize my behavior Saturday night was born of more than mere drunkenness. While Christine might tolerate my inclinations because they were not focused on her, Griffin would surely feel differently.

"Dinner first?" Griffin asked.

I nodded, and he called out the address of a restaurant to the cabbie, who set off at a smart pace.

With any luck, Griffin wouldn't realize I had any feelings for him outside of simple friendship. And if he did…

Well. I would worry about the moment when it came. In the meantime, I would try to simply enjoy his company. If I could have nothing more than this, then I would cherish it for as long as it was in my possession.

But, God, I would miss him when the case ended, and there was no longer any reason for us to meet. That I could not deny.

A few hours later, a cab let us out a block away from our destination on the south side of the river. This section of town had long fallen from its glory. Most of the buildings were once fine houses, each several stories tall and set back from the street, surrounded by formal gardens and high brick walls. But those days had been a century ago; now, most were broken up into squalid tenements which made my poor apartment seem like a palace. The remaining private residences seemed to have taken on an oddly furtive air, lurking behind overgrown hedges and rusted gates, their windows covered with grime until they resembled cataract-stricken eyes.

It was not a place I would have ventured to on my own, certainly. As the carriage rolled away, I shifted my stance from foot to foot. "It's nearby, then?"

Griffin nodded. "Yes. The property is abandoned, at least according to city records. But I've found the official records in Widdershins seldom describe reality."

"Do any of them?" I asked wryly, expecting an answer about bureaucratic incompetence.

"Some." His brow furrowed. "Most, when compared to here."

The wind seemed to take on a colder edge, and I tugged my overcoat more tightly around me. "Is Widdershins very different?"

"Perhaps. Or perhaps I'm simply unused to New England ways." He thrust a hand into his pocket. "We should light our lanterns, as I don't think the street lamps will be of much help."

This I could do. Before he had the chance to pull out his matchbook, I whispered the secret name of fire. His police lantern caught flame.

Griffin let out a little hiss of alarm and almost dropped the lantern. "You might have warned me."

"Sorry," I said, a bit smugly.

He looked at the lantern, then at me, his expression somber. "Whyborne, promise me you'll be careful with anything you learn from that book."

I'd expected him to marvel at my accomplishment, and instead he chastised me. My heart sank, and I pressed my lips together tightly. "It's only a beginner's spell. Nothing with any real power."

"I know. But the man or men who wrote the book didn't necessarily have your best interests at heart. The Brotherhood has used it or something similar to do monstrous things."

"A gun can be used to defend or to murder," I said. Why had I expected a man of action such as him to praise my scholarship? "The things contained within the book are no different."

"Perhaps." He looked away, his shoulders slumping a fraction. "I'm not asking you to stop studying it. Just…be careful. For me."

My pulse quickened. For him? What did he mean by that? "What if I promise to ask your opinion before I undertake any more rituals or, er, spells from the book?"

He turned back to me, and his expression lightened. "That would set my mind at ease."

"Then I shall."

The lantern lit his face from beneath, giving it strange shadows. The flame I'd conjured reflected warmly in his eyes, drawing out hints of rust amid the green. I wished they were windows to the soul in truth, so I could look into them and know his thoughts.

Or did I? He seemed to be studying me with the same intensity. Did I want to know he reflected on my crooked nose, or my too-thin upper lip, or the way my hair insisted on sticking straight up no matter how I tried to tame it?

I bent my head and began to fumble with my lantern; he'd procured a replacement for the one I'd lost in the warehouse. "See? I'm using matches."

He cleared his throat. "Yes. Thank you, Whyborne. Shall we continue?"

CHAPTER 13

THE HOUSE HE led me to was the most ill-favored of the lot. A wall of crumbling brick surrounded it on three sides, while the back overlooked the Cranch River. At one time, perhaps, it had been a pleasant place to spend a summer day. Now even in winter the faint reek of sewage and dead fish wafted from the water. In July the stench must be appalling.

The rusted gate was held in place by a suspiciously-new padlock. I expected Griffin to employ his lock picks, but instead he led the way past the gate and into a narrow lane, which separated the property from its neighbor. No lights showed in any of the houses, and no footsteps marred the thin layer of snow in the lane.

We came to a place where the upper portion of the wall had been knocked away, perhaps due to a fallen branch. "Can you climb?" Griffin asked.

I stared up at the wall. Although the missing bricks lowered its height slightly, it might as well have been a hundred feet tall. "No." I couldn't look at him. "I don't believe I can."

"Let me give you a boost," he said, unperturbed. Dropping to one knee, he cupped both hands in front of him.

Not at all sure this would work, I nevertheless set aside my lantern. Taking a deep breath, I put one foot in his hands, and did my best to push off with the other.

I ended up with my arms sprawled over the wall, the edge of the mortar digging into my breastbone, and a bruise on my chin where I'd clipped the brick. Somehow, I managed to get a leg over the wall and scramble around sideways.

"Here," Griffin whispered from below, and passed up first one lantern, then the other.

I set them on top of the wall, then more or less fell off onto the other side. A moment later, Griffin passed the lanterns down, then hopped to the ground beside me, his overcoat flaring around him.

We stood on what had once been a lawn, now filled with the dry, dead stalks of weeds and brambles. The hedge bordering the drive was vastly overgrown, and some of the shrubs planted near the house were tall enough to obscure the windows. The house itself had once been grand, before slowly settling into ruin. From the outside, at least, it did not look as if anyone had been there in a very long time. But the padlock had been fresh; that alone suggested some recent activity.

A few flakes of snow fluttered down from the sky. The night seemed very dark, the stars and moon covered over by heavy clouds. The air had grown bitterly cold, excoriating my lungs with every breath. I should have worn a warmer hat.

We made our way across the yard, our shoes crunching softly in dead weeds and snow. My imagination insisted the unkempt bushes were actually the twisted shapes of Guardians, just lying in wait for us. Griffin led the way slowly around the house, as if studying it from all angles. Eventually, we circled around to the front. There were no prints to be seen in the snow covering the drive, thank goodness. If this site was used by the Brotherhood, it didn't seem to be occupied at the moment.

"What do you expect to find here?" I asked, keeping my voice low just in case.

"I'm not entirely certain," he murmured back. "Madam Rosa told me Philip Rice was seen a few days before his murder in the company of one Buckeye Jim, a notorious river rat."

"Odd company for the son of a wealthy industrialist."

"Quite. Some further inquiries showed Buckeye hasn't been seen in his usual haunts as of late, but instead has taken employment of some sort, which apparently includes the delivery of large numbers of cattle and goats to somewhere along this stretch of the river."

I looked around. "Cattle and goats? *Here?*" Even in its rundown condition, this was a residential area, without the space to keep a herd of any sort.

Griffin nodded. "I had the same thought. Earlier today, I took out a boat. It probably wasn't obvious to you in the dark, but there is a path beaten along the back of the property to a large cellar door, as if a number of animals had been herded along it."

"And where are they now?" I asked, although my mouth had gone dry. "Surely they couldn't be kept inside the house, could they?"

Griffin shook his head grimly. "No. They couldn't."

My skin crawled, and I tried not to think what might have happened to the cattle, or what we might find inside. "The *Arcanorum* suggests the Guardians have great appetites for raw flesh."

He was close enough I sensed a shiver pass over him. "Under the circumstances, I can't say I'm happy to hear that."

I rather understood how he felt. "Shall we enter through the back?"

"No."

"No?"

Griffin's breath steamed in the frigid air. "Hopefully any evidence of the Brotherhood's intentions will be in the more hospitable part of the house, such as it might be."

"But we'll have to look in the basement eventually."

"Perhaps." Why did he sound reluctant?

He led the way up the drive and onto the porch. The snow had begun to fall in earnest now; with any luck, it would continue throughout the night, and obscure our tracks so no one would be any the wiser as to our visit. Griffin started to reach into his coat, presumably for his lock picks, then changed his mind and tried the door instead.

It opened easily. Someone had oiled the hinges in the not-too-distant past, for there was no accompanying creak such as one might expect from an old house.

We exchanged a glance. We didn't have to speak to know that neither of us liked this conveniently-unlocked door.

But like it or not, we had to investigate. Griffin drew his revolver and held it ready in his hand as we stepped inside.

The light from our lanterns revealed a hall running the length of the building. A few pictures had once hung on the walls, but they were now on the floor, the glass broken and the frames curiously gnawed. A wide doorway on the right led to a parlor, where lurked shrouded furniture, as if the original owner had intended to return some day.

The house stank of mildew and stale air, underlain with the cloying sweetness of rot. No doubt mice had died in the walls…but great numbers of cattle had presumably disappeared into the cellar. There was no stink of manure or of penned animals, but rather something far more fetid.

I left the door open behind me; the idea of a quick avenue of retreat appealed. Griffin glanced back but made no objection.

Old cobwebs hung from the corners and ceiling, but the dust on the floor had been disturbed by many comings and goings. Griffin stepped into the parlor and scanned the room carefully. A gas lamp jutted out from the wall near the door; he reached over and turned the valve. The hiss of escaping gas rewarded him.

"Do you think it likely the gas company forgot to turn it off when the house was abandoned?" I asked, as he shut it off.

"Not really."

The wind rose outside, and snow swirled more violently against the great bay window overlooking the lawn. The beams groaned in response, but beneath the sound, there was an odd scraping, as of something large being dragged over a hard floor.

"Did you hear that?" I whispered.

"The wind?"

"No." But now I was no longer certain. "Perhaps."

Griffin led the way back out into the hall. The kitchen was unremarkable, and seemed not to have been used in decades. Mirrors once hung on the walls of the dining room, but they were all smashed into fragments, which glittered in the light of our lanterns.

We made our way upstairs, the steps creaking beneath our feet. Two of the rooms were completely empty, and the third had only the same sheet-covered furniture as the parlor downstairs.

"I suppose it's the basement, then," I said, as we went back down the steps. We'd seen the door to the cellar in the kitchen, but hadn't opened it.

Griffin drew a deep breath and let it out forcefully; it steamed in the frigid air. "I suppose."

I drew close and noted how pale he looked. Was he ill? "Are you all right?"

"I'm fine." Then he let out a resigned sigh. "Actually, no. I don't care for underground spaces."

"Claustrophobic, are you?" He'd entrusted me with his weakness, and I wanted him to know I sympathized. "I understand. I don't care for water, myself." The thought of setting foot on a boat made my skin crawl; I wasn't even fond of going over bridges. Not anymore, at least. "I hope visiting my office hasn't put you out terribly?"

"What? Oh, no. Not at all." He straightened self-consciously. "There's nothing for it. Let's…let's go to the basement."

I took the lead, hoping it might make things a bit easier for him. Once again, the door was unlocked, and the hinges moved more silently than might have been expected.

I paused at the top of the short flight of stairs and shone my lantern around. The basement was dark and dank, just like most cellars. Built into the steep hillside carved by the river, its wide door must open onto the back. Surely any cattle were driven inside here.

So where were they now?

I cautiously began to descend the steps. Griffin remained at the top of the stair, the beam of his police lantern sweeping the confines of the room. The walls appeared to be rough stone, but the floor was concrete, no doubt a newer addition.

In the center of the floor was a trapdoor. All around it were chalked symbols and circles, many of which I recognized from the *Arcanorum*.

My skin crawled, and not just from the icy air of the basement. Griffin came down one step, then another, then stopped.

"We have to go down." His voice was hollow, like something from a grave.

"No." I shook my head and backed up a slow step, then another, until I was abreast of him. "No. Something isn't right here."

"What do you mean?"

"The symbols, the chalk…nothing is smudged. The way one would expect if there had actually been a ritual performed." I glanced at him. "And if you had this entire house to yourself, would you do a complicated ritual down in the dark basement? Or on the upper floor, in a spacious room, with gaslight to see by?"

His eyes widened in alarm. "Oh hell. This is a trap, isn't it?"

From above our heads came the sound of the front door slamming. I jumped—then jumped again when it was answered by the opening of the trapdoor below us.

A suffocating cloud of stench rolled out of the open trapdoor: wet fur, mildew, fish slime, and above all the putrescence of rotting flesh. A swarm of horrors boiled out behind it, every one of them howling like damned souls vomited up from the bowels of Tartarus itself. Guardians, in every shape and form madness could conceive: hybrid monsters mixing reptile, amphibian, and mammal with the shapes of men, side-by-side with things which had once been human, but were now shockingly, hideously *incomplete.*

My muscles froze in place, my brain scrambling to categorize these things even as they loped and crawled and flopped up out of the basement. Their suffocating stench burned my nose and throat, and I clutched dizzily at the stair rail.

"Run!" Griffin shouted. He seized my coat, and hauled me up with him, even as the first of the Guardians reached the bottommost step.

My paralysis broke. Griffin and I stumbled out of the basement; I slammed the door and threw the bolt. It wouldn't hold them long.

We ran out of the kitchen and down the hall; from behind us came a storm of insane howls, accompanied by the heavy crash of bodies against the fragile wood. The front door was shut, and for a moment I prayed the wind had simply blown it thus.

Griffin seized the doorknob, but it refused to turn. "Damn it!"

"Just unlock it!"

"I can't! It's been jammed shut!"

The sound of splintering wood came from the kitchen, accompanied by howls of triumph. "Come on," Griffin commanded.

He led the way into the parlor, just as the first of the Guardians emerged into the hall. The sight of them seemed to thicken the blood in my veins. There were too many—how could we hope to evade them?

"Close the door!" Griffin ordered as he ran into the parlor. I followed him, shutting the door behind us—and was knocked aside as a Guardian hit the wood from the other side at the same moment.

I went to the floor. The abomination loomed above me: it looked to have been made from two separate men, their faces half-fused together into a distorted mass of two mouths, two noses, and three eyes. Multiple arms flailed at me, and bile burned my throat as I scrambled back across the dusty floor.

Griffin's revolver roared, and the Guardian jerked back. It started to howl—then abruptly collapsed into the same gray-blue dust as the one in the museum.

More of them forced their way through the door. Griffin kept shooting, emptying his revolver. "Whyborne! The window!" he shouted, drawing his sword cane. "Get out!"

A half-crocodile Guardian lunged at him. He ducked aside, and it struck the gaslight with such force the lamp sheered off. Gas jetted out of the broken pipe with a loud hiss.

I ran to the bay window. Whipping the cover off a smallish chair, I heaved it with all my strength, through the window in a shower of broken glass and snapped wood. Snow swirled in, along with a blast of frigid air.

I turned back. Griffin battled the monsters with his sword cane, his overcoat swirling around him, his lips drawn back from his teeth in a grim expression.

"Griffin! Come on!"

"Go!" he shouted over his shoulder. The Guardian lunged at him, all snapping teeth, and my heart skipped a beat, certain its jaws were about to close on his arm. In a quick move, he kicked it in the gut, shoving it into its fellows, where they formed a scrum in the doorway. The one beside it seemed to perceive an attack; it turned with a wet snarl and bit the first creature savagely.

"Damn it!" I ran back to Griffin, taking advantage of the few seconds of space the struggle brought. Before he could lunge at the creatures with his sword cane, I seized him by the arm and pulled him in the direction of the window. "Move!"

"I told you to run!" he exclaimed, as we both pelted back toward the window.

"I ignored you. By the way, I'm about to use the fire spell."

"What—?"

I stopped just in front of the broken window. The Guardians had recovered; the crocodilian one lay slumped on its side, panting miserably in a pool of thin blood. As their hungry, mad eyes turned on me, I knew exactly how the rabbit feels before the pack of hounds.

Griffin's arms wrapped around me, dragging me backward, but I kept my gaze focused on the air beside the Guardians as I whispered the ritual words.

Then we were falling backward out the window, even as the cloud of gas escaping from the broken pipe ignited.

CHAPTER 14

THE EXPLOSION WAS deafening; a huge cloud of fire rolled out the window after us, its immense heat brushing against my face as we tumbled into the snow.

We hit the ground and rolled. Flaming debris from the house came down around us; Griffin shoved me flat on my back, covering us both with his heavy coat.

The echoes of the explosion reflected back across the river, then slowly dwindled away, like dying thunder. The leaping flames threw warm light onto the falling snow, turning it into a storm of sparks pouring down from the heavens.

Griffin started to push himself off of me, then stopped. His hands were braced to either side of my shoulders, his legs twined with mine. My heart pounded, my palms sweated, and I was suddenly, acutely aware of how close his face was to mine.

"You're a madman," he whispered. "An utter madman."

"Perhaps," I allowed. "But it worked."

The leaping light from the burning house painted his features in gold, highlighting his patrician nose and finding the threads of brown and blue in his green eyes. His pupils widened, the irises contracting to slivers. "Whatever am I to do with you?" he murmured.

The warmth of his breath feathered over my skin. Heat collected in my groin, my lips. My mouth was dry, my voice hoarse, and perhaps he was right and it was madness when I whispered, "Whatever you want."

A shiver went through his body, perhaps because we were lying on the cold ground. But instead of getting up, he leaned closer, his overlong hair tumbling over his forehead. He paused, his mouth almost touching mine, his eyes seeming to ask a question.

It was madness; it was folly; it was sheer selfishness. I was delusional, misguided, wrong, out of control. I needed to pull back, to say something sane, to re-establish mastery over myself. I could not do this. I could not take this risk.

Later tonight, I'd relive this moment in my lonely bed and wonder if I'd done the right thing. But at least that would be familiar, would be something I knew how to cope with.

And yet the very thought felt like dying.

I surged forward, crossing the final, tiny gap and pressing my lips to his. It was awkward and desperate and frantic, but the feel of his mouth against mine sent a bolt of electricity straight down my spine. Just a moment, just this one kiss, surely that would be enough…

Then he kissed me back, and it would never be enough, a thousand years of this would not be enough. His mouth was hungry and insistent, his tongue probing my lips, asking for greater intimacy. I granted it, tongues swirling together, mine following his when it retreated and tasting him in return.

There came the clanging of bells in the distance, the fire company alerted to the explosion. Griffin drew back a fraction. His breath was as ragged as mine, which left me dazed with wonder.

"My dear," he whispered against my lips. Then he swallowed convulsively. "We should leave, before the fire companies come."

"Y-Yes." It was amazing I managed that much coherence.

He closed his eyes and leaned his forehead against mine, our breaths mingling. "Will you come home with me?"

Was he asking…? "Yes." Oh, God, yes.

His lips curved into a smile. Then he was on his feet, reaching down to help me up.

I took his hand; he hauled me up, shook the snow from his trousers, then scooped my hat from the ground and handed it to me. "We'd best go along the river," he said. "Otherwise, I fear we'll walk right into the fire companies and the police, who might have some awkward questions to ask."

I nodded dumbly. He headed to the riverbank, and I followed, shivering in the lack of his warmth.

We walked along the river for a distance, skirting houses both inhabited and not. When the glow from the fire grew faint against the low clouds, Griffin led the way down an alley, then along the street, where he hailed a cab.

We climbed in and sat beside each other. I clasped my hands between my knees, unsure what to do. What did he expect from me? We were in a public conveyance. It would be foolish to make any overtly affectionate gestures even in the dark…wouldn't it?

Griffin settled back against the seat, apparently at ease. "You were very clever," he said.

Did he expect me to be as casual? He was no doubt a man of the world, whereas I was anything but. "Wh-what?" I asked, then cursed myself for stuttering.

"With the gas," he clarified. His mouth pressed into a thin line at the memory. "I wouldn't have thought of it."

I shrugged awkwardly and looked away. "I couldn't simply flee. And I'm not…well. I can't fire a gun, or use a sword cane, or box, or anything really useful."

"Don't be ridiculous. You saved our lives. Not to mention you were the one who realized it was a trap."

Was this really what he wanted to speak of? What if I had mistaken his intent? What if he had invited me back to his home to review the case, not to do anything more intimate?

Fortunately, it wasn't long before we arrived in front of Griffin's house. My stomach roiled as the cab clattered away: I couldn't quite tell if it was from anticipation or nausea. My mouth felt dry, and my palms sweaty.

Griffin, on the other hand, seemed perfectly at ease as he unlocked the gate and led the way to his porch. Saul awaited us there, sitting tucked back from the snow, his ears flattened grouchily.

"Poor Saul," Griffin crooned, pausing to pat his head. Saul meowed imperiously and went to the door, pressing his face into the crack until it opened.

"Come in," Griffin said; perhaps he imagined I needed the encouragement. Perhaps I *did* need the encouragement. "Do you mind reviving the fire in the study upstairs while I feed Saul?"

"Of course not," I said, glad to have something familiar to do. While he followed the orange tabby to the kitchen, I went up the stair and into the study.

The fire was well-banked; I knelt down in front of it and stoked the embers, adding a few logs, until the flames snapped and popped cheerfully. Snow built up against the windows; it would be hard for me to get home if it kept up this way.

I could still do the sensible thing and scurry back to my apartment while the weather allowed. But I couldn't forget the kiss. The way Griffin pressed against me, the way he made my heart pound and my thoughts scatter…

…Was dangerous. I'd spent so many years in control, never yielding, and yet he walked into my life and suddenly I had no will to resist the desire enflaming my skin and stiffening my groin. The high wall I'd built around me had fallen, and I didn't even know if I wanted it back.

Footsteps sounded on the stair behind me. I climbed to my feet and stood staring at the fire, not quite daring to turn around.

"Would you like something to drink?" he asked.

I considered it, but after my disgrace on Sunday, I couldn't bring myself to risk it. "No. Thank you."

He came up behind me, pausing only scant inches away. My body trembled from his nearness, and my lips ached with the need to be kissed again. What would he do? Would he touch me?

His breath stirred the small hairs at the nape of my neck. "Have you ever been with a man?"

I wanted to laugh; surely he was being generous. "No. I-I've never even been kissed before." He might as well know what he was getting into.

He drew in a soft sip of breath, and I braced myself for mockery. "Truly?" he murmured, sounding awed. "Am I really the first to look beneath the cold exterior and see the passion seething within?"

I closed my eyes. His description had nothing to do with me; it couldn't. "I don't know what you mean."

He chuckled softly, and a shiver ghosted over my skin, because he still touched me only with his breath. "Don't you? You blind me, my dear, with your fire. Carefully controlled, directed only into the outlets you allow, but otherwise left to boil beneath the surface. You're like a bottle of fine champagne, yearning to be opened. Year after year, the pressure building slowly, with no release. And ever since I met you, all I could think was what it would take to make…you… pop."

A groan escaped me as I turned to him, my lips seeking his even as his arms twined around me. He had removed his suit coat and tie, and the heat of his body soaked through the fabric of his shirtsleeves. He kissed me deeply, before pulling back and nipping at my lower lip, then plunging in again.

He went to his knees on the carpet, pulling me down to straddle his lap. My hardened member pressed against one equally as stiff, and I gasped at the sheer eroticism of it. To know he wanted me the way I wanted him, to feel the exquisite pleasure of pressing my erection against his and know he experienced the same, was more than I had ever imagined, and I clung to him helplessly.

He shoved my coat impatiently off my shoulders, and I let it fall, beyond caring whether it became creased or not. He pulled away just far enough to fumble at the buttons of my waistcoat, before stripping it off and attacking the rest of my clothing. His lips were like fire against the skin of my throat; I arched my head back to give him access.

His kisses fell on my skin like rain on drought-stricken ground, soaking up every caress and thirsting for more. He pulled up my undershirt, sliding his hands over the exposed skin of my sides, every finger a brand against me.

Griffin paused, a shudder going through him as he mastered himself. "Is this what you want?" he whispered, his lips moving against the sensitive spot between my neck and shoulder. "If this is too much, too soon, we'll stop."

I shook my head frantically. "No, please, I-I want this." If he rejected me now, I'd shatter into a million pieces.

He moved—and suddenly I found myself on my back in front of the fire, with Griffin above me. His eyes were dark with lust, his kiss-swollen lips parted. "As you like," he murmured, then bent his head to my chest, closing his mouth around one nipple.

I gasped and arched my back, my fingers digging helplessly into his shoulders. Dear lord! He sucked hard, then nibbled lightly, and every touch of his lips sent a wave of heat straight to my groin. Suitably encouraged by my moans, he worked his way down, kissing and licking over my ribs to my belly, until he came to my trousers.

The brush of his hand across the cloth tented over my erection made me twitch. I clenched helplessly at the rug as he undid the buttons and slid his hand inside to free me. The touch of his fingers was nearly my undoing. I closed my eyes and fought for control as he drew my length out.

"Mmm." His breath brushed against my member and I let out an involuntary whimper. "Have you really been hiding this fellow away? What a tragedy."

There was no possible response. I settled for whimpering instead.

"Look at me," he commanded, his fingers closing around the base of my shaft. Unable to gainsay him, I did as he asked. He was on his knees between my legs, his head bent low. My aching member jutted at him obscenely, the length flushed dark with desire, the sensitive tip of the glans protruding past the hood, a pearl of moisture gathered on the slit.

Without breaking eye contact, he lowered his head and flicked out his tongue. I let out a gasp, my hips jerking involuntarily. "Please..."

He gave me a sultry smile. "Please what?"

I could barely think, let alone speak. "I-I can't—"

Mercifully, he didn't press the issue. Instead, his hand slid up the length of my shaft, then wrapped around it, gently retracting the hood, a moment before his mouth closed around me.

Yes. God, yes! His mouth felt warm and hot and wet. All of my defenses were stripped away by the wave of exquisite pleasure. His lips slid down my length, sucking hard, then drew back, and there was no possible way I could stand another repetition.

My back arched, and I pushed at him blindly, trying to get him off before I lost all control. But he slid all the way down again, *moaning*, and it was the end of me. My scrotum tightened, and a wave of white-hot pleasure pooled at the base of my member, surging up and out as I spent myself into his mouth.

He gently let my softening length slip from his mouth, before stretching out beside me while my breathing slowed. His lips were slick with my spend when I turned my face to accept the kiss he offered. I expected to be repulsed by the taste of myself in his mouth, but it proved oddly erotic.

His eyes were still dark with desire, his cheeks flushed and his member hard as he pressed against my hip. "Come to bed?" he asked.

I licked my lips and nodded. "Yes."

He took my hand and led me to the bedroom. My other hand was occupied with keeping my trousers from falling down about my ankles. The bedroom was cold, and I winced in anticipation of icy sheets—although no doubt they would warm up quickly with Griffin beside me. He turned to me beside the bed and pulled me close, kissing me deep. I let go of my trousers to return his embrace, and they slipped away, leaving behind only drawers, which he divested me of quickly enough. His hands shaped my buttocks, pulling me tight to him.

When our mouths parted again, I set myself to the buttons of his vest, wanting nothing more than to feel the burn of his skin on mine. My hands shook, making me even more clumsy than usual. He didn't seem to mind, shedding his clothing as I worked through the layers. A light dusting of hair covered his broad chest, and a darker trail led from his navel down, to disappear beneath his trousers.

He was handsome as a Grecian statue, his body strong and nicely muscled. A strange scar wrapped around his right thigh; the skin there looked almost melted, as if he had been splashed by acid.

I forgot about the scar at the sight of his member: thick and well-formed as the rest of him, the hood drawn back and the tip glistening with liquid. My greedy length stood up again at the sight.

What if he thought me a sex fiend?

Fortunately, he seemed to approve of my renewed passion. He eyes roved over me, and he licked his lips, before swallowing thickly. "How I want you, my dear."

"I'm yours," I whispered, kissing him.

He threw back the covers on his bed and pulled me down into it with him. The feel of his skin on mine, with nothing separating us, drew an involuntarily groan from me. "Tell me what to do," I begged.

"What do you *want* to do?"

I didn't know what to say, what to ask. Seeing my uncertainty, his smile took on a slight wryness, and he cupped my face in his hands. "There's no wrong answer," he said gently. "There's nothing to fear."

Of course there was: failure, disappointment, my own poor judgment. But it was hard to remember that when he pressed his body against mine, his length hard and hot against my stomach, his mouth at my ear whispering: "Tell me what you ache for. Tell me what has kept you awake at night, alone and yearning in your bed. Show me the secret fire in your heart."

"Let me touch you," I panted. "Please."

He rolled onto his back, his eyes smoldering along with his smile. "Have your way with me, then."

CHAPTER 15

I ROLLED ON top of him, kissing him fiercely, before trailing my lips down his throat. His skin tasted salty, and his masculine scent fired my nerves. His chest invited exploration, and I ran my hands over the finely-sculpted muscles, over the little buds of nipples. He sighed in pleasure when I touched them, so I bent and kissed the one, then the other.

"Yes." He arched against me. "Use your teeth."

A gasp and a twitch of his member were my rewards. I kissed and licked and nipped my way down, making him jump once or twice when I found unexpectedly sensitive places. I wanted to explore every inch of his skin; I wanted to learn everything he liked.

His member distracted me from the task; hard and leaking with need, it bobbed and twitched in response to my mouth on his belly, as if asking for attention. I sat back and ran my fingers up and down the shaft, exploring.

"Mmm, yes," he gasped, his hips jerking slightly against me, as if he couldn't keep still.

My mouth watered, and I licked my lips nervously. "May I…?"

"Do you want to suck my cock?"

Stupidly, his language made me blush, even though I was on my knees between his legs, naked and erect, having already spent myself into his mouth. "Y-Yes."

"Then do, or else you'll have me begging."

I wanted to devour him like a starving man, but somehow I held back, tasting him with my tongue, lapping up the liquid seeping from his slit, swirling around the head, sucking lightly on the hood.

"My dear, please," he whimpered, his hips flexing again. "Before you drive me mad!"

I closed my mouth around him, careful of my teeth. I tried to take the thick column of flesh entirely, as he had with me, but the brush of the head against the back of my mouth almost had me gagging. "I'm sorry," I said, after I'd hastily drawn back.

He shook his head. "Don't be. What you're doing feels wonderful."

Wanting to give him as much pleasure as I could, I wrapped my hand around the base of his member and put my mouth to work on the upper part. His moans and pants were encouraging, even interrupted with the occasional "more tongue—oh!" or "less teeth."

Eventually, he reached down and tugged me away. "Kiss me," he said breathlessly.

I kissed him, and he rolled me onto my side, so we lay facing each other. Our lengths rubbed together, and I let out a small gasp at the sensation. To know he was hard, needy, for *me*, to feel his erection against my own, was powerfully arousing.

He flung one leg over my hip, rubbing his full length against me. "My dear," he whispered, but anything further seemed beyond him.

"Yes." I gripped his shoulders with my hands and thrust against him.

A shiver ran across his skin in response, and a sigh escaped him. One of his hands curled around both our lengths, and his leg tightened over my hip, as if seeking to draw us even closer. We writhed against one another, pushing and rubbing and thrusting, until suddenly his body stiffened, his member twitching against mine.

"Yes, yes, please, Ival, yes—"

Hot semen jetted out against my belly, even as his face contorted with ecstasy. And, oh God, I had done this to him, *me*, and I couldn't possibly hold back any longer, body tightening and a second surge of pleasure pulsing through my member, even as I shuddered and whimpered and bit at the smooth skin of his shoulder.

Eventually, my mind pieced itself back together from the shattering ecstasy. We lay curled together, his leg still loose across my hip, our mingled spend cooling on our bellies. His breathing was ragged from exertion, as was mine. His eyes were closed, his forehead pressed to my shoulder.

What was the etiquette of the situation? Was I to thank him, gather up my things, and leave? Yet again, I had no idea what he might expect from me.

As if he'd heard my thoughts, he nuzzled his lips against my skin. "Stay the night?"

My heart gave a happy little lurch in my chest. "Yes. If it's not inconvenient."

He chuckled warmly. "You are anything but an inconvenience, my dear."

I liked hearing him call me that. But it brought up a question I couldn't hold back. "When you, er, you called me…"

He drew back, and to my astonishment, a light blush spread across his cheeks. "You said you didn't like Percival or Percy, and Whyborne seemed terribly formal for the throes of passion. I thought perhaps you wouldn't mind Ival too much. If you hate it, of course, I won't—"

"No, not at all." But it didn't sound as if he'd invented it on the spot. "Do you mean to imply you've been contemplating what to call me in the 'throes of passion,' as you put it?"

He laughed, but it seemed directed at himself. "Well, yes. I had to have something to call you when I dreamed about having you in my bed."

Did he mean to say he'd imagined this? Perhaps even brought himself to release thinking about me? Even as spent as I was, my member gave a twitch.

"Me? "I asked, baffled. "Why me?"

"Because I want you," he said simply.

"Then why… the other night, after we went to the brothel…you didn't…I mean, you might have…"

He propped himself up on an elbow, looking down at me quizzically. "You were *drunk*, Whyborne. I couldn't have lived with myself if I'd taken advantage."

Oh. "I thought you hated me," I confessed.

He collapsed beside me again with a sound halfway between a sigh and a laugh. "Why on earth would you think such a thing? I didn't hate you, and indeed I felt rather guilty for being as tempted as I was. And if you must ask 'why' again, as I suspect you will, then because I preferred to have you in my bed because you wished to be there, not because you were too drunk to know any better."

I could hardly argue with such a sentiment. Still, it made me feel warm, all the way down to my toes. "I'm glad," I said softly.

He glanced at me, and whatever he saw in my face made him smile. "As am I."

His body fit snugly against mine, his head resting on my shoulder, one arm tossed across my chest and his legs tangled with mine. I closed my eyes, thinking this couldn't possibly be true. I'd wake tomorrow in my lonely little bed, with nothing but my drab, colorless existence around me. Griffin's presence in my life would have been a dream altogether, something I longed for but could never have.

He let out a little sigh of contentment, and his arm tightened around me as sleep claimed him. I turned my head just enough to press my lips against his forehead, and silently strove to memorize the smell of his skin, the weight of his limbs.

Outside, the snow piled up against the windows, but our bed was warm and safe. Holding Griffin against me, I let myself slip away into sated sleep.

I slept poorly, mainly because I was unused to sharing a bed with another. Every time Griffin shifted or snored or rolled over, I awoke with a jolt. At some point during the night, Saul wandered in, and, finding his master's bed otherwise occupied, curled up at our feet and began to purr. It would have been soothing, if he hadn't chosen to change position every ten minutes.

I finally fell into a deep sleep some time shortly before dawn. When I at last awoke, my first groggy thought was it all must have been a dream. But I was naked under the sheets, a state I had never before slept in, and the scent on the pillow beneath my cheek was of Griffin's shampoo.

I opened my eyes and blinked a few times. Griffin was no longer beneath the covers with me; instead, he sat on the edge of the bed, fully dressed, one hand resting lightly on my leg.

There was a damp patch on my pillow; I'd been drooling. Hoping he hadn't noticed, I sat up, pulling the covers with me to keep out the cold air, and to keep from revealing my nakedness. Not that he hadn't already seen all I had to offer, but it put me at a bit of a disadvantage, sitting there without a stitch of clothing, while he wore everything but his suit coat.

"Good morning," he said with a warm smile. "I was just going down to make breakfast. Would you like something? I have eggs and cold cereal."

We'd just spent the night together: was I supposed to acknowledge it at all? Pretend it had never happened? Kiss him?

"Breakfast sounds wonderful," I said.

He took his hand away from my leg, and his expression grew more guarded. "Is everything all right?"

I'd given away my anxiety. "Er, yes, at least I think it is. I haven't looked out the window, but I suppose the world continues apace? And you seem to be in good health, and reasonably cheerful, so…perhaps?"

He stared at me for a moment, before tossing back his head and laughing. "My dear Whyborne, every time I think I know what's going on in that head of yours, you manage to utterly confound me."

Oh. He'd thought my fears more commonplace ones. "Forgive me, I… everything is fine. I have no regrets about last night."

His laughter trailed off into a wicked grin, and his hand strayed back to my knee. "I'm very glad to hear it. Perhaps you would consent to a repeat performance?"

My length showed its approval by rapidly forming a tent in the covers. Griffin's smile grew wider at the sight, even as my face heated. What must he think of my complete lack of control?

"Would you be so kind as to pass me my drawers?" I asked. Still grinning, he did so, and then watched as I readied myself for the day. Had he dressed first and quietly as a way of steeling himself against rejection, should I harbor regrets or shame about our actions? Certainly it would be easier to take such a thing dressed and at a distance, instead of naked in bed with the fellow. But someone as accomplished, worldly, and handsome as Griffin would have no fear of rejection from, well, someone like me, so that couldn't be it.

"Will you tell me why you expected disaster, simply because you lost control over your passions?" he asked, as I knotted my tie.

I hesitated. What would he think of me, when he heard my story? Would he regret sleeping with me?

"There was a boy," I said at last. "A dear friend. Leander Somerby. He was two years older than me, the son of my godfather. Our fathers were great friends from their school days. I knew him my entire life."

I paused, but Griffin only said, "Go on," in a gentle tone I didn't deserve.

I drew a deep breath, struggling to steady the beating of my heart and the sourness rising in my stomach. "We grew up together, more or less. We explored the bounds of Somerby Estate every chance we got: wading through its streams, riding through its fields, and skipping stones across the lake behind the house."

Griffin smiled. "I must confess, I rather imagined you were the sort of boy to be happier reading indoors than running about outside."

"Yes, well, you have the right of it for the most part," I admitted. Would he think less of me for it? "Leander was always the leader in our exploits. Left to my own devices, I would have chosen the library."

"I see."

"One spring, Leander became convinced someone was performing blasphemous rituals on the island in the center of the lake. It was boyish nonsense, of course, but reading too much wild fiction had fired our imaginations. It seemed to have all the makings of a grand adventure.

"Leander came up with a plan. We would take his boat out on Walpurgisnacht—May Eve, the so-called witches sabbath—which seemed a natural time for any evil-doers to return to the island. He dreamed of the praise we would receive, having thus proved ourselves men. As for me, I imagined crouching in the little boat beside him, huddled under a blanket to hide ourselves from any observers, our thighs pressed together in the close quarters."

"Heh." Griffin's smile hinted at memories of his own. "And rather more than that, I assume."

"You assume correctly." What a young fool I had been. "When the night finally came, it was nothing like my fevered dreams. A storm arose with the sunset. Rain and wind lashed the lake into a cauldron of thrashing water, and lightning danced off the surrounding hilltops.

"I should never have agreed to go out on such a night. It was madness, and I knew it. But I didn't want him to be angry, or to scorn me for a coward. I wanted him to l-love me as I loved h-him."

The smile vanished from Griffin's face. Moving to my side, he put a hand to my shoulder. "What happened?"

"Disaster, of course. The boat capsized." I rubbed at my arms, trying to warm them. God, the water had been cold. "I managed to get the boat turned back over, with me in it, more by luck than anything else. Leander didn't have enough strength left to pull himself back in, though. I grabbed his hands, but the cold…I could barely feel my fingers even though I'd only been in the water a few minutes. I-I hung on for as long as I could, but…The last I saw of him was his pale face, staring up at me in despair as the water closed over him."

Griffin put his arms around me, pulling me against his chest. "I don't recall anything else until waking up in bed with pneumonia," I said. "Uncle Addison had pulled me out of the boat, unconscious and cold as death. Th-they had to drag the bottom to find Leander."

"The blame isn't yours," Griffin murmured against my hair.

"If I hadn't loved him, if I hadn't *wanted* him, I would never have gone along with his scheme. I might have talked him out of it, or at least not been so desperate to-to prove myself to him. I couldn't let it happen again, so I tried not to think of, er, such things. To remain in control."

His arms were warm around me. "What changed your mind?"

"I didn't," I admitted. "But it seems there is something about you I find irresistible."

"Careful: your compliments will go to my head."

Perhaps I owed him the truth. "Your kindness," I said, not daring to look at him.

He regarded me with a mixture of warmth and puzzlement. "I don't understand."

"You're…well. You're an ex-Pinkerton. You foil bank robberies and chase down outlaws, and carry revolvers and a sword cane, for God's sake. And you would have been far above me even if you were hideous, but of course you had to be terribly handsome on top of everything else, and-and I assumed you would be condescending, or cruel. A situation I know how to handle. But you weren't, you were kind. You didn't laugh at me, and you didn't act like I was useless, even when I behaved foolishly. How could I defend myself?"

Dear heavens, how pathetic. I twisted my hands together and hoped the floor might open up beneath me.

His hands twined around mine, stilling them. I stared at the buttons of his vest, breathing in the smell of sandalwood. "I haven't had much of any schooling, you know," he said, apropos of nothing. "I grew up on the Kansas prairie, where the orphan train left me. There was a small schoolhouse with a few books, where I learned to read and do sums, but little else. Once I arrived in Chicago, I taught myself to speak and dress properly, and copied the manners of wealthier men until I made those manners my own. I read as often as I have free time, but I must admit to preferring novels to scientific treatises. How do you think I felt, going to the museum with the object of asking help from a man with a *real* job, who could speak a dozen languages—"

"Thirteen. But I can read more."

He laughed. "Thirteen languages and can read more, *and* is the son of a railroad magnate to boot—"

"That doesn't matter," I objected.

"My point is you were raised with manners and books and servants, while I was hitching mules and milking cows. I was intimidated; I rather worried you'd sneer at me, and was very grateful when you didn't."

"Oh," I said. Griffin, intimidated by me? Even given his reasoning, it seemed ludicrous.

He brushed a kiss across my lips, there and gone before I could gather myself to respond. "Come now, my dear. Let's have breakfast."

"Yes." There was a golden bubble in my chest, pushing out against my ribs. "Thank you for being patient with me."

His smile turned the gloomy morning to pure sunshine. "You're worth it."

CHAPTER 16

THE SNOW OF last night had piled up in deep drifts all around the house. "At least my absence at the Ladysmith this morning won't be remarked on," I said, peering out a window while Griffin enthusiastically scrambled eggs. "Not to suggest it would be otherwise."

"I thought the Ladysmith was a well-oiled machine, every cog working together to make it 'the best' museum in America," he remarked, in a fair imitation of the director's voice.

"More like a cabinet of curiosities—the staff, that is, not the museum." I returned to the kitchen and sat down at the small table. There was a larger dining room, but I preferred this more intimate setting. It reminded me of all the meals I'd had with Miss Emily, when the rest of the family had been too busy for me. "The museum's philosophy is to leave us alone to encourage our brilliance, which actually does produce results for the most part. The downside is, I could probably expire from a gas leak in my office, and if Christine were in the field, no one would notice for weeks."

"You and Dr. Putnam are good friends?" Griffin asked. Although his tone was studiedly casual, he seemed to be giving the eggs far more attention than they required.

"She's my only friend, besides you, I suppose. I would say she's like a sister to me, except I was never at all close with my older sister."

Was it my imagination, or did Griffin's shoulders relax just a fraction? Certainly he seemed less intent on the eggs. "She seems very…driven."

"She knew what she wanted from life, and she took it," I said, although the words were far too simple to encompass the battles she'd fought. But the story was Christine's to tell, not mine. "If she makes it in to the museum today, she might notice my absence, although she'll probably just assume the snow kept me home. She isn't really one to worry."

"Well, then, we shall thank the snow gods for the chance to have a lazy breakfast," Griffin said, neatly dividing the eggs onto two plates.

We had coffee and cold cereal in addition to the eggs. Griffin took the newspaper at home, and courteously offered part of the morning edition to me. We sat together comfortably, with our food and coffee, perusing the news. I couldn't recall a better breakfast.

"Last night," Griffin said, after cleaning a good portion of his plate.

From his businesslike tone, he doubtless meant the investigative portion of the evening. The investigation of the house, that is, not one another.

"It was a trap." The words had even more weight now, in the light of day. "They knew we'd be there. Or someone would."

He nodded, his mouth pressed into a tight line. "Yes. The question is how."

"Did you speak to anyone? You said you'd asked around. Perhaps the Brotherhood knew someone was looking for this Buckeye Jim character?"

"Perhaps," he allowed. "Or perhaps it was planned from the beginning."

"You mean, er, Rosa?"

His gaze rested on nothing, as if he didn't see the warm little kitchen, but rather some far colder and lonelier place. "Madam Rosa, yes. She was the one who gave me Buckeye Jim's name and linked him with Philip Rice."

"But you said she was your best informant. Surely she wouldn't have betrayed you."

Griffin looked down at his plate. "I learned a long time ago not to rely on other people," he said tonelessly. "I paid Rosa. If someone else paid her more, why wouldn't she turn on me?"

"Because you were kind to her?" I suggested.

He glanced up, blinking as if he'd half-forgotten I was there. "I tried to be. But kindness isn't always enough." Don't be naïve, in other words.

"I see." My cold cereal had been reduced to a puddle of milk; I put the spoon down carefully. "If you're right, the Brotherhood knows your identity. Why set up an elaborate trap instead of simply finishing you off here?"

Griffin shook his head. "You forget—I always go to the docks in disguise. Rosa doesn't know my real name."

"Very foresighted of you."

"It's habit, to hide as much of the truth as possible." His mouth tightened, as if at remembered pain. "There were times working with the Pinkterons, when I could barely remember who Griffin Flaherty even was."

It didn't sound as if his memories were pleasant. I touched him lightly on the back of the hand. "If you ever need reminding again, I will assist." My stomach clenched around my breakfast; when had I grown bold?

Griffin's pensive expression melted into a smile, and he turned his hand palm-up, linking his fingers with mine. "I'll hold you to that, my dear."

I ducked my head, unable to suppress the silly grin stretching my mouth. My eyes chanced across a headline on my neglected newspaper.

"VIOLENT ATTACK ON GOOSE TEMPLE ROAD LEAVES ONE DEAD, ONE INJURED," it read.

Within a few sentences, I had snatched up the paper. "Griffin, listen to this! *'Yesterday, early risers found two men lying to the side of Goose Temple Rd. One had already expired from his injuries, but the other remains in desperate straits in the charity ward. According to relatives, the men were in the habit of drinking together late into the night, and must have been met their assailant while walking home from the saloon.*

'The widow of the dead man, one Gerald Dalton, insists he was partially eaten and covered with human bite marks. Police, however, deny her claims and say the two revelers met with a wild dog rather than any human assailant. They also deny any connection between the attack and the disappearance of Miss Ashley Moore, last seen in the same area five days ago.'"

Griffin regarded me with a thoughtful frown. "Do you think they ran afoul of the Guardians?"

"Perhaps, but most of them wouldn't leave a human bite. I suspect something else. Some*one* else." I dropped the paper and pulled the *Arcanorum* from my breast pocket. A hasty perusal brought me to the passage I needed. "Here we are. According to the book, anyone raised from the dead *'must have it red'* for three months after."

"And you don't think they're referring to wine."

I glared at him from under lowered brows. "It means raw meat and blood, I'm sure of it. Perhaps cattle might do for the likes of the Guardians, as they've merely been built from the parts of dead men and animals, but for someone who had truly been resurrected, only human flesh would do."

Griffin's hands clenched convulsively on the table. "Blackbyrne?"

"Blackbyrne. It must be."

The snow melted throughout the afternoon, until only a trace remained on the soggy ground. Griffin spent the day immersed in newspaper clippings and notes on the Brotherhood, cursing and muttering to himself as he scratched down ideas and wild speculations on a notepad. Sifting back through the newspapers, which he kept copies of in his study, he found reports of other unexplained attacks going back to the beginning of November, when Blackbyrne's grave had been violated. It seemed more and more likely that our guesses were correct, and the Brotherhood had stolen Blackbyrne's body and resurrected him toward some unknown purpose.

"I wonder…if Philip Rice was a member of the Brotherhood, did he begin to have doubts?" Griffin murmured, half to himself.

"After resurrecting a cannibal? Who then perhaps set about making the Guardians, or giving the instructions to do so? I'd think that would be enough to give anyone second thoughts," I said. "Do you believe they killed him for it?"

"Maybe." Griffin rubbed tiredly at his eyes. "Without more evidence, all we can do is speculate."

When the alarm clock went off the next morning, before the sun had even risen, a number of curses in several languages went through my mind. Dragging myself out of Griffin's warm bed and into the icy dawn was tortuous, a procedure made no easier when he sleepily tried to pull me back under the covers with him.

Only my need for a change of clothing before work impelled me out the door and back to my apartment. None of my neighbors seemed to have noticed my absence, which didn't surprise me. I certainly wouldn't have noticed theirs.

I walked up the steps to the Ladysmith's entrance a short time later, surrounded by other staff members rushing to get to their desks on time. I'd washed, shaved, and attired myself in clothing not rumpled from being left on Griffin's floor, and yet I still felt marked. It seemed as if any of them would know what I'd been up to with Griffin simply by looking at my face.

None of them gave me a second glance, however. The phalanx of suspicious-eyed guards hired to protect the exhibit did glare at me, as if certain I'd committed a criminal act of some kind—but they glared at poor Dr. Leavitt the same way, and he was over ninety years old and had never done anything more savage than collecting the Lepidoptera which formed his study.

Miss Parkhurst gave me her usual smile as I passed by her desk. "Good morning, Dr. Whyborne. Did you enjoy your snow day?"

My ears grew hot. "Er, I-I suppose." It occurred to me I ought to respond in kind. "Did you? Enjoy your day, that is."

"Oh yes!" Her smile was big and bright. "I went out with some of the other girls who live in the same boarding house, and we had a bit of a snowball fight." She blushed lightly. "I suppose such things must sound rather silly to you."

"It sounds delightful," I answered. And it probably was, if one had enough coordination to actually hit anything with a thrown snowball. I'd watched my brother and his friends play in the snow as children, only to be laughed at and told to go back inside when I asked to join them.

Her smile had flagged; now it returned full force. "It was, sir. Would you like me to bring you some coffee?"

"If it isn't too much trouble—"

"Not at all, Dr. Whyborne. You're never any trouble."

I sat at my desk for a while, uselessly shuffling papers and putting off the inevitable. Perhaps if I went to the library and searched for more references to Nyarlathotep? Or found Christine and pried her away from the exhibit long enough to discuss what Griffin and I had found?

All of which I needed to do…and all of which was simply an excuse to avoid the most urgent, but most unpleasant, task.

"Nothing for it," I said aloud, as if hearing the words would bolster my courage. "Best to get it over with quickly. Like an amputation—just one fast slice."

Dear heavens, maybe I was going mad, talking to myself in the confines of my office. Not to suggest I was the only one; I sometimes heard my colleagues muttering to themselves as I passed by their open doors. Still, the habit wasn't a pleasant one, and I wanted to be normal, for Griffin's sake.

I'd never cared what anyone thought of me before. Everyone already considered me odd, but I'd accepted my fate even before I reached adulthood. I wasn't athletic enough, or competitive enough, or manly enough; I was too bookish, too quiet, too awkward.

And that was fine, really. Or, if not fine, at least tolerable. Survivable.

Before Griffin had come along, I'd been living inside a photograph: just a facsimile of life, without either color or depth. Could I go back to it, now that I had seen the alternative?

I took a sip of coffee. It had gone cold while I sat there wool-gathering. Or delaying, to be honest.

Swallowing the coffee, I squared my shoulders and left my sanctuary. Unfortunately, by the time I'd reached Bradley's office, my determination had faded, and I was back to slouching and tucking my elbows in. Suppressing a sigh, I knocked on Bradley's door. His voice distractedly called for me to enter.

His office was the opposite of mine: absolutely neat, with nothing on the desk except for an expensive pen set, a leather blotter, and the latest issue of *The American Historical Review*. Bradley had been busy reading an article; he glanced up, and his eyes widened to see me standing in his door.

And with good reason. I'd never been in his office, never having had the slightest desire to interact with him beyond what was absolutely necessary. Or beyond what he forced, given he had no such inhibitions about barging into *my* office.

"Percy?" he asked in obvious puzzlement. "What are you doing here?"

No *"How can I help you?"* or *"Good to see you, old fellow, how did you make out in the snow yesterday?"* I hadn't expected anything different, but it would have been nice to be proved wrong.

If only I could turn around and leave, but it was too late. Taking a deep breath, I said, "Bradley. I need your help."

A satisfied smirk crawled across Bradley's blandly handsome face. "Well, well, got something your dusty scrolls can't answer, eh?" he asked. He was joking, I was sure of it—but the cruel edge in his voice was no less real.

He'd marked me the first day we'd met, greeting me with a finger-crushing handshake and a snide remark about those dainty professors I'd studied under at Arkham. Both of us had known our respective places immediately. Bradley was an adult version of the boys who had tormented me at school, just as I took the role of the boys he'd no doubt tormented. He was a man's man, despite his vocation; after all, he studied *American* history. A litany of red-blooded patriots, fighting savages and redcoats alike, taming the wilderness, proving their worth with bulging sinews and roaring guns.

How I fit into his narrative, I wasn't certain. Probably as some quivering coward, sniveling behind the stockade walls with the women, while pseudo-Bradleys shot Indians and wrestled bears.

"Er, y-yes," I said. He didn't offer me a seat. I hovered near the door, unsure what to do with my hands. "That is, I, er, I was w-wondering—"

"Oh ho, come to me for advice, eh?" Bradley's smirk turned into a leer. "Looking for tips on how to get little Maggie Parkhurst to crack her thighs?"

"I, er…what?"

"Don't bother, if you ask me. She's frigid." Because of course any of the secretarial staff who didn't welcome his advances must be frigid; the fault couldn't possibly be his. "A few years ago, I would have said just drag her into one of the storerooms, but those days are over thanks to your friend Christine."

I swallowed back my revulsion and tried not to imagine the clammy touch of his hand anywhere on my bare skin. "N-no. I wanted to ask about Theron Blackbyrne."

"Ah, because of the grave-robbing! Dreadful business—the newspaper wanted a quote from me about it, you know." He puffed out his chest slightly.

"Oh. Yes, exactly. I just wondered…I don't know much about him, you see, and I was curious…"

"You've come to the right man, Percy. I know more than anyone else—and don't listen to the old biddy at the county library, either. She doesn't have access to source material I do."

Of that, I had no doubt. If nothing else, the museum would have bought anything truly valuable the library had on hand, not wanting the competition. Still, it seemed rather petty to feud with an elderly public librarian. "Oh no, you're—" I swallowed against bile "you're quite the expert. So, er, is it true Blackbyrne dabbled in the occult?"

Bradley burst into laughter. "Only you, Percy," he gasped out between chuckles. "Has all the ancient nonsense you study turned you into an occultist?"

"No, no, of course not." I pasted an idiotic smile on my face like an ill-fitting mask. "It was just, ah, I'd heard he'd been accused, and…"

"Oh yes, he was." Bradley's speech took on a lecturing aspect, for which I was grateful. "Superstitious rubbish, of course. He supposedly met with other alleged witches in the woods outside Salem to perform dark rites."

"Yes, very silly," I said, before he could begin to recite the long litany of names, too many of which were of innocents who had ended up dangling from the end of a noose. Stories of the witches who had met such a dreadful fate had haunted my nightmares as a child. "Still," I forged ahead, "I was told the accusations didn't end with Salem."

I'd been told no such thing, of course. Fortunately, Bradley needed no prompting.

"Oh yes, yes. Blackbyrne spent time in Europe. Of course lesser minds used his absence to claim he was seen in or near various castles and manors in Bavaria and Transylvania; places of legend, where superstitious peasants huddle around the fire and pray not to be carried off by the devil in the night. They even claim he joined some kind of cult while over there." He leaned forward, as though imparting some secret knowledge. "Some diaries even hint he left instructions behind on how to resurrect him."

My heart quickened. "Really?"

"Supposedly, he and the other families who followed him to Widdershins were all in on it together." Bradley shrugged carelessly, but I recalled the odd arrangement of the graves and shivered. "About sixty years ago, it was all the rage to try to trace some kind of hidden message in the very streets of the town—ignoring the fact some of the streets have been realigned, and the city has grown considerably. As I said, it's all balderdash. I'm rather disappointed another staff member would even express interest in such nonsense." He paused and watched me slyly. "But don't worry. I won't mention it to the director."

I wanted to tell him. I wanted to speak the secret name of fire. I wanted to summon up a Guardian with blood and thunder, and laugh when he wet himself in terror.

The *Arcanorum* would let me. If I'd understood its hints aright, I could call up a plague of psychopomps: whippoorwills in summer, crows in winter, which would dog him and haunt him until they snatched his soul from his lips.

My breath caught in my throat. Dear heavens, what was I thinking?

Griffin had warned me against the book. He hadn't warned me against myself.

I forced my breath past the obstruction. "Thank you," I said through lips gone numb. "I-I have to go."

"Of course," he called as I groped for the door handle. "Come back any time you want to make a fool of yourself."

I slammed the door behind me and fled.

CHAPTER 17

I TRUDGED BACK to my office, my mind reeling. My heart pounded, as if I'd run a race, and the last dregs of anger left bitter acid in my veins. I'd loathed Bradley from the moment we'd met, but I'd never imagined doing him actual harm.

Then again, I'd never before been in a position of power over him before. Over *anyone*. Given the chance, would I become the very thing I hated?

No, of course not. I couldn't actually carry out the acts I'd fantasized.

Could I?

Maybe Griffin had been right. Maybe the *Arcanorum* wasn't good for me.

I'd been walking quickly without paying attention to where my steps took me; when I came around the corner and found Griffin himself standing in front of Miss Parkhurst's desk, I was even more surprised than I would have been otherwise.

The sight of him stole my breath. The waves of his hair tumbled over his collar, and the cut of his coat showed off his physique to good effect. He hadn't said anything about coming by, when I'd left him earlier. Actually, he hadn't said anything more than a mumbled: "Come back to bed."

The memory made my ears grow hot—along with other parts. The balm of his presence spread over the sandpaper scratches Bradley had left behind, and the knot in my stomach relaxed.

And perhaps Bradley, in his crudeness, had given me an idea. He would in no way approve of my twist on it, which made it all the sweeter.

I tried to keep my expression professional yet friendly, and tamp down on the overly-joyful smile which wanted to burst onto my mouth. "Griffin?"

He turned, and I caught a glimpse of a more intimate grin before his expression settled into something suitable. "Ah, there you are, Whyborne! I was just looking for you."

"I'm sorry, sir, but you weren't in your office," Miss Parkhurst said.

Bradley had said such foul things about her; my blood threatened to boil. I forced a stiff smile onto my face. "No need to apologize. I certainly don't expect you to keep track should I decide to wander off. Thank you for taking the time to assist Mr. Flaherty."

She blushed slightly and glanced down. Had she fallen for Griffin's charms as well? I could hardly blame her. "It's no trouble, sir."

Griffin watched me approach, his head cocked slightly to the side, as if he sensed something had unsettled me. "I had hoped you and Dr. Putnam might be free for lunch."

"Yes. Er, I am. But there's something I need to show you first."

I felt certain my face betrayed me, but Griffin only looked curious. "Oh? By all means, then."

Instead of leading the way down to my office, I chose a more well-lit route, taking stairs to the third floor, then following a labyrinthine series of hallways, until we came upon a seldom-used storeroom. I'd been inside only a time or two myself; it contained mainly fragments of cuneiform tablets too small to piece into a coherent whole.

I ushered Griffin inside. He looked around in polite puzzlement. "What was it you—"

I threw the bolt with a loud click.

Griffin turned to me swiftly. His back was to a desk used to examine the tablets; at the moment, it was free of any clutter. Arching a brow, he settled his hip casually against the desk and crossed his arms. "I see. Want to show me something, do you?"

His lazy grin was out-shone by the hungry gleam in his eye. I crossed the room in two strides and clasped his arms tightly.

"Perhaps," I murmured, my lips a breath away from his. "Or perhaps you might show me something."

He kissed me with utter abandon: sucking hard on my lower lip, before plunging his tongue deep. My member swelled in response, pressing against the jut of his hip as I ground against him.

I pulled away long enough to draw my handkerchief from my pocket. Griffin shot me a curious look; I ignored it in favor of spreading the white cloth on the ground, to protect the knees of my trousers.

Suitably arranged, I unfastened his trousers. His breath came short and fast, and his length pressed against his drawers, as if desperate for release.

"What are you going to do to me?" he gasped, his voice ragged with lust.

Surely he had to know. I was on my knees in front of—oh. He knew exactly what I intended. He just wanted to hear me say it.

I could say it, in a dozen different tongues, if he wanted. But yet, simple English seemed the hardest.

"Are you going to suck my cock?" he cajoled. His hips twitched as I pulled him free of his clothing.

I swallowed hard, not sure why the words brought a heat to my face, far beyond the act itself. "I…yes."

"Say it."

"I-I want to suck your cock."

His eyes went heavy-lidded, and he made a soft sound of desperation, thrusting his hips forward. His…cock…jutted out proudly: thick and veined and utterly, utterly delicious.

I wrapped my lips around it with a moan. He tasted divine: salt and musk and a trace of sandalwood soap. I wrapped one hand around the base of his erection and set myself to sucking the rest with gusto, even as I pumped him. My other hand I used to unfasten my trousers and draw out my own aching member.

I pulled back to nibble lightly at the head, before sucking on the slit itself, lapping up the slick fluid with my tongue. His soft moan let me know he liked what I was doing. I tongued harder, was rewarded with a gasp of raw pleasure.

I stroked him with my hand, then fastened it around the base of his cock, pointing it up at his belly to give me access to the underside. The wrinkled skin of his sack was drawn up tight, and I licked lightly at it before taking one side into my mouth. His skin was salty and heavy with his scent.

"Whyborne," he whispered, his voice cracking. "Damn. Feels good."

I trailed my tongue back up along his shaft, before taking it into my mouth again. He thrust against my face, and I let him. Every moan, every whimper, every movement from him fired my blood and stiffened my own erection. I'd never imagined being this utterly aroused before I met him; now, I couldn't imagine living without it.

"Yes," he whispered. His fingers twined through my hair, anchoring my head loosely while he pushed his cock into my mouth. "Yes, please, feels good, don't stop."

Hearing him beg, tasting his arousal on my tongue, feeling his thick cock fill my mouth: was there anything better in the world? I whimpered encouragement, tugging frantically on my own member. What would it feel like if he had his mouth on me at the same time…?

It was almost enough to send me over the edge. I clung on, determinedly, sucking harder. Griffin's rhythm shifted suddenly, and his fingers clenched in my hair.

"Oh God, yes, Ival, please, don't stop, please…!"

His cock seemed to stiffen and swell further, before he released into my mouth. He tasted bitter and musky and wonderful, and I swallowed, aflame from the idea of taking his spend into me, desperate to have it all. He moaned and twitched as I milked the last drops from his softening organ.

He pulled away, his slit leaving a slick trail across my lips. I arched, tugging hard at myself, and his eyes fastened on my erection, his lips parting hungrily. "Yes," he whispered huskily. "Yes, do it, now, I want to see…"

I closed my eyes, then forced them open when he whimpered, even as white-hot pleasure gathered at the base of my cock. My sack tightened, and everything clenched, my spine bowing inward as I found release with a final few strokes. White gobs of semen spattered against the floor, and I groaned aloud.

Spent, I slumped momentarily against his legs. His hand slid through my hair, and a soft chuckle escaped him. "You will be the death of me, my dear."

I wanted to lose myself in drowsy happiness, but his words worried me. "I…I'm sorry."

He laughed and crouched down, pressing a kiss to my semen-slick lips. "For what? It was not meant as a complaint. I wanted your passion. I still want it. Watching you just now, with your lips swollen and your mouth…God. I have no words. You confound me; you drive me mad, and I cannot get enough."

What did he mean I confounded him? Perhaps it didn't matter; enough to know he viewed it as a good thing. "I can't get enough of you, either," I confessed.

"Mmm." He kissed me again, then drew away. "Say you will spend the night again. Or, if it seems unwise, perhaps I can visit you?"

Warmth spread out from my chest, penetrating even to the tips of my fingers and toes. "No one will notice my absence," I assured him. "I'm yours, as you want me."

Had my declaration sounded too premature? Too needy?

If so, Griffin didn't seem to notice. "Excellent," he said as he began to put himself back into order. "In the meantime, however, there is still the matter of lunch. Are you…up…for it?"

I rolled my eyes. "You've seen to that," I said, as I climbed to my feet. The handkerchief which had protected my trousers served to clean off any remaining traces of my passion, and I reordered myself smartly.

Griffin's eyes were dark with desire, the rusty threads turning the green into something warm and welcoming. "I'd say you've seen to me," he murmured, his fingertips ghosting across the front of my trousers. "But never fear, my dear: I fully intend to return the favor."

Marsh's was almost deserted when the waiter led us to a secluded booth. I'd caught a glimpse of the cook when we came inside; his hairless head and staring eyes made me uneasy. We were a bit early for the lunch rush, but a group of clerks laughed and talked at a table near the front window, and a man and woman sat in deep discussion at a booth. The woman looked as if she might burst into tears; perhaps her companion had chosen this public location in the hopes she would restrain herself.

Griffin slid into the booth across from Christine and me, just as he had before. To think, when last we'd been here, we hadn't yet become…whatever we were. Lovers? Partners-in-crime?

We'd waited a few minutes before leaving the storeroom, giving our breathing a chance to even out and our lips to look a bit less freshly-kissed. Or other things, in my case. I blushed at the memory and hid behind the menu, hoping Christine didn't notice.

She didn't. "Your expedition," she said briskly, after we'd given our orders to the waiter. "I assume it turned out satisfactorily?"

I gave her a suspicious glance, but the question seemed innocent.

"Not quite as expected," Griffin said. "You read about the gas explosion in the papers yesterday?"

"Good gad, you don't mean to say you were involved?"

"I'm afraid we were." Our meals came. I had gotten the fish sandwich again, and proceeded to cut it up into neat squares, a practice of which Christine heartily disapproved.

For once, she didn't accuse me of misunderstanding the entire purpose of a sandwich, being too engrossed in Griffin's recounting of our evening. Or a heavily-censored version of the evening, anyway, which did not involve anything more improper than blowing up a house full of Guardians.

Once Griffin was finished, I told them what I'd gleaned from Bradley this morning, leaving out the unpleasant details. Christine could probably imagine them easily enough, and I didn't want Griffin to realize Bradley had inadvertently inspired our time locked in the storeroom together.

Griffin's expression grew more and more somber as I spoke. When I was done, he let out a long breath, as if he'd been bracing himself against more bad news. "It seems Blackbyrne planned for this."

"But why didn't they bring him back to life right away?" Christine asked. "Why wait two hundred years? Surely he would have wished to return sooner."

"Maybe," Griffin allowed. "But possibly the person most interested in Blackbyrne's return was Blackbyrne himself. If you were his second-in-command, say, would you be eager to hand power back over to him? Or would you keep it for yourself?"

"Which doesn't answer the question: why now?"

"Perhaps he has something the modern-day Brotherhood needs or wants? Sorcerous expertise, maybe?"

"No reason we come up with will be more than speculation," I pointed out. "We don't have enough facts to guess what their motive might be."

"Well, one thing isn't speculation," Christine said. "The gala is tomorrow night. We must all be there and on the lookout."

Griffin nodded. "Indeed. The snow yesterday disrupted my plans, but this afternoon I'll track down the caterer and pretend to be looking for work. Barring that, most of the guards recently hired probably don't know one another. If I can put together a convincing uniform—"

"Don't be ridiculous." Christine settled back in her chair, smirking in a way I didn't like. "As a mere woman, I am expected to have an escort with me. Normally Whyborne accompanies me, but you need an invitation and he doesn't."

I opened my mouth, then closed it again. I didn't have any objections to the idea…well, none I could speak aloud. After all, it would be pure foolishness to be jealous because Griffin could appear on Christine's arm, but not my own. Still, my jaw ached from clenching my teeth together.

For his part, Griffin seemed pleased. "An excellent suggestion. This way, I won't have to hide my identity. Most people don't look beyond a uniform, but posing as a caterer would still have meant some risk."

The waiter came to clear away our plates. We paid, then departed to stand awkwardly on the sidewalk. "I will see you both later," Griffin said, with a little bow, as if he and I had made no plans involving his bed.

Perhaps I was getting better at deception, because I managed not to flush too badly as I said my good-byes, and kept from watching his trim form stride away for more than a moment. When I turned back, Christine wore a smirk on her face.

"Well, Whyborne," she said slyly, "planning on what to wear tomorrow?"

"Don't be absurd." I only owned one formal suit, after all.

"I don't know. I rather think you and I shall have to duel over my escort."

"Christine!"

She only laughed at me. "Oh, come along, Whyborne, there's work to do. Like as not we'll both be stuck at the Ladysmith until dawn, finishing up for the gala."

Griffin's scream woke me from a deep sleep.

The sheets tangled around my flailing arms, and my heart raced in my chest. We were under attack, but from where?

The moonlight streaming through the window silhouetted Griffin's form beside me. He sat upright, arms wrapped around his torso, his head bowed and his shoulders hunched forward. Nothing else stirred in the room, and my heart began to settle again.

"A nightmare?" I asked. It must have been a terrible one, to cause him to cry out.

Griffin didn't acknowledge me. A low, soft moan stole from his lips: the sound of a wounded animal.

Was he still asleep? "Griffin?" I said, loudly enough to wake him. When he didn't respond, I lit the night candle with a word.

The soft light bloomed, throwing a golden glow across the rumpled covers and gently highlighting the muscles of Griffin's torso and back. He shivered in the frigid air, every muscle stiff and tense.

"Griffin?" I hesitantly touched his shoulder. "Can you hear me?"

He whimpered at the brush of my fingertips. "What is it?" His voice was harsh and cracked with horror. "God in heaven, what is it?"

My hands trembled and my stomach clenched. I leaned over, trying to get a glimpse of his expression.

He stared straight ahead, his eyes like glassy orbs, seeing nothing. "His face is gone," Griffin whispered. "God. Oh God. It's gone, it's gone, he doesn't have a face, I can't; I can't; I can't…"

"Griffin!" I knelt on the bed in front of him, clasping both his arms in an attempt to force him to look at me. "It's not real! It's just a dream."

He blinked slowly, but still didn't seem to actually see me. "It isn't real?"

"No. You're here, old fellow, in your own bed, safe and sound."

Griffin swallowed convulsively. "Please don't make me go back to the madhouse."

CHAPTER 18

GRIFFIN HAD BEEN in a madhouse?

Goosebumps pricked my skin, and not just because of the icy air. What was it he'd said the night we'd found the Guardian in the warehouse and he'd told me of his last case with the Pinkertons? "...*They said I'd broken under the strain. I was mad.*"

Had they sent him to the asylum? Told him the things he'd seen in that accursed place were the result of a fractured mind? Dear God, I'd heard the stories of what went on behind the walls of such places. Had they locked him in? Restrained him in a straightjacket? Used injections or ice-water baths to "cure" him?

My gorge rose, and my muscles tensed with the need to do something, anything, to protect him. But of course it was far too late.

Nor would anger help the situation now. Leaning forward, I pressed a kiss to his forehead. "Of course not, darling," I said, as tenderly as I could form the words. "No one will make you go anywhere you don't want, ever again."

"I'll be good; I promise." He closed his eyes and his shoulders slumped in defeat. "Please. Just let me go home."

I slid my arms around him; all resistance was gone, and he let me pull him back down and cover us both in the blankets. His skin was like ice; I wrapped my legs around him as well, trying to warm him. "You are home," I whispered into his ear. "The monsters are real, but they aren't here now. You're safe."

He buried his face against my neck, dampening my skin with hot tears. I closed my eyes, stroking his brown curls rhythmically. Seeing him in pain was like swallowing broken glass.

I wanted to do more than just hold him. I wanted to take away every hurt he'd ever suffered. I wanted to find whoever had sent him to the asylum and pummel them senseless. I wanted to hide him away from every cruelty in the world, somewhere safe and warm and happy.

I couldn't do any of those things. So I did the only thing I could and held him close, murmuring words of comfort into his ear. Eventually, the small tremors and occasional whimper subsided, and he fell into an exhausted sleep. But I lay awake until dawn, on guard in case the terrors of the night returned to claim him again.

When I next awoke, I found myself alone. The early sunlight streamed through the window, and frost traced fanciful patterns on the panes. I slid a hand over to Griffin's side of the bed and found the sheets had gone cold.

Had he awoken disoriented again, trapped in the past? He'd dressed at least, and the washbasin had been used, so hopefully he had recovered from his fit.

I slid out from under the sheets and dressed hastily. The water of the basin had a thin crust of ice on it; I decided to heat some water in a kettle to shave, as I had no desire to freeze my neck and face.

I went out into the hall and made for the warmth of Griffin's study. He sat in his wing-backed chair, staring out the window, with Saul curled up on his lap. There was a snifter in his hand and a bottle of whiskey on the floor beside him.

"I don't blame you for not wanting to stay," he said without turning to look at me. The words were hurried and sounded rehearsed. "I hope you'll agree to continue our association in a professional capacity until the case is done, but I understand if you don't wish to."

Had he been sitting out here alone for hours, convinced I would leave at the first opportunity? I'd done nothing to give him that impression, I was sure of it. Perhaps he simply couldn't imagine anyone would stay with a man who wasn't entirely whole. Who had been broken, and hadn't managed to put all the pieces back together.

I cleared my throat. "I certainly hope your detective skills are normally sharper than this," I said briskly. "Otherwise you will soon be out of business."

I crossed the room and took the snifter from his unresisting hand. "Although this is surely not helping anything," I added. I opened the window, tossed the whiskey out, and shut it again hastily as a wave of cold air poured in.

I turned to find Griffin sitting forward, his eyes wide. Saul meowed grumpily and hopped down off his lap. "You're staying?" The words were spoken softly, as if saying them too loudly would somehow make them untrue.

I put down the snifter and crossed my arms over my chest. "Do you truly think me so inconstant?"

Griffin's lips tightened and he slumped back in his chair. "I was in an asylum. I have fits, as you saw last night. I should have mentioned it before we became involved, but I chose the coward's path. If you left, it would not in any way reflect on you."

I knelt beside him and laid my head in his lap. "I hope you realize you have my highest regard and-and affection," I said. Strange, how much harder it was to expose my heart than it had been my body. "You can confide in me without fear."

"But I am afraid." I could feel his fingers trembling as he rested them against my hair. "What if you change your mind, once you hear?"

"At least give me the chance to prove I won't."

"Yes. And…you deserve to know. It was the last case, as I said. We split up." Griffin's voice was low, tremors cracking the words. "Glenn and I. They called us G&G at the agency."

"Was he…were the two of you…?"

"He was married. Four children, and another on the way."

At least they hadn't been lovers. "Still, I'm sorry."

His fingers stroked my hair, smoothing the stubborn locks. "I did a quick search of the upper floors of the house, while he went into the basement. There was nothing upstairs, so I followed him into those damnable depths." A shudder went through him. No wonder he had been alarmed at the prospect of going through the trapdoor in the abandoned house.

"It was dark," he went on. "And it stank. God, the smell! I couldn't stand the thought an innocent girl might be down there. I held my breath and pressed on. There were rooms burrowed down into the earth itself, and I swear some of them were far older than anything built by human hands.

"I don't know what I might have found, had I gone all the way to the bottom of that rotting pile of ancient, hollowed stone. There was a hall—and a room—and Glenn—and a *thing*."

His fingers curled in my hair, his entire body shivering now. "I don't know what it was. It was slime and eyes and ropy tentacles, and it had Glenn. No. It was *digesting* Glenn. It had him, and his face…it was gone. Melted off, down to the skull. But he was still alive. Still screaming."

Dear heavens. My mind shied away from picturing it. How had Griffin endured the sight? Even worse, what must it have been like for poor Glenn? Of all the horrible ways to die.

Griffin let out a long shuddering breath. Was he weeping? I kept my cheek pressed against his leg, not wishing to embarrass him by seeing his tears.

"I shot him," he said, his voice raw with grief. "There was nothing else to be done. I killed him, and then I emptied my revolver into the thing, and it didn't even seem to notice. One of its tentacles whipped out and wrapped around my leg. You've seen the scar. It was cold, beyond cold, like the darkest night ever known, and yet it burned at the same time. I think I screamed. How I pulled loose from it, I don't know. Perhaps it was still busy absorbing Glenn. Or maybe it was nothing but blind, stupid luck. A sort of cosmic joke, where one of us lived and one died, with nothing but random chance to say which was which.

"I don't recall fleeing the house, although I must have. The next thing I knew, I was strapped to a gurney in the hospital. I told my boss everything. But he said I was wrong. The police had come, and there was nothing left of Glenn but a pile of bones. He said the culprits had tried to dissolve him in acid. They'd thrown acid on my leg, and the pain had unhinged me. And when I screamed he was wrong, everyone said I was mad."

Griffin let out a bitter laugh utterly devoid of humor. "I *was* mad. For a little while at least. Screaming, clawing-at-the-walls mad. But I wasn't wrong."

"No," I said quietly. "You weren't."

"I ended up in the asylum. It was…bad. I don't…I can't talk about it. I thought I would die there. But my father came and insisted they turn me over to him."

"Your father?" I asked. "Weren't you an orphan?"

"Yes. Sent to Kansas on the orphan train after my parents died. Adopted on the platform by a couple who couldn't have children of their own. They didn't even try to give me a new name, which happened to most of the orphans. They were good to me, and I never felt like anything less than their son. At least, not until I was caught with the son of the neighboring farmer."

"Oh," I said. Had the boy been Griffin's first love? "What happened?"

"I left town, and he stayed behind and married the girl he'd already been engaged to, and everyone agreed I was a devil who'd tempted him off the Christian path." Griffin's voice grew rough with old anger and hurt. Then he sighed. "But Father came for me, when I had no one else. He removed me from the asylum and took me home. I don't know what he thought of me; I didn't dare ask, and he didn't offer. But he and Mother gave me a safe place to come back to myself, and for that I am eternally grateful."

"And you moved here?"

"Eventually, yes. I wanted somewhere different, somewhere I could forget. And yet the past refuses to go away."

I opened my eyes to avoid the visions of a stormy night on a lake, which threatened to play out against my lids. "It has a way of doing that."

"Yes." He sighed and stroked my hair again. "I won't pretend I wasn't unhinged by what I saw. I still suffer from fits, as you now know. If…if you decide to leave, I understand, and will not think you faithless."

My neck was developing a crick, but I didn't want to move. "I am where I wish to be," I said at last, not sure how else to make him understand.

His body hitched slightly, as if against tears, and his fingers coiled in my hair, tenderly.

I had dedicated my life to words. But sometimes, words are not needed. We sat together quietly in the warmth of the fire, and watched snow drift past the window, for as long as we were able.

~ * ~

That night, I put on my tuxedo suit and removed my silk top hat from its box. I gave more care to my appearance than usual as I dressed. When I was done, I added the gold pocket watch and diamond cufflinks which had been my eighteenth birthday present from my father, before he realized I meant to defy him. Normally I considered them too fancy, but perhaps Griffin would like them. I even managed to induce my hair to lay flat, through the judicious application of oil.

I was as well put together as possible for me. Now all I had to do was go down to the street and wait.

Fortunately, the evening was comparatively mild for December, the clouds rolling away, the stars shining in their multitudes against the velvet sky. A few people walked about in the early evening, moving through the streets on their own business. None of us made eye contact or greeted one another. Would Griffin think it strange, or did the people of Chicago or Boston mind their own business just as assiduously?

The clop of hooves heralded the approach of a cab. I caught a glimpse of Christine's face at the window as it pulled up, and she flung open the door for me. It was always odd to see her in an evening dress; this one had the usual froth of skirts and sleeves so wide she might have concealed an arsenal of handguns in them. Knowing Christine, she probably had. "Hello, Whyborne. Ready for an exciting evening?"

"As ready as one can be," I said, climbing into the cab. Then I saw Griffin, and couldn't catch my breath to speak further.

He was always handsome, but in his tailcoat and top hat, he looked resplendent. His brown curls were neatly brushed, and his elegantly tailored clothing showed off his lean form to best advantage. He sat beside Christine, leaving the rear-facing seat for me. I was glad for it, because I hadn't appreciated just how difficult it would be to keep my hands from him. I wanted to kiss him hello, to strip off his gloves and press my lips against his fingertips, to—

The cab started with a lurch, and I nearly fell on Christine. "For God's sake, Whyborne, sit down," she said irritably.

Griffin gave me a smile, his eyes warm. "The tuxedo becomes you," he said.

My face grew hot. "I, er, thank you."

"You never put forth such an effort for me," Christine said.

"Not true," I objected, although of course it was. Christine rolled her eyes.

"We should lay our plans for tonight," Griffin said. "Whyborne, I would like for you to circulate as you see fit. Keep an eye on anyone who seems odd or suspicious. Christine, as the excavator of Nephren-ka, you are most in the spotlight. It would make sense for you and I to remain close to the mummy at all times, before and after its unveiling. I understand refreshments and dancing will precede the reveal. Will it seem suspicious to do no more than a single turn around the dance floor?"

"Call it a refreshing chance to have even a single turn," she said. "It's impossible to drag Whyborne out of whatever spot he finds to hide in."

"You could always find someone else to escort you," I replied stiffly.

"Bah, the rest of them are useless. At least with you I'm assured of intelligent conversation."

"I'm flattered," I said in a tone meant to indicate the opposite.

Griffin held up a white-gloved hand in front of his mouth. I suspected he was trying very hard not to laugh.

The Ladysmith was brightly lit for the occasion; I hated to imagine the gas bill once the night was over. A line of carriages, hired and otherwise, waited in front of the museum. Uniformed attendants greeted each carriage as it pulled up to the curb. When it came our turn, Griffin climbed out, then offered his hand to Christine and helped her down. Although he said he'd been raised a farmer, he'd learned fine manners well, every gesture impeccable as she took his arm.

There was no reason to feel any jealousy whatsoever. But our first night together, Griffin had asked me if I'd ever been with a man, as if allowing the possibility I might have been with a woman. And I'd heard some of those who visited the bathhouses went home to a wife and children.

I hadn't the courage to ask him if he'd ever made love to a woman, just as I hadn't the courage to ask him about any of the men he'd obviously been with. Acid crept along my veins as I pictured those other men, those potential women. No doubt they were all handsomer, smarter, and more desirable than me. How long would it take Griffin to remember he could do better?

I trailed after Griffin and Christine as we went up the stairs to the entrance, where there was a small scrum, as all the new arrivals vied to check hats and coats. In the confusion, Griffin slipped to my side and leaned in to whisper in my ear.

"You look very handsome, my dear. A good thing Christine was with us, or I would have had a difficult time restraining myself, and you would have arrived in a far more disheveled state."

The tips of my ears went hot, even as other parts roused. "Not here," I whispered back.

The look he gave me smoldered. "If we didn't have a job to do tonight, I'd have you in the storeroom right now."

I didn't dare move, for fear of showing the rigid outline of my erection through my trousers. It would be utterly mortifying to be noticed in such a state…and yet his boldness only fed my arousal. I didn't say anything, but my expression must have given me away; he gave me a sly, promising smile before turning to the coat check.

Damn him. Did he have to flirt, knowing we could not act on it in even the smallest way? And now I was distracted, thinking about what I wanted to do to him after the gala, instead of worrying about the Brotherhood.

Apparently, my priorities weren't quite as noble as I'd hoped.

"Come along, Whyborne," Christine said impatiently.

The path to the coat check was clear. I hurriedly handed over my hat and coat. No one seemed to find anything out of the ordinary, except for Griffin, who insisted on smirking at me.

As soon as we passed into the grand foyer, however, he became all business. A buffet lay beneath the looming hadrosaur, while waiters in immaculate uniforms circulated with trays of champagne balanced on their fingertips. A number of chairs and tables encircled the outer reaches of the room, while in the center a string quartet played a waltz. To the left, the drapery across the exhibit hall entrance had been removed, although the mummy itself was still under guard and hidden from view. The idea, as I understood it, was to allow the guests to see the other artifacts, while prolonging the mystery of beholding Nephren-ka himself for a while longer.

"Dr. Putnam!" Dr. Hart exclaimed, swooping in from one side. She and Griffin stopped; I slipped around them and did my best to blend into the crowd.

And it was quite the crowd; everyone who was anyone had been invited. Uncle Addison conversed with Mr. Rice, Griffin's employer. The owner of the canning factory danced with his wife; rumor had it they were in fact first cousins, and their identical, oddly-bulging eyes seemed to confirm it. The publishers of all the local newspapers were there, alongside various other captains of industry. My family was among the few not represented.

I wandered over to the buffet. Bradley stood there, heaping his plate full, which greatly diminished my appetite.

"Ah, there you are, Percy," he said heartily. "Here alone, are you?" He glanced across the room, and a decided smirk formed on his mouth. "I see Christine has thrown you over for that detective fellow. It must rankle, eh?"

"No," I said flatly. Not in the way he imagined, anyway.

Fortunately, Mr. Farr wandered up. "I say, Bradley, what about the portrait of…"

With Bradley distracted, I fled. A quick glance around showed nothing out of the ordinary, with the exception of Christine and Griffin waltzing elegantly across the dance floor. I snatched a flute of champagne off the tray carried by a passing waiter and downed half the contents in a single gulp.

Eager to get away from the dance floor, I scurried into the exhibit hall, clutching the remnants of my champagne. A few others circulated here already, looking at the lesser exhibits, but it was clear the bulk of the crowd had come to see the mummy. Uncertain what to do, I followed my natural inclinations and went to the darkest, most secluded corner. Perhaps I could keep an eye out from here.

An unrolled scroll lay beneath the glass case I ended up standing beside. I'd not had the time to translate it, thanks to the demands of Griffin's case, but as I looked at it, my mind automatically picked out certain hieroglyphs.

Immortality. Opening the way. Those from Outside.

Nyarlathotep.

"Fascinating, is it not?"

I jumped, my champagne glass falling from my hand. Long, white fingers caught it before it hit the ground. How could anyone move so fast? I started to thank the man, or apologize, but my voice died in my throat.

He rose from a crouch, standing uncomfortably close to me. A smile played around full, sensual lips as he lifted the flute to them and took a sip. His golden hair curled in ringlets about his face. His perfect cheekbones, high forehead, and straight nose made him seem almost impossibly handsome.

Those eyes. There was no rational way to know, yet I felt certain they were the same which had stared at me from beneath a hood in the Draakenwood. Their gaze trapped me like a pin through a butterfly: burning and intense, as if he knew the whole of every secret desire.

I needed to run, to tell Griffin, to raise some alarm. But I found myself unable to move.

Then he looked away from me, directing his gaze to the scroll instead. He lifted my champagne glass again, his nails long and filed into points. "Most of those present are dazzled by the mummy," he said. His accent was strange; I could not place it. "And yet I can't help but feel it is here, in these words, where true knowledge lies. Would you agree?"

Did he know I recognized him? Did he care?

Afraid he would turn his gaze on me again, I hastily put my back to him and focused on the scroll. It was a mistake; he took the opportunity to move closer to me, until I fancied the heat of his body reached even through the air between us. It reminded me uncomfortably of Griffin's seduction in front of the fireplace.

"It's all important," I said. At least my voice didn't tremble too badly. "But, yes, in many ways I agree."

"I thought as much." His breath stirred the hairs on the back of my neck. The odor of rot and mold wafted over me—from him? Or from some other source? "You are a man of learning, as am I. The gold, the jewels—all meaningless baubles, distracting lesser minds from the only source of real power: knowledge."

A shiver ran over my skin, and I had to lock my knees to keep from bolting. "Who are you?"

But I already knew the answer, didn't I?

"A man who shares your interests," he said. His low voice was like a soporific smoke, making my thoughts heavy and slow. The ends of his fingernails traced the length of my spine, from shoulders to seat, and a wave of unwilling pleasure sent blood rushing to my groin. "Several of your interests, I suspect."

My resolve broke. "Excuse me," I said breathlessly, and walked away on trembling legs, half-afraid he would give pursuit.

He didn't. And when I risked a glance back over my shoulder, he was gone.

I hurried out of the exhibit hall, into the swirl of mingling guests. Some of the trustees nodded to me in vague recognition. Uncle Addison called my name, but I pretended not to hear, ducking on the other side of a flock of ladies in colorful dresses.

Griffin and Christine loitered near the hadrosaur, heads together in conversation; anyone else might have thought they were courting. But it would be hypocritical to be jealous, when I was the only one who'd been targeted for seduction tonight.

Something in my expression must have betrayed me, because they both straightened as I approached, and Griffin looked alarmed. "Whyborne? Is everything all right?"

"No," I said. "It's not. Theron Blackbyrne is here."

CHAPTER 19

CHRISTINE'S FACE PALED, but she asked, "Are you certain? The man's been dead for centuries, after all."

"I'm sure. I've walked past his portrait in the art gallery a thousand times." True, the painting didn't come close to doing him justice, mere paint on canvas couldn't convey the strange magnetism he exuded. "And even if I hadn't, the man I spoke to was the same I encountered in the Draakenwood. I'm absolutely certain of it."

Griffin didn't question me, for which I was grateful. "They must be ready to make their move. Where is he now?"

"I don't know." I looked away, unable to meet his eye. "He slipped away."

"Let us know if you spot him again."

Christine muttered a curse in Arabic. "We have to stay close to the mummy."

"Agreed," Griffin said, and started in that direction, Christine at his side.

Something Blackbyrne had said nagged at my mind. Actually, *everything* he'd said nagged at me, like little worms wriggling in my brain. I'd spoken to a man who had *died*, who had *been dead* for almost two centuries, whose body had rotted to dust, and yet was now walking and talking as if he'd merely lain down for a nap.

I hadn't really understood the power contained in the *Arcanorum* until now. If such a thing could be achieved…what were the limits? Did any limits exist?

A bell rang, its high, silvery peal cutting through the rumble of talk. Mr. Mathison had taken his place in front of the black drapes still concealing Nephren-ka's sarcophagus. He beamed at the crowd, as if he'd personally arranged every detail, from the excavation to the layout of the exhibit.

"And now, the moment you've been waiting for," he said. Mathison wasn't known for his originality. "If you'll all come close, we shall unveil the mummy! For the first time in four-thousand years, human eyes will once more look upon Pharaoh Nephren-ka's face!"

Which wasn't at all true, of course. Christine's team had opened the sarcophagus in situ and shipped it over in multiple crates, to be lovingly reassembled for the exhibit. But a smattering of applause broke out in response, along with a surge of excited voices as the crowd moved into place.

What was it Blackbyrne had said? Something about the mummy.

"Most of those present are dazzled by the mummy…it is here, in these words, where true knowledge lies."

Blast.

I caught sight of Griffin and Christine; they'd almost made it to the mummy. The guards had drawn back, but all their attention was on the crowd. I didn't see anyone moving in the rear of the exhibit hall, and it seemed impossible a thief would try anything while such a gathering stood only feet away, but I knew I was right.

Even if I had called out to Griffin, he would never have heard me over the noise, which swelled louder as Mathison reached to grasp the cord to release the drapes. I had to act quickly.

I shoved my way to the edge of the crowd, receiving several angry looks and at least one muttered oath. One of the guards noticed and moved to intercept me, as I made my way along the wall. If I could convince him to help instead of hinder, perhaps we could get to the back of the exhibit before it was too late.

"I give you: Nephren-ka!" Mr. Mathison declared loudly, and pulled the cord.

Every light went out at once.

The hall erupted into screams.

A few voices shouted for calm, but they were lost in the general uproar. Bodies bumped into me, and I struggled to keep my footing. Devil take it, where was Griffin in all this?

Light gleamed near the back of the exhibit hall: the directed beams of police lanterns, much like Griffin used, reflecting from glass-fronted cases.

The Brotherhood.

I shoved recklessly through the crowd, not caring who I trod on or pushed aside in the process. "The back of the hall! Thieves!" I shouted at the top of my lungs, hoping to direct the attention of the guards, but the general din swallowed up my voice.

I broke free from the press, tripped over some irregularity in the floor, and barely kept my feet. Ahead of me, a shadowy group lit only by their shielded lanterns headed for the staff entrance.

I collided with a guard, who was striving to light a lantern of his own. Snatching the lantern from his startled hand, I lit the wick with a word and ran for the closing door.

"Whyborne!" Griffin shouted, but the door shut behind me, cutting him off.

The hallway was narrow, and the light from my lantern threw great, moving shadows on the bare plaster walls. A steep, narrow flight of stairs dove down, letting out onto a hall near the library.

The library.

The stacks were silent and deserted, but the odd acoustics amplified the hoarse breaths and muttered words of my quarry. I ran after the thieves, my heart pounding and a stitch forming in my side. What would I do when I caught up with them? I had to get the scroll back, but how?

And why the library? Why trap themselves in a dead-ended catacomb beneath the museum, where they would surely be cornered?

The answer awaited me when I reached the farthest room of the labyrinth. Part of one wall stood open—a secret door. Had the mad architect put it there?

I slowed in front of the passage and held up my lantern cautiously. A dank set of steps dove into the earth. I saw the walls here were rough brick, and the breeze blowing up from the depths reeked of rot and slime. Hopefully the thieves would wrap the scroll to avoid exposing it to such conditions. Then again, perhaps it would be better if the papyrus disintegrated at this very moment.

I hesitated, but really, there was nothing for it. Taking a deep breath, I headed down the stairs.

The arched ceilings of the vaults below reminded me of some ancient wine cellar or catacomb, far older than the museum above. After a few such vaults, the decaying brick came to an end, giving way to rough-hewn stone. The voices of the thieves echoed back from just a short distance in front of me.

I passed through an entrance barely wide enough for my shoulders—then froze. Theron Blackbyrne looked back at me from the adjoining vault, his wickedly smiling face illuminated by a lantern.

God, he was beautiful. His dark eyes pulled at me, an almost hypnotic suggestion pressing against my mind.

"No," I whispered aloud.

His smile grew wider, and he gave me a little nod, as if from one professional to another. Then he turned away, and a thuggish man armed with a gun took his place.

I barely had time to register the weapon pointed at me, before the roar of the revolver echoed through the catacomb.

My lantern hit the ground and went out. I flattened myself instinctively against the wall, still alive. The thug had missed.

Why was there something warm and wet trickling down my arm?

I looked down to see a ragged hole in the left shoulder of my coat. The pain hit an instant later: a hot, angry burn across my upper arm, near the shoulder. I clapped my other hand over the wound instinctively, even as I pressed my back tighter against the rough, stone wall.

No more shots followed, and the footsteps receded into the distance, taking the light of their lanterns with them. I considered chasing after them again, but doubted I'd fair nearly as well against the next bullet. Instead, I relit my lantern and groped my way unsteadily back to the stair. A wave of faintness came over me, and I sagged against the wall, then slid to the floor.

"Whyborne?" Christine's voice echoed from above.

"I'm here," I called. My arm throbbed in time to my heartbeat.

The rustle of skirts and vitriol of curses preceded her. At the sight of me, however, her face went pale as chalk. Gathering up her skirts, she rushed to my side. "Move your hand, Whyborne," she instructed, even as she hoisted up her dress to reveal her underskirt.

I looked away quickly. "Your dress—"

"Devil take the damned dress." There came the sound of ripping cloth, and a moment later, she pressed part of the underskirt against my wound.

I winced at the pressure but didn't object. "It was a scroll. They were after a scroll. I didn't realize soon enough—"

"Whyborne? *Whyborne?!*" Griffin's voice echoed down the stair from above. A moment later, he appeared, his face white and his sword cane held out in front of him, trembling visibly. He was terrified of underground tunnels, and yet he'd come down here into the dank earth after me.

"I'll be right there," I called, hoping to spare him.

His eyes widened at the sight of me, and the last vestiges of color drained from his face. Ignoring my words, he ran down the final steps and dropped to my side.

"My dear?" he asked, voice shaking. He clasped my hand in one of his, while stroking my cheek with the fingers of the other. "Are you all right? We'll call a doctor for you; I swear, you'll be fine, you'll see—"

"Dear God, man, get ahold of yourself!" Christine snapped. "You may not care for your reputation, but think of Whyborne's!"

Griffin shot her a furious look, and for a moment it seemed they might end the evening with a brawl. "I'm fine," I said hastily, even though my arm stung abominably. "It's just a scratch, Griffin, truly."

His green eyes shifted to me, searching for the truth of my words. Whatever he saw must have comforted him, because he nodded and let go of my hand. "I…yes. Let's get you upstairs, shall we?"

There came the sound of many feet on the stairs, accompanied by startled exclamations concerning the existence of the hidden door and tunnels. Griffin rose to his feet, giving my good shoulder a quick squeeze. Striding to the bottom of the stair, he met the astonished Mr. Mathison and Dr. Hart, at the head of a large contingent of guards, trustees, and other men who had decided to investigate.

"Is there a doctor?" he called. "Dr. Whyborne has been shot!"

Christine let out a snort. "Men. Always so damned dramatic," she muttered, as the crowd descended on us.

The next few hours passed in something of a blur.

I was rushed upstairs, despite my protests, as if I'd been gravely injured. Three of the trustees were medical doctors; all insisted on examining my wound, to the detriment of my coat, shirt, and dignity.

The wound itself was quite shallow. The bullet had merely grazed me, removing a divot of flesh just deep enough to bleed profusely. I was subjected to cleaning with alcohol, which stung rather more than the bullet itself. Then I had to be bandaged, and offered laudanum, which I refused. The entire time, Dr. Hart hovered around rather alarmingly, as if worried I might suddenly expire. Mr. Mathison pumped my good hand with gusto, blathering something about loyalty and the museum, to which I could only nod and smile rather fixedly. Then they both went into a long diatribe about what a disaster this was for the Ladysmith, reinforcing one another's list of woes, until finally one of the doctors forced them out of the small side room in which we'd taken refuge.

Once they left, Addison appeared. "Are you all right, my boy?" he asked, taking my hand in his.

"Percival! Where is Leander? Where's my son?"

...A hand let go, and water closed over...

I focused relentlessly on the here-and-now. "I'm quite fine," I reassured him. "I have three doctors, and none of them have tried to amputate yet."

A small smile flickered around his lips. "I'm glad you can face this with a sense of humor."

"I know it's a terrible embarrassment to the museum," I said carefully. It was a blow to far more, but there was no reason to trouble him. "I don't mean to suggest otherwise."

"I know. I know." He hesitated, and for a moment his watery blue eyes fixed on mine, as if he strove to impart some message. Then he sighed and patted my hand. "Things will work out in the end, though, Percival. You must believe it."

I hadn't believed anything of the sort once I was old enough to leave the nursery, but I nodded anyway. "Of course, Uncle Addy."

He left, and I was extremely glad to see Griffin and Christine were my only other visitors. One of the doctors secured the final layer of gauze and snipped it off with a pair of sharp scissors.

"There you go," he said briskly. "Now, is your wife here? Tell her to change the dressing in the morning and make sure there's no sign of infection."

I glanced down. "I, er, no. I'm a bachelor."

"I'll look after him," Griffin said with perfect ease, as if he were simply a friend interested in my wellbeing. "I have a spare room. Whyborne can stay with me tonight, and I'll keep an eye out for fever."

The doctor nodded. "Good, good. I don't expect any trouble, but one can never be too careful, yes?"

He left, taking his kit with him. I considered asking Griffin how close an eye he intended to keep on me, but Christine was there, and I found I couldn't manage it. "Can we leave?" I asked instead.

It came out rather more plaintively than I intended. Griffin arched a brow at me. "Are you sure? You're the hero of the hour. The newspapermen will want an interview."

I turned scarlet and looked down. "I-I know I failed, but…"

"Oh no, Griffin is quite serious," Christine said. When had they decided to use each other's first names? "You were the only one to realize what was going on and actually give pursuit, despite the 'small army' Mathison hired."

"But I didn't—"

"You tried," Griffin said. "And you came a great deal closer to foiling them than the rest of us." His fingers brushed my cheek lightly, before withdrawing. "Come. You look exhausted."

It had been a trying evening, to say the least. I nodded mutely and followed him out. The gas was back on, and every light in the grand foyer burned, perhaps to reassure everyone order had been restored. Most of the attendees had left already; those who remained were either museum staff or reporters. Mr. Rockwell lined up the hired guards, roaring imprecations at them. Christine took my good arm and glared daggers at anyone who tried to approach us.

The air outside revived me somewhat, although it also heightened the pain in my arm. A hired cab hurried to retrieve us; Griffin gave the driver Christine's address, then his.

"Well," Christine said, when the cab had pulled away from the curb and we were more or less alone for the first time, "that was a damned mess."

"It was my fault," I said miserably. "I realized what Blackbyrne was after, but not until it was too late."

Griffin sat directly across from me, his gaze fixed on my face, as if nothing else in the world mattered at the moment. "You didn't fail. I should have questioned you more closely about the conversation with Blackbyrne. You were the only one who acted quickly enough to even come close to catching them."

"And after the Brotherhood resurrected Blackbyrne, the mummy wasn't a bad guess," Christine put in. At least she'd managed to keep my blood off her dress, although her underskirt would have to be replaced.

"Do you know what was on the scroll they took?" Griffin asked.

"No," I admitted. "Nyarlathotep was mentioned, though."

"Blast," Griffin said, his jaw tightening.

I hunched into my overcoat. "I'm sorry."

"It isn't your fault, Whyborne," Christine said, staring out the window at the passing street lamps. "It isn't any of our faults."

Perhaps she was right. But if so, it was a cold comfort indeed.

CHAPTER 20

WE LET CHRISTINE off in front of the boarding house in which she resided. Griffin offered to see her to the door and received a pointed glare in return.

Once she was gone and we were alone in the dim interior of the cab, he moved closer and took my hand. We rode in silence until the carriage pulled up in front of Griffin's house. Saul waited for us on the porch, as usual. It was good to be home after a trying evening.

Except of course this wasn't my home. Even if it had begun to feel like it.

Griffin locked the door behind us, before turning to me. "Are you truly all right, my dear?" he asked. His hands brushed my forearms lightly, as if he wanted to reassure himself but half-feared to touch me.

"I'm perfectly fine. The wound aches a bit, but nothing more."

He didn't look entirely sure he believed me, but took my hand and led me up the stair. I hoped his bedroom was our destination, but instead he stopped in the study. "Would you like something to drink?" he asked.

"Please." I walked to the fire and stoked it absently.

"I'll get the fire. You should rest."

"I'm fine, Griffin. I'm not even using my injured arm."

Since there was no sensible answer, Griffin handed me the measure of brandy he had poured in exchange for the poker. I suppressed a sigh and took a large swallow of the alcohol. Since I'd never had the chance to eat dinner from the buffet, its warmth spread quickly through my veins.

Griffin finished with the fire and went to pour himself a drink as well. I stared down at the flames, remembering the first time I had stood here.

Remembering, also, the way Blackbyrne had come up behind me, the feel of his nails against my spine and the scent of decay on his breath.

I shivered. "Are you cold?" Griffin asked.

"No. Just thinking about Blackbyrne."

Griffin slid his arms around my waist. "You're positive it was him?"

"Yes. It was him in the Draakenwood as well."

"And he approached you? Spoke to you?"

"I…" Surely he wouldn't be jealous, would he? There was no reason. "Perhaps I'm mistaken, but it seemed as though he meant to seduce me."

Griffin's fingers tightened on my hips, pulling me back against him. "Did he?" There was an odd, low note to his voice I couldn't identify.

"I know it sounds mad, but yes. Perhaps I should have lingered and tried to learn more."

"No," Griffin growled, and nipped at the back of my neck while pressing his erection against my buttocks. At least he was no longer treating me like a fragile vase due to my injury, although his reaction made little sense.

"No?" I echoed. "If I'm not mad to even think it, if he truly was interested, perhaps I could have prolonged our interview and learned more—"

He spun me around and pressed a kiss to my lips: possessive and heated, almost bruising in its intensity. "No," he repeated in between kisses. "I can't stand the thought of anyone else's hands on you."

His unexpected words sent my blood racing. Did he mean it? We hadn't discussed our relationship, but it sounded as if he wished it to be something more than a few casual encounters.

God, please let him want that.

I pulled away to look into his eyes. They were dark with lust; his lips parted and swollen from our kisses, his expression one of such intense desire I'd do anything he asked just to keep it focused on me.

"Tell me what you want," I begged.

Griffin ground his erection against my hip. "Get in the bedroom. Now."

I was more than happy to comply. We left a trail of shed clothing behind us on the way, eager to find skin. My shirt was already ruined; I didn't object when Griffin ripped it off in a shower of buttons, his mouth fastening on one nipple, then the other, before trailing down my belly in a series of sharp nips and hard sucks.

I tried to give back the same in kind, but he shoved me onto my back in the bed, climbing on top and pinning my good arm with his hand. I might have been able to struggle free, but I gave only a token resistance. The sight of him above me, wild with desire, the feel of his stiff cock against mine, made my head spin.

He let out a soft growl and bit my neck, right at the base where it joined the shoulder. I yelped and bucked against him, stiff and ready. Instead of rubbing against me as I expected, he pulled back. His eyes were half-hooded, gleaming as they watched me. "Get on your knees."

I swallowed hard and complied. I'd never seen this possessive side of him before, never imagined it would stiffen me until my cock was hard as a rail spike, aching to be driven.

"Face the other way. Legs spread and hands on the headboard."

I couldn't seem to get enough air into my lungs, but my entire body craved his touch as I turned my vulnerable backside to him.

"Don't move," he whispered, the mattress flexing as he leaned over to rummage in the nightstand. A moment later, he took out a jar of petroleum jelly. Had he kept it there just in case?

I bit my lip. Would I enjoy this? Would it hurt? Would it change things between us, somehow?

Griffin settled behind me again. His hands traced my back, then suddenly pulled me tight against his chest, his teeth grazing the nape of my neck. I whimpered incoherently and pressed against him.

"Ival," he whispered into my ear, low and intimate. He pulled away for a moment; when he returned, it was to slip one hand between my legs. One slick finger pressed against my fundament. "Say you're mine."

It was clear what he was really asking. His finger circled the puckered flesh, pressing lightly and sending sparks of pleasure straight into my cock. "I-I'm yours," I gasped.

"Good," he murmured, and pushed his finger inside.

The sensation mixed the strange and familiar, and an involuntary gasp escaped me. He worked me slowly, sliding his finger in and out, letting me grow accustomed, and I relaxed. Then he discovered a certain spot and pressed. I moaned, my entire body quivering in response.

His breath caressed my neck, and his free hand tugged hard on my nipple, adding yet another dimension to the sensations devouring me. He paused to add more lubricant, but resumed with two fingers instead of one. I gasped at the additional stretching, but pushed back helplessly, wanting more.

"I'm going to take you," he whispered hoarsely. "I'm going to bugger you until you don't know anything but my cock up your ass, until that clever tongue of yours can't shape any word but my name."

My member was swollen to bursting, and I whimpered, beyond caring about anything except how badly I needed him.

"Ask for it," he whispered huskily, and, oh God, three fingers now, and I couldn't possibly take much more and I didn't care. "Beg me to fuck you."

My face flamed in reflexive embarrassment, despite the fact he held me in his arms, fingers buried in me. "Griffin, please!"

"Please what?"

"F-fuck me!"

He nipped me again at the base of my neck, then withdrew for a moment. I glanced back; he slicked his cock generously, the velvety skin glistening in the candlelight. Catching me watching, he grinned and stroked his length deliberately. "Want to see what's going to be splitting you open?"

"Unh," I said, because there were no words left in my brain.

He kissed the base of my spine, before settling one hand lightly on my hip. The broad head of his member pressed against my hole, and I gulped for breath past the bands threatening to tighten my throat.

"Ival," he groaned; the ends of his hair brushed the skin of my back. Then he pushed into me.

I moaned and pressed back at the same time. God, he felt twice the size I knew him to be, the thick head of his cock breaching me, stretching me to limit even though he'd prepared me well. Then suddenly the head was inside me, and he made a small sound of such pleasure I almost lost all semblance of control.

"Are you all right?" he asked; his voice was thick with lust. "I'll stop if—"

"Damn it, Griffin, fuck me," I growled.

He moaned, a sound of pure ecstasy, and pressed in slow and steady. It burned a little, but I didn't care. I didn't care about anything but this: his body in mine, opening me, filling me, pressing against the spot which sent a blinding shock of pleasure straight into my cock.

I rocked back against him; our bodies collided again and again. I wanted this; I craved it; I couldn't get enough of it. I cried out wordlessly every time he thrust, and his fingers tightened on my hips, hard enough to bruise.

"Say you're mine," he gasped; he sounded close to release. "Are you, Ival? Are you mine?"

I bit the pillow in blind lust. "God, Griffin, yes, yours, no one else's, just yours, please." I didn't even know what I begged for, except *more*. More everything: more of him, more of his cock, more of his hands on me, more of his heart.

"My dear, yes, yes—"

His voice roughened with urgency, and his thrusts took on a different tempo. "Do it," I groaned. "Take me; take me; make me yours—"

A hoarse cry tore its way out of him; he jerked into me hard, then went still, his cock twitching inside me. I dropped my hand to my own, hyper-sensitized length, and a single tug was enough to make my entire body clench as I spent myself onto the bedding. Griffin let out a startled sound of pleasure, pushing hard against my bottom, my contractions milking a final sigh out of him.

I collapsed facedown into the bedding, my arms limp as cooked noodles. Griffin pressed himself against me for a moment, then gently pulled free. The sound of his footsteps padding to the washbasin barely penetrated the sated haze cocooning me. A few moments later, he returned to the bed. "Spread your legs, my dear," he said gently.

"Again?" I asked, and got a soft chuckle. The washcloth was damnably cold, but there was something fine about being attended to.

When he crawled back into bed, I had just enough energy to roll onto my back. Griffin tucked his head against my shoulder, and we held each other in sleepy contentment.

"Are you all right?" he murmured, ever the gentleman.

I smiled. "Better than all right, I think."

"And your arm?"

"A bit achy, but I assure you I didn't notice it at the time."

He was silent a long moment; then his arm tightened across my chest. "When I saw you injured…"

The words trailed off into nothing.

I hesitated, but it was night, and words spoken in the dark can always be forgotten come the dawn. "You came into the underground tunnels after me. Thank you."

"If something had happened to you, I would never have forgiven myself," he admitted softly, as if afraid someone might overhear.

"But it didn't." I pressed my lips against his forehead.

"Not this time."

"Shh." I wrapped my good arm around him, wanting closer contact, and he obliged. "Don't dwell on such things. We're here, now, together. That's what matters."

"Yes." His lips brushed my skin, then settled again. Curled together, we lay a long time in contented silence, before sleep claimed us at last.

The sound of a fist pounding on the front door woke me. I blinked, bleary-eyed and rolled over. Only the faintest gray light showed through from outside the window.

Griffin sat up, his body stiff with alarm. Even if whoever was outside meant us no ill, we were in a rather compromising position. My heartbeat sped, and I sat up as well, casting about for my discarded clothing.

The cadence of the knock changed to a succession of smart raps. "It's Christine," I said, relieved and appalled in equal measure.

Griffin's green eyes widened. "Christine?"

"Er, yes. I'll see to her."

I fumbled on my clothing hastily. I had nothing to wear except the ruined suit from the night before, as my original intent had been to return to my apartment after the gala to preserve appearances, before joining Griffin later. Not only was the sleeve torn and bloody, but the shirt was missing most of its buttons thanks to Griffin's enthusiasm. I swore silently and buttoned up my coat to conceal as much of the damage as possible.

Christine waited on the stoop, dressed in her usual sensible boots, skirt, and shirtwaist. "Dear God, man, don't tell me you were still lazing about in bed!" she exclaimed at the sight of me.

Blood rushed to my face, but I pointed at the sky. "It's isn't even dawn yet. What on earth are you doing here?"

"I had an idea," she said, brushing past me and into the house, without waiting for an invitation. "There might still be a way of reading the scroll those bastards stole."

"You're making no sense," I said, rather shortly. Blast it, if she was going to spout nonsense, she could at least have waited until a decent hour. My head ached, and my arm ached, and other parts of my anatomy ached, although at least the latter pains I had obtained in a pleasant undertaking. "Shouldn't you be on your way to Egypt?"

"Don't worry, old man, I intend to spend the day finalizing arrangements. With any luck, I'll be steaming away from Widdershins on Wednesday. Now fetch Griffin; I don't want to repeat myself."

It really was far too early for this. "Wait here," I said. Leaving her in the parlor, I hastened back upstairs. Griffin was knotting his tie when I reappeared; he cast me a questioning look with more than a little worry in it.

"Christine claims to have come up with some idea as to how we can know what the scroll said, even though it is no longer in our possession," I said, sitting down on the edge of the bed. "Honestly, I think she couldn't sleep and decided we shouldn't, either. I'm sorry."

"It isn't your fault."

"No, but she is my friend, and I feel I ought to apologize for her behavior."

"She knows about us." It wasn't a question.

I clasped my hands between my knees and looked down. "She knows about me," I clarified. "We have been friends for a long time, and she…well, she notices things. It's one of the reasons she's good at her job."

"She would have made a fine detective."

"Don't be daft. She'd be a terrible detective. No subtlety whatsoever." I watched as he put his coat on, straightening it in the mirror, his every movement stiff. He'd been run out of his small Kansas town after being caught with another man; of course he would fear discovery. "Don't worry. Christine is my friend, and yours too, I think. She won't tell anyone. That isn't her way."

The set of his shoulders relaxed slightly, and he let out a rueful chuckle. "Christine seems more the type to shoot you in the chest than stab you in the back."

"Quite." I stood up and caught a glimpse of myself in the mirror. "Dear heavens, I'd best stop by my apartment. I look like I've been mugged and beaten."

Griffin's expression sobered. "How are you feeling?"

"A bit sore, but nothing too troublesome. Or were you asking about my arm?"

He laughed and closed with me, cupping my unshaven jaw with one hand and kissing me softly. "I have indeed corrupted you. The Whyborne I met would have never made such a jest."

"I might have, but only in my thoughts."

"No complaints concerning last night's activities, then?"

His need for reassurance made me smile. "None at all."

"Perhaps we shall try it the other way about next time."

It took a measure of will not to press my stiffening member into his hip. "You will have me in a state, and Christine is downstairs."

"You started it," he reminded.

There was no arguing, so I kissed him instead: hard and deep, a promise for later. His arms wrapped around me, holding me against his broad chest for just a moment.

"Come down when you're ready, my dear," he murmured, before hurrying out and down the stair, as if unsure he could resist the temptation to do more, should he linger.

Another look in the mirror made me question what he might find irresistible, however. My hair stood up as usual, but this morning the spikes clumped together from both the application of oil and a night pressed against a pillow. Purple shadows encircled my eyes, and the bandage on my arm showed through the gaping, blood-stained holes in my sleeves. I'd have to call a cab; if anyone saw me on the street like this, they'd summon the police.

A comb and a quick wash and shave restored some of the damage, at least. I went downstairs to find Christine and Griffin on either side of the desk in his parlor. Saul had jumped up between them and was accepting Christine's attentions with a complete lack of feline dignity, his purr loud enough to hear from the hall.

Christine and Griffin fell silent at my approach; Saul kept on, obliviously happy. Had they been talking about me?

"How's the arm?" Christine inquired gruffly. Perhaps she'd been asking Griffin about my health. Or threatening to dismember parts of his anatomy, should he break my heart. Either seemed likely.

"Stiff, but I'll survive," I said. "Would you care to enlighten us as to your revelation of this morning?"

Christine looked uncomfortable. "Whyborne, I…well. If I've been too blasted hard on you, I apologize. I rushed over here without thinking about your wound, or, er, anything."

What on earth had Griffin said to her? "We're friends because of who you are, not you who aren't. Think no more of it."

Griffin kindly fetched another chair for me, and Saul abandoned Christine to jump into my lap. "Well?" I asked, stroking his fur, "are you going to explain or not?"

Christine leaned back in her chair. "The scroll is gone, and unless you gentlemen come upon a clue soon, it seems likely it will remain lost. However, while we were setting up for the gala, the director had all of the exhibits photographed for posterity."

I sat up sharply, dislodging Saul from my lap. "Are you saying there's a photographic record of the scroll?"

"I'm saying there might be," she cautioned. "Even if there is, I don't know if they would have captured the entire thing, or only parts of it. Thanks to the disaster last night, the director will no doubt be in his office today, even if it is

Sunday. I'll ask him to deliver the photograph to you for translation immediately, assuming it exists. If he wants to know why, I'll tell him it's a way of putting a small bandage onto the wound the museum's reputation has suffered."

I could not keep myself from shaking her hand. "Brilliant, Christine. Truly brilliant."

"Dear lord, don't go all maudlin on me," she said, pulling her hand away. "It may come to nothing, if the photographer didn't do his job properly."

"Of course." I hastily composed myself. "Still, it's worth a try."

"Precisely. Well, I expect by the time you arrive at the museum, I'll be at the docks, discussing the finer points of loading my equipment onto a steamer. Never fear, though, I'll be by the Ladysmith again before I leave, and you can inform me of your progress then."

Griffin and I escorted her to the door. "I'll accompany you, if Whyborne has no objection," he said to her. "If Dr. Hart balks, I'll invoke Mr. Rice's name and hint at the connection with my case."

She regarded him for a moment, then nodded. "A sensible suggestion. Come along, then."

We parted at the sidewalk, and I watched them walk briskly away. Hoping Christine didn't say anything too terribly embarrassing about me, I turned in the other direction and headed for the nearest corner to hail a cab.

CHAPTER 21

IT DIDN'T OCCUR to me the theft would be the focus of every newspaper in New England, until I alighted from a cab in front of the Ladysmith and found a crowd of newsmen loitering on the steps. I started past them, assuming they waited for someone more important than me to speak with, and was surprised when the entire pack rushed to surround me.

"Dr. Whyborne! Is it true you tried to apprehend the criminals?" one of them demanded, while another cried: "Do you think the police are doing enough, Dr. Whyborne?"

"Is it true your father doesn't contribute the museum? Does he think it isn't safe?"

"What sort of artifact was stolen?"

"Show us where you were shot!"

"I, er—no!" I exclaimed. Clutching the collar of my overcoat against the cold wind, I hurried past them.

Rockwell glowered from his post in front of the doors, which no doubt explained why the reporters had gotten no farther. As I started past him, he laid a meaty hand on my upper arm, directly on top of my wound.

I winced, but bit back a gasp. "Good morning, Mr. Rockwell."

"Think you're better than us, do you?" he asked in a low voice. His hand tightened on my arm, sending a throb of pain through the trail left by the bullet. "Trying to show us up? Running after the thieves like you think you're some kind of hero and we're nothing?"

"I-I, no," I said, barely holding back a gasp of pain. Hot blood trickled down my arm as the scab broke under his grip.

"If I were you, sir, I'd keep to my place."

Hidden in my office, out of sight and mind. God knew it's what I would prefer. "Y-Yes. I will."

His eyes assessed me for an uncomfortably long minute. Then he gave a curt nod and let go. My arm throbbing, I fled past him and into the museum.

I didn't slow until I'd reached the safety of the hall leading to my office. Damn the man. If he'd only done his cursed job, he wouldn't have to fear a thin, weak scholar would show him up. Every beat of my heart sent a pulse of pain through my arm, and I shifted my shoulder uncomfortably, trying to get my coat to hang less heavily on the bandage. I could not afford to ruin another shirt.

The book in my coat pocket tapped lightly against my breast, dislodged by my movements. If he knew the power the *Arcanorum* could give me, Rockwell would never dare lay a hand on me again. Bullies like him were only strong while assured of victory; when faced with anyone more powerful, they turned into fawning sycophants, desperate to prove themselves. I could—

Could what? Turn into Blackbyrne, commanding a secret army of men and thugs and monsters? The idea was so absurd as to be laughable.

Wasn't it?

The smell of coffee greeted me as I approached my office, and I entered to find Griffin seated in the spare chair. A large box of photographs occupied the center of my desk.

"The director jumped at Christine's suggestion," he said, nodding at the box. "Unfortunately, although the photographs were developed, they haven't been sorted yet. Christine has left for the docks. Have you eaten?"

"No," I said, closing the door behind me.

"I suspected you wouldn't take the time, so I brought you a donut. It's there beside your coffee."

His thoughtfulness brought a smile to my face. "Thank you." I reached for the coffee with my off hand, then winced when the wound pulled.

Griffin was instantly alert. "Are you all right?"

"Yes. Mostly." He gave me a narrow look, though, and I relented with a sigh. "I had a bit of a run-in with Mr. Rockwell."

I tried to make light of the account, but by the time I finished, Griffin's brows were pulled down in a threatening scowl. "Damn the man. He had all the guards he should have needed, not to mention every reason to suspect something would happen last night. He should have positioned his men better. If this had been a Pinkerton job—"

He caught himself with an effort, his lips thinning. "Well. There's no sense in what-ifs. But if the man is weak enough to bully you because you performed his job better than he did, then your security is ill-served. I will mention the matter to Mr. Rice."

I was sorry I'd said anything. "Don't, please. I don't want to cause trouble."

"He's a wretch."

"He's afraid of losing his job."

"As he should be!"

I toyed uncomfortably with a pencil. "I know, but I don't wish any conflict with him."

Griffin looked at me closely, before letting out a sigh. "Very well, my dear. I won't mention it to Mr. Rice. But I won't forget about it, either."

I sat down and pulled the box of photos closer. "Help me sort these," I said, hoping to distract him. My dignity wouldn't survive Griffin thrashing Rockwell on my behalf.

We spent the next hour combing through the photographs. Eventually, I found a single image of the stolen scroll. The angle and lighting were poor, and I wasn't certain I'd be able to make out enough detail. I took out a pad of paper and a magnifying glass, and set to work.

Some hours later, I sat back in my chair. My neck and back hurt from leaning over the desk, and squinting through the magnifying glass left me with a headache.

"Well?" Griffin asked.

I glanced at him guiltily. How long had he sat there while I ignored everything but the picture before me? "I don't have a complete translation. The photograph is too poor to make out some of the hieroglyphs. But I do have the gist of it. I'm afraid the news isn't good."

"And here I'd hoped it would be an ancient birthday party invitation," he said dryly.

"I mean this is bad news even for the Brotherhood," I clarified. "I can't imagine what they'd want with it."

"Who is translating for them?" Griffin asked.

A question I hadn't considered before. "I don't know. Mummies are cheap enough, and there were plenty of Greeks who spoke both their own language and Egyptian, who might be resurrected and forced to translate. Perhaps not from the same era, but close enough to read the hieroglyphs. If the Brotherhood could raise Blackbyrne, they—or he—might be able to raise a mummy. Assuming Blackbyrne didn't learn to translate hieroglyphics during his earlier occult career."

"What does it say?"

"The scroll speaks of raising the dead, which the Brotherhood already knows how to accomplish. But it takes things a step beyond. It talks about the path to immortality."

"Immortality," Griffin repeated, but he sounded oddly resigned. "Of course. If you're a society of powerful, wealthy men, what's left?"

The next words stuck in my throat, but I forced them out. "True, but…it's immortality at a cost. Listen: *'Lo, he has come into being; the man who was dead has come into being; the container has come into being. Then shall you call on the Beyond-One, saying, "You who are All-in-One and One-in-All, the God Behind the Veil, who open the gate and are the gate, Yog-Sothoth, let Those from Outside see and rejoice, let this container be filled." Then say to the one who is summoned, 'I have called you while the stars stand at…'* I can't make out the rest of the incantation, I'm afraid, so I don't know where the stars are supposed to be. It picks back up at: '*…the container will be yours to command, and lo shall it make the rivers into deserts, and the desert into ocean, and lift up the land or cast it down as you say.'*"

The silence after seemed very great, as if we weren't surrounded by a city, or were the only living beings in the whole of the museum

At last Griffin stirred. "What are we looking at if we don't stop them?" he asked quietly.

I met his gaze. "The end of the world."

"Someone paid off Rosa," Griffin said.

We had sat in silence for several minutes, during which my thoughts spun in useless circles, like a machine with a slipped gear. "What?" I asked.

"Rosa. The madam. The Brotherhood either paid her to betray me, or fed her false information. I'm guessing the former, as she's too savvy for the latter. If she knows someone in the cult, or at least someone who works for them, perhaps we can chase them to ground."

"It's worth a try," I agreed.

Griffin rose to his feet. "Shall 'Weatherby' and 'Flannery' make their triumphant return?"

Considering my last experience, "triumphant" hardly seemed appropriate. Still, I nodded and said, "If you think my presence will be of use, then of course I'll go."

"I knew I could count on you." He came around the desk, leaned down, and brushed his lips across mine. "I have some things to look into. I'll meet you at seven o'clock outside your apartment."

I spent the rest of the day hunched over the *Arcanorum*, making notes and attempting to match certain passages to the information on the scroll, in hopes of building a fuller picture. I made a few brief trips to the library; on one of them, I overheard Mr. Quinn discussing the secret passage and old tunnels the thieves had fled into the night before.

"Has anyone looked into them?" I asked.

Mr. Quinn turned his unnerving stare on me; he didn't seem to blink quite as much as normal people. "Mr. Rockwell took a troop of men into the vaults last night," he said in his sepulchral voice. His long hands twisted together like a pair of white spiders. "The thieves collapsed part of the tunnel behind them. The director has had work crews tramping through the library all morning, trying to move the rubble. Mr. Bradley is quite put out he was not informed there were ruins beneath the museum."

"Did anyone know about them to tell him?"

"Oh no, no." Mr. Quinn smiled dreamily. "Imagine, a secret passage in the library. How often we all walked past it without knowing. Anything could have been on the other side. Watching."

The hair on the back of my neck stood up. "Er, yes," I managed, "well, if that's all, I have, er, things. To look up."

"Of course, Dr. Whyborne. Do let us know if you need any…assistance."

Somehow, I didn't want to bring up the name Yog-Sothoth to Mr. Quinn.

My research revealed nothing more. Many rituals depended on astronomical phenomena. The winter solstice was fast approaching, but there was no guarantee it was the celestial event to which the ritual was keyed. The rise of a particular star, or a certain conjunction of planets, were just as likely.

We didn't know when, or where. Or who; some poor devil would have to serve as the 'container' of the entity called through, after all. No doubt the Brotherhood would choose one of their own, but other than Blackbyrne, we didn't know the identities of the living cult members, let alone dead ones.

Perhaps the madam would be able—and willing—to shed some light on our opponents. We needed something, anything, to give us a chance.

That evening, Griffin met me in front of my apartment building. He strolled up the street in his dockworker's garb, and I was shocked at my sudden desire to embrace him. Such a display would only end up with us both in jail, so I tucked my hands into my pockets to keep from touching him.

"Hullo, Weatherby," he said affably. "Nice night. Fancy a stroll?"

"Don't mind if I do." I fell in beside him. "Your day was well?"

"Well enough. Yours?"

"Unproductive."

"Ah."

I glanced at him. There were dark circles under his eyes, and a drawn look around his mouth. He was under a great deal of strain, and had been for a long time. He'd lived with the burden of having seen things most people wouldn't credit; he'd been called mad; he'd endured knowing the Brotherhood was out there, plotting God-knew-what insanity, and been unable to do anything about it. Poor Philip Rice had already lost his life by the time Griffin came onto the case, but he was still responsible for bringing peace to a grieving father.

And now I told him failure meant the possible destruction of the human race, or at least its enslavement. No wonder he looked troubled.

"We'll stop them," I said quietly. The mix of snow and mud on the sidewalk squelched under our feet.

"We have to. For all our sakes." God, he sounded bleak.

I badly wished to take his hand. Instead, I said, "Buck up, old fellow. We haven't lost yet."

He cast me a small smile. "You're right, of course." Turning his gaze back to the fore, he added, "I'm glad you're here with me."

Despite the circumstances, his pronouncement filled me with warmth. I ducked my head and tried not to smile too ridiculously.

I was better prepared for the brothel's atmosphere this time. It looked much as it had on my first visit: full of bad whiskey, bad breath, and badly-dressed women.

With the addition, it would seem, of bad tempers. My partners at cards were there; catching sight of me, they rose menacingly to their feet.

"Didn't think you'd show your face around here again, Weatherby," said the gap-toothed dealer.

"Aw, no, ye're not sore losers, are ye?" Griffin asked, slinging a friendly arm around me.

"To hell with you, Flannery," another man said. "You're the one as brought him here. Guess you got a part of the cut?"

"I didn't cheat," I said, affronted. How dare they suggest I was a cheat?

"I'm here to see Rosa," Griffin said, his tone going short and businesslike. "Weatherby, wait outside."

"You can just go with him," said Nelly, who had been perched at the bar. "Madam Rosa ain't seeing no one. She said we wasn't to let anyone disturb her."

Was Nelly telling the truth, or had Rosa just left instructions to turn Griffin away? If she had knowingly sent him into a trap, she certainly wouldn't want to face him again.

Griffin's face took on a harder cast; probably he'd had the same thoughts. "Sorry, Nelly, but this canna wait."

Nelly hopped down off the bar. "Ain't nothing she can do for you as you can't get from any other girl here."

A laugh escaped Griffin, but it was oddly flat. "'Tisn't that kind of business, girl. I'll tell her ye tried to stop me; ye willna get in trouble." He started for the stairs.

The bouncer stepped in front of him. The man was a wall of muscle, his arms straining at the seams of his coat, and he wielded a short, stout cudgel. "You ain't going nowhere if you know what's good for you."

Griffin's mouth thinned. "I don't have time for this."

The bouncer lunged at him; Griffin sidestepped neatly, seized the man's arm, and twisted. One moment, the bouncer was attacking, and the next he was on his knees, his elbow at a horrible angle, bellowing in agony. Some of the other men started for Griffin, but he drew his revolver and turned to them coolly.

"Back off, boys," he said, no longer trying to disguise his voice with a false accent. "I don't mean Rosa any harm, but I *will* speak with her now."

No one moved. Griffin nodded and turned to the stairs. "Come along."

I hurried after him. "Do you, er, think anyone will summon the police?" I whispered as we went up the stairs together. Being arrested in an ordinary brothel would be only marginally better than being arrested in a bathhouse.

"Not without Rosa's order," Griffin replied. His words were clipped, his eyes watching the doors we passed, the corners, the shadows, anywhere an assailant might hide. "I'm surprised she hasn't yet come out. She must truly not wish to face me."

I winced. "Not looking good for her innocence, then." I wouldn't have cared, except it was obvious Griffin did.

"No it isn't," he agreed flatly.

The madam's room lay at the very end of the hall. Griffin didn't bother to knock, only grabbed the knob and tried to open it. It was locked, of course.

The furrow between his brows deepened. "Rosa?" he called, pitching his voice to carry through the door. "I know you're in there. I just want to talk."

I pressed my ear to the door. Someone within was eating dinner, as unlikely as it seemed, given the disturbance downstairs. The sound of chewing and slurping was loud, interrupted by an odd crack every now and again. And there was a sort of leathery slither, accompanied by a gelatinous burp, which sent a frisson of atavistic horror down my spine.

I took an alarmed step back. "We need to get inside. Now."

CHAPTER 22

GRIFFIN SWORE AND rammed the door with his shoulder. The cheap lock gave in the space of two blows, and the door flew open. Griffin charged inside, revolver in hand, and I could do nothing but follow.

The stench rolled out to greet us in a wave: graveyard rot and sickeningly-sweet perfume twined together into a hellish blend. I reflexively touched the *Arcanorum* where it lay in my breast pocket, like a talisman.

The layout of the rooms was reversed from what might normally be expected. In a hotel or apartment, the sitting room would greet the visitor first, then the bedroom. But in this place, it was the sitting room which was the private space, tucked in the back where the clients wouldn't see.

The bed dominated the room. The garish red pattern of the comforter seemed odd, even for a brothel.

No, wait. It wasn't a pattern, or at least not a deliberate one.

Madam Rosa's remains sprawled across a coverlet soaked in her blood. Her head dangled over the edge of the bed, her sightless eyes seeming to stare accusingly at me. A misshapen thing crouched over her; it looked up at Griffin's horrified gasp, and its bestial face was smeared with blood and fluid. It had been *feeding* on her torn-open body.

Griffin fired his revolver. The monster lurched clumsily away, making for the open window. Like all of the abominable Guardians I had seen, it was partly human and partly something else, in this case a hellish admixture of bat. Its ears were huge, and its face so creased and wrinkled it barely seemed a face at all. Slimy flaps of skin hung in gigantic folds from its arms, rippling and stretching as it extended its hideously elongated fingers to drag itself across the floor.

Griffin shot again, and it let out a scream and collapsed to the ground, flopping horribly. I cast about for a weapon, but before I could do anything, Griffin fired a third time.

The bullet caught it through the skull, endings its torment. With a last, fading shriek, it began to crumble back into the constituent salts from which it had been formed.

Silence fell within the little room. From outside came the sounds of revelry and the clop of hooves. The laughter and catcalls seemed strangely far away, as if they echoed from some other universe entirely.

Griffin's face was unreadable as a granite statue as he gazed down on the remains of Rosa's corpse. My hands were clammy and bile stung the back of my throat, but I managed to say, "If you want me to search her room…"

"No." He closed his eyes briefly, as if at some pain. "Wait outside. I'll…I'll take care of things."

I walked out into the hall and waited silently. No one challenged me, for which I was grateful.

Before much time had passed, Griffin rejoined me. "Nothing," he said, and, God, he looked distant. Cold.

"I'm sorry," I said. "What should we do with the, er, the body?" There wasn't much point in summoning the police, I supposed.

Griffin rubbed at his eyes. "I…I don't know."

I touched his elbow lightly, steering him toward the stairs. He came with me without argument. On the way out, I caught Nelly's eye.

"I'm sorry," I said. "We were too late. Your mistress has been murdered."

She let out a small cry, pressing her hands to her lips. I wished there was more I could do, for her, for Griffin, even for poor dead Rosa.

We went out into the night and walked back toward the more reputable part of town. When we came to the intersection which would determine our path, to his home or my apartment, Griffin came to an abrupt halt. His fists were thrust deep into his coat pockets, his jaw set firmly. "Whyborne, I…I'm not sure I would be good company tonight."

"What was she to you?" I asked, even though I wasn't at all sure I wanted the answer.

He passed a hand over his face, then tucked it back into his pocket, as if afraid it might wander on its own. "She was a friend. My first friend in Widdershins. I thought she was, anyway." He laughed bitterly. "Of course, she never even knew my real name. Oh, how we delude ourselves."

How selfish was I, to be relieved even as I sympathized with his pain? "Do you not want my company, or do you think you won't be good company? Because those are two very different things."

"I'm not really in the mood to entertain."

"That wasn't my question." When he looked uncertain, I let out a sigh. "Have we not already had this discussion? Or do you still believe my regard for you to be purely venial?"

He hesitated visibly, as if caught between two prongs I could only guess at. The glance he stole at my face seemed to decide him. "I would be grateful for your presence."

I fell in beside him, and we walked silently back to his house. We undressed with a minimum of speech, and I took him into my arms, holding him against me.

Although my body was not insensate to his presence, the sweet wave of arousal was less urgent than usual, and I ignored it as I cradled him. More important was making sure he understood he was not alone. The death tonight had shaken him, whether because he'd known Rosa, or because she reminded him of the girl he'd failed to save, or some other reason, I didn't know.

I held him close, hoping I could offer some comfort by my presence, by the press of my skin against his, simple and undemanding. Because I didn't want him to hurt, or to be afraid, no matter how bad things looked.

Because I wanted him to be happy.

Because I loved him.

I closed my eyes and pressed my lips against his brow, and held him long after his breathing had lapsed into sleep.

I was in a dark mood when I arrived at the museum the next morning Griffin's sleep had been interrupted by a fit, which had left him shaking uncontrollably in my arms until almost dawn. Although he seemed largely restored by the time I left, the strain was wearing on him.

He wasn't the only one. How were we to stop a group of powerful men, one of them raised from the grave itself, from doing exactly what they wanted, especially since we had no idea when or where they would act? Our best chance of finding a link to them had died with Rosa, and I had not the slightest idea what to do next.

Griffin had said something vague about tracking down some of the local resurrection men, but I doubted he would have much luck. Widdershins didn't boast a large medical school like Arkham, and although there seemed to be enough inhabitants who wanted bodies dug up to keep a healthy sideline going, surely there couldn't be very many employed full-time in the business, as it were.

A knock came at my office door shortly after noon. I called a brusque command to enter; Miss Parkhurst timidly opened the door halfway and stuck her head inside. "A message came for you, sir," she said.

My heart sank into the basement at the sight of the wax seal on the envelope. "Thank you," I forced myself to say. She was only the messenger, after all.

"Of course." Still, she lingered in the doorway. "How is your arm, if-if I might ask, Dr. Whyborne?" Her face turned bright red, as if the question had been in some way personal.

"I, er, quite well, Miss Parkhurst," I replied.

"Oh, the other girls will be glad to hear it! None of us were there, of course, but we heard, and well, you were very heroic."

My face was surely as red as hers. "Oh. N-not really. I didn't…didn't get the papyrus back, you see, and, er."

"Still, it was more than anyone else did, wasn't it?" She twisted her hands together. "If you need anything, just let us know. We wouldn't want you reopening your wound, after all."

I tugged at the knot of my tie. "Th-thank you, Miss Parkhurst. And please, extend my thanks to the other ladies as well. Your concern is appreciated."

She blushed again, but smiled as she left. I must not have sounded as idiotic as I feared.

Once she had gone, I laid the unopened letter on my desk, as reluctant to touch it as if it had been penned in poisoned ink. But poison was far too subtle for my father; with an effort I picked it up and broke the wax seal bearing our family crest.

The enclosed note was short and direct; I would have expected nothing else. My older brother Stanford was in town, and I was directed to dine with them tonight.

No *"How are you, son?"* no *"I heard from Addison you were shot, and wanted to make sure you're doing well."* No *"We haven't spoken since your mother's birthday, ten months ago."* Not even a damned *"Merry Christmas."* Just a command to present myself for dinner at 7 o'clock.

I didn't have to go. I didn't owe my father anything. Mother had sold her own jewelry to pay my tuition at Miskatonic, and I'd lived on my small museum salary ever since, without any assistance from him.

But what if this summons concerned Mother? The old dread stirred in the back of my mind, like lead seeping into my veins, turning my heart sluggish. She'd been ill for a very long time. If the end were near…well, Father wouldn't say it in a message. He probably wouldn't even say it face-to-face. I'd have to see for myself.

I put down the brief letter and pressed my fingertips against my closed eyes. I had too much to do…but at the moment, unless Griffin found some new clue, we were at an impasse.

If Mother had taken a turn for the worse, and I didn't go…

Stifling a sigh, I hurriedly penned two notes. One was to Father, accepting his invitation, as if he'd left me some choice. The other was to Griffin.

That one I lingered over, unsure how to phrase things in a way he would understand. *"My father has ordered me to come to dinner, and I intend to accept because I worry about Mother's health. I shall most likely be out quite late, and miss our appointment this evening."*

I folded the note carefully, then, on impulse, pressed the paper lightly to my lips. God, I would miss him tonight. I craved him, like an opium addict craved the pipe: the sound of his voice, the touch of his hand, his mere presence in the same room.

How had this happened? How had I lost my heart this badly, after having such control?

Had I ever really been in control? Or had merely fooled myself? Perhaps I'd never been truly tempted, until someone came along to engage all of me: a desire of character, intellect, and carnal dimensions.

I needed to pull myself together. Addressing the note to Griffin with a firm hand, I took both missives up to the Miss Parkhurst's desk. She turned pink again for no reason I could discern, and took them to post.

The rest of the day dragged on. Griffin sent a message back, saying he'd made no progress which required my presence and wishing me a good evening with my family. His final line suggested we reschedule our "appointment" for tomorrow night. That alone gave me the strength to face the prospect of dinner tonight.

After work, I stopped by my apartment long enough to freshen my appearance a bit. Then, like a gladiator walking into an arena he expects to leave bleeding and wounded, I summoned a cab and returned home.

Unlike some other old families, who aspired to an actual estate, the Whybornes had occupied an enormous house on High Street almost since the founding of Widdershins. Let the Somerbys have their grounds and forest and lake, Father had always said, usually within hearing of Addison. The Whybornes remained where they could keep their fingers on the pulse of commerce.

Then Addison would laugh, and tell Father he was missing the *point* of having money in the first place, which was to pay other people to do that sort of thing for you.

At any rate, the house dated back to colonial times, although it had been extensively renovated both within and without. When I knocked at the door, the butler, Mr. Fenton, admitted me without comment. At one time, we'd been on speaking terms, but when I'd pursued a career in philology against Father's wishes, I'd apparently committed high treason in Mr. Fenton's eyes.

Fortunately, not everyone on the staff viewed me with such disfavor. "Well, if it isn't Master Percival!"

I grinned, genuinely happy for the first time that day. "Miss Emily," I said fondly, embracing my old nurse. It shocked me how aged she looked; in my mind, time had stopped the day I'd walked out of the house, Father's admonishments ringing in my ears. Even though I'd seen her since, my visits had been infrequent enough to preserve my image of her younger self, like an insect in amber.

She drew back and inspected me carefully. She'd helped Mother with all three of us, of course, but when Mother had taken ill shortly after my birth, her role had shifted from maid to nurse, of me and Mother both. She had one child, a daughter, and no husband. Her daughter could be my half-sister or cousin, but I cared for Miss Emily too much to ask for the truth, if she didn't offer first.

"How is Mother?" I asked.

Miss Emily waved a wizened hand. "Fine, fine. Same as she has been, thank the Lord."

Tension left my shoulders, and my knees went weak. Mother was fine. This dinner was nothing but another bizarre ploy by Father to bring me into line. "Will she dine with us?"

Emily's mouth pursed, revealing a forest of wrinkles. "Probably not. You might want to see her first."

I nodded. I would have embraced her again, but Mr. Fenton was already scowling at us, no doubt to carry tales to Father. I didn't want Miss Emily to get into trouble, so I excused myself and made my way up to Mother's room.

As I trod the familiar, dark-paneled halls, it seemed in some ways as if I'd never left. Nausea squirmed in my belly; I half-expected to be called to face Father in his study, or to bear the brunt of my brother's pranks, or catch sight of my sister and some giggling friend of hers, pointing and laughing at me.

"Percival!"

Hunching my shoulders instinctively, I turned to the source of the greeting. My brother had changed little in the three years since I'd last seen him. He was smartly dressed in the height of Fifth Avenue fashion, where he lived with his wife and three boys. His vest encompassed an expanding waistline, and the slight chubbiness of his face made his eyes look even smaller and meaner. He'd taken after our father: big, burly, and athletically inclined, at least in their younger days. My sister and I had both inherited Mother's willowy frame, which was acceptable in Guinevere, but certainly not in me.

"Stanford," I said by way of greeting. I wanted to run, like a mouse trapped in front of a cat, but there was nowhere I could go.

No. We were adults now; Stanford wouldn't lock me in a closet, or hit me with a stick, or dangle me over the upstairs balcony until I begged for mercy. Those had been the product of boyish high spirits, at least according to Father. Stanford had been praised for his conduct, and I told I needed to learn to fight back. The world was "red in tooth and claw," as Tennyson said, and Stanford and his friends were doing me a favor by teaching me a valuable lesson.

Now that we were grown, he could only sneer. "How are you, dear brother? Still fondling books all day?"

"Yes, quite," I said with a pale half-smile. "I trust Darla is well? And the boys? I'm surprised you came to Widdershins without them this close to Christmas."

"And pry Darla out of New York? Never happen." He snorted in disgust. "Women have no ambition, Percival, but at least it keeps them out of trouble. She made some noise, but I gave her money for a new dress, and that was the last I heard of it. Be glad you don't have to worry about such things. I don't suppose many women are throwing themselves at poor librarians, are they?"

My blood boiled in my chest, but I kept my expression neutral with a lifetime's worth of practice. "I'm not a librarian."

"You work with books, don't you?" he asked with a shrug. Stanford never cracked a book if he could help it, which was the one way he differed from Father, who at least believed in the power of knowledge.

I had to get away, or else I might be tempted to…what? Yell? Strike him? Show him just what a book could do?

God, no wonder Bradley had gotten under my skin with such ease. He was nothing but a stand-in for the real thing. How utterly pathetic, for Bradley and myself.

"I wish to call on Mother," I said with a curt bow. "I'll see you at dinner."

He waved a languid hand, and I turned on my heel and left. How I would eat at all, I didn't know; my stomach churned with acid, and my legs trembled with remembered powerlessness. If only Griffin were with me, perhaps I could bear this.

But then he would see how weak I truly was, and that I could bear even less.

CHAPTER 23

MOTHER'S CHAMBERS WERE on the uppermost floor, where the windows allowed her to look out over the neighborhood. I hurried up the stairs, confronted at every turn with a painting from colonial times, or a musket fired by my great-great-great grandfather during the Revolutionary War, or some other artifact testifying to the greatness of our dead ancestors. Living here had not been like growing up in a museum, but rather a mausoleum.

I'd had one refuge within the house, where I might retreat without fear of censure. Thank goodness; I might have gone mad, otherwise.

I knocked on the door at the top of the stairs, and was bid enter by a muffled voice within. I walked in without attempting to conceal my smile.

The room was much as I remembered, although it had been ten months since I'd been there last. Bookcases lined the walls, and spacious windows let in the sun during the day and looked out on the gaslit street at night. A huge fireplace dominated the long wall opposite the doorway; above it hung a beautiful painting of the Lady of Shallott. The Lady's face had been modeled on the woman who now sat in front of the fire, bundled in layers of blankets, a book in her hand.

"Percival," she said, and her joyful smile pricked my conscience. It really had been too long. "Your father said you would visit this evening. Come, sit with me."

I seated myself on the ottoman at her feet and took her hands. Her skin was thin, translucent, and her grip weak. Her glorious hair had gone gray, and wrinkles marked her lovely face. But her eyes were still sharp and fierce, the eyes of a hunting hawk, even if one trammeled in a mew.

"How are you?" I asked.

"Well enough. But what of you? How is your job at the museum? I heard there was a robbery of some sort, but Niles wouldn't let me see the papers. He worried it would upset me."

Damn Father, treating her as a child instead of a grown woman. Still, I should have sent word around, telling her I was all right. "There was a robbery, yes."

I launched into my tale, starting with my first meeting with Griffin and leaving out only the most personal details. I even lit a candle for her using the secret words, and her exclamation of delight warmed me as little about the case had.

It was only fair. She had been the one to introduce me to wonder, after all. She'd shared her love of books, and, when I proved interested, taught me Greek and Latin, in order to read the great works as closely as possible to their original forms, rather than as bloodless translations censored to match the modern idea of morality. We'd spent hours discussing every aspect of the classics, wringing meaning from every line, each word. We'd mused together on the gods, and she'd laughed when as a boy I made little altars to Pan and Bacchus.

"I can't believe it," she said, touching her chest when she saw the flame spring into being. "Oh, Percival, this is wonderful! And it's truly no slight-of-hand?"

"It's real," I assured her. I hesitated to speak of the Guardians, because there were things of horror as well as wonder hidden beneath everyday life. But I could not condemn Father for treating her like a child and then do the same myself.

We sat together for a long time after I'd finished. She mulled my words and asked pertinent questions. Eventually, her hand tightened on mine. "I would tell you to be careful, but you already know that."

"I try," I assured her.

"I'm glad," she said with sudden fierceness, and her raptor gaze unexpectedly pierced me. "Even if nothing lurks beneath the surface of the world but madness, I'm glad to know there is something more. That this isn't everything."

She'd spent half her life trapped in these chambers, too sick to venture out. No need to wonder why she felt as she did. "It's why I told you," I said.

She nodded, then added, "Your Mr. Flaherty seems a clever sort."

My ears grew hot. Of course I hadn't spoken of our relationship, but I couldn't leave Griffin out of the account, either. "He is. And very kind. A good man."

"I'm glad you've found a friend," she said. "I should like to meet him sometime. Perhaps in the new year, when your father is out of town on business?"

"Yes. I'd love to introduce you."

There came a polite rap on the door. Mother's lips thinned, but she called, "Come in."

Mr. Fenton opened the door. "Dinner is served, Master Percival. Mrs. Whyborne, I believe Emily will be up shortly with your repast."

I wanted to stay and talk to her, not sit through some horrible meal with Stanford and Father. But I was here at Father's whim, and although I didn't care if I ever set foot in these halls again for my sake, I refused to let him cut Mother off entirely from the outside world.

I squeezed her hands. "Shall I visit on Christmas?"

"If you have the time," she said. "I don't wish to take you away from your friend's side."

I didn't know how Griffin intended to spend the holiday—assuming we even survived to see it, and Blackbyrne and the Brotherhood didn't unleash horror on the world before then. "I'll make time," I said, and hoped my promise wasn't in vain.

I followed the butler down to the grand dining hall. The long table looked utterly ludicrous, with my father at the head and a single place set to either side of him, the rest of it bare. But I couldn't find it in me to laugh; this was how I'd spent most of the dinners of my childhood.

Dinner with Leander and Uncle Addy had been different. We'd eaten in a smaller room, full of light and warmth, laughing together. God, no wonder I'd fallen in love with Leander. He was an Apollo to my Hades: a being of golden light and life, while I was something growing among the shadows of the dead.

Niles Foster Whyborne sat at the head of the table, regarding me silently as I approached. His dark hair had gone iron gray, along with his neatly-trimmed beard, and there were more wrinkles on his face. But his straight bearing and trim form were not much altered from my youth.

"Sir," I mumbled in the direction of my feet.

"Percival." My name was short, clipped, and held the edge of disappointment inextricably associated with it. "Sit down."

I sat across from Stanford, careful not to look directly at him. I might as well have been eight again, or ten. Or eighteen, explaining to my plate that no, I was not going to attend Father's alma mater, or go into business, or any of the things he wanted me to do. And, yes sir, I understood a real man wouldn't study comparative philology, except perhaps in his declining years after he'd made his mark in business and could no longer do anything useful.

The three of us sat in uncomfortable silence while the servants laid out our dinner. Once they had withdrawn to stand along the wall, Father said, "Stanford, how are things in New York?"

Stanford launched into a long tale discussing the various cutthroat deals he'd made, seguing into his ideas of the proper way to handle striking workers—shooting the lot of them in cold blood seemed to sum it up. Father nodded, putting in his own advice on occasion. I half-hoped neither would speak to me, and I would escape unscathed. Unfortunately, just before the dessert course was served, Father turned to me.

"I hear there was some excitement at the museum gala," he said. For him to even acknowledge the museum existed was a rare thing, unless he was making a point about how I was wasting my life on womanish frivolity.

Dessert. Served, I cut my slice of chocolate cake into squares, using the motion to give me somewhere to direct my gaze, even as it bought me time to think. "Yes," I said at last, seeing no way to avoid it. I did not volunteer anything further.

"Addison said you were injured."

Why was he bringing it up? Not because he cared. "A scratch, only."

Stanford let out an ugly laugh. "What happened—fall down while you were running away?"

My fingers tightened on my fork and knife. I carved the cake into increasingly smaller squares, trying to disguise the shaking of my hands. "I was struck by a bullet."

"While trying to apprehend the thieves, Addison tells me," Father said. Out of the corner of my eye, I saw him give Stanford a quelling look. As for myself, I kept my gaze fixed on the plate and cut. And cut.

"I was performing my duty to the museum," I said. My throat tightened around the words, and I had to push them out.

"Such a duty belongs to the guards, not you." Ah, now we came to it. He believed I'd brought shame on the family, acting like a common watchman.

"The guards were confused," I said carefully. Cut. Cut. "I saw the miscreants and acted. Isn't that what you want, Father? For me to be a man of action?"

"Not if the result is your death," he said, sounding annoyed. No doubt my demise in such a fashion would be a horrible embarrassment, especially if it made the front page of the paper. What a disappointment I was, unable even to die correctly. "I don't want you behaving in such a reckless fashion again."

"Yes, Father," I said, not because I meant it, but because it would prevent an argument over the dinner table.

He nodded, pleased, and turned back to Stanford to talk business again. I stared down at my plate. Surely I should feel some shred of guilt for lying to him. He was my father; I owed him some respect, didn't I?

But I lied all the time. My life had been nothing but a fable, told to keep society happy, or at least keep it from noticing me. I'd lied about my feelings for Leander, I'd hidden away any spark or sign of passion after coming to manhood, and now I pretended Griffin was merely a good friend. What did one more lie matter?

When we were done, the servants came and removed our plates. My cake had been reduced to a pile of tiny crumbs, but I hadn't eaten a single bite.

Griffin answered my knock on the door.

He was in his shirtsleeves, and the warm gaslight shining out from behind him revealed his expression of surprise. "Whyborne? I thought you were going back to your apartment." He stepped back and motioned me inside. "Come in, my dear, out of the cold. Is everything all right?"

I couldn't summon the words. They were lost somewhere behind me, buried in shadows or mired in the dust of Whyborne House. I stepped forward, shut the door behind me, and kissed him: deep and raw and needy, my tongue pushing impatiently past his teeth to explore his mouth. He tasted like whiskey and tea. His fingers gripped my lapels, his skin almost painfully warm against my cold hands when I buried my fingers in his hair.

God, he smelled good: of male skin and sandalwood. He was alive, real, bright, utterly unlike anyone I'd ever known, a streak of color in a world of drab browns and grays.

He pulled back, his broad chest heaving. "Is everything all right?" he asked.

I captured his lower lip with my teeth, worrying at it until he moaned and plunged his tongue into my mouth. I sucked at it, hard, rhythmically, even as I pressed my erection into his hip.

When we broke apart again, I leaned into him, sliding my hands into the gap between his trousers and his shirt to cup his buttocks. "I need you." The skin of his neck was warm, just above the collar, and he shivered when my breath touched it. "You make me feel alive. Everything else is just a role, but this is real."

"Let me lock up," he said huskily. "I'll meet you upstairs."

I hurried to the study on the second floor. A stack of notes and folders sat beside one chair, along with a half-empty tumbler of whiskey. He must have been going over the particulars of the case, looking for some hint, and perhaps I should have been responsible and offered to help. But I didn't want to be responsible, not right now.

The room was warm and cheery thanks to the fire. I took off my coat and hat, and had unfastened my vest by the time he joined me. Thankfully, he didn't ask me again what vexed me. Perhaps he already understood from my words, from knowing where I'd been, even though I'd never spoken in detail about my family to him. He crossed the room and caught me to him, kissing me with bruising passion. The rough stubble on his jaw scraped my skin, wonderfully masculine. He shoved his thigh between mine, and I pushed against him, desperate for more, for the feel of skin on skin.

I pulled back and resumed unbuttoning my clothing as fast as I could. He did the same, his fingers clumsy with desire. The warm light of the fire dusted his skin in gold and found unexpected highlights of red in his hair. I traced the lines of muscle revealed by the soft light with my tongue, working my way down until I was on my knees.

There was no finesse to what I did, only animal need, wrapping my lips around his cock and sliding my mouth down until I reached the root, my nose pressed into the curling hair at the base.

"God!" he exclaimed, surprised by my tactics. His fingers clenched in my hair, and the muscles in his thighs shook as he fought not to thrust into my mouth. I clutched his taut buttocks, hard enough to leave finger-shaped bruises, pulling my mouth back almost to the tip, then sucking him back in again and again and again.

With a sharp gasp, he pushed me back. "Stop, stop," he said, voice shaking.

I let out a whimper at being denied. The taste of him filled my mouth, and I hungered for more, for the tang and salt of his release. "Did I do something wrong?" I asked. "Tell me and I'll do better, I swear."

"You've done nothing wrong." He knelt in front of me to put us on a level, cradling my face in his hands, his fingers tracing my swollen lips. "I just didn't want it to end yet." His smile turned sultry. "I like seeing this side of you."

Our lengths slid together when he pulled me to him, and I moaned and thrust against him. His hands shaped my back, then slid to my shoulders as I kissed and nibbled and bit my way from the base of his throat across his chest. I licked first one nipple and then the other, trailing my lips back up his neck to find his mouth again. I longed to rub against him like a cat, to spread his scent all over me.

"Ival," he whispered, his lips against my ear, sending shivers of delight across my skin. Hearing the lover's name made me feel like someone different, someone new: not Percival or Whyborne or any of the other masks I'd constructed to protect myself. Here, I could just be me.

"Tell me what you want," I begged.

He kissed my cheek, then nipped at my lips. "Lie down on your side."

He lay down as well, only opposite, placing our cocks on the level of each other's mouths. I eagerly caught hold of his length and pointed it at my lips. He was hard and red and leaking, as if my desire had enflamed him, and—

And his tongue licked down my length, from slit to base: warm and wet and very, very good. "I won't last," I warned him.

"Then don't," he said, his breath cool against my heated skin. He took me into his mouth, lips sucking on the head, before sliding down to the root.

I did the same for him. The sensation of his length in my mouth was heavenly, much better than any of the furtive, pale longings I'd had in my youth. I took as much of him as I could, swallowing so my throat worked around him. His legs were spread for access; I took his sack in one hand, tugging and rolling his balls until his thighs started to tremble.

He could hardly warn me with his mouth full of my organ, but the tension in his body and the way his hips twitched with the need to ram into me were warning enough. I moaned in greedy anticipation, and an instant later, his rod swelled and spasmed, spilling the hot, salty, bitter cream into my mouth.

His cries were muffled by my cock. Letting his length slip from my lips, I closed my eyes and clung to his thighs, pressing my face against them as I jerked and thrust into the hot wetness of his mouth. The tremors started in my own legs, and I arched my back and started to groan even as my balls tightened. At the last instant, he suddenly shoved a saliva-slick finger into my passage—and that was it, white lights exploding behind my eyes, my cock swelling, my body clenching hard around the intruding finger, and dear lord it kept on cresting and rising until I had no air left in my lungs, until I was completely and thoroughly and utterly spent.

CHAPTER 24

I COLLAPSED BACK onto the carpet, beyond sated. I'd probably have rug burn on my hip and shoulder tomorrow, but at the moment my nerves sang with the last aftershocks of pleasure.

Griffin sat up and looked down at me fondly, the firelight haloing his hair. "Well. You seemed to enjoy that."

I glanced away, uncomfortably aware I'd behaved like a wanton. "Yes."

As my heated blood cooled, I began to shiver. Griffin noticed and pulled the throw from the back of the couch. He stretched out beside me on the floor, wrapping us both in the heavy cloth. "Do you want to tell me what's wrong?"

His fingers trailed gently along the side of my face. I kissed his fingertips, then rolled over onto my back to stare at the ceiling.

"I just want to be myself," I said at last. "But no one else wants just me, except for you."

His hand slid over the curve of my hip, the touch gentle and reassuring. "Dinner with your family didn't go well?"

I swallowed back a laugh more desperate than amused. "At least I could leave when it was over. At least I didn't have to go back to my room after and stare out the window, wondering if I'd ever escape. At least Father gave up on calling me into his study for lectures after I went to Arkham."

"What happened? You don't have to tell me, but I'm curious. What led to your falling out?"

"There was no falling out on my part," I said eventually. "Perhaps because there had never been any 'in' to fall out of. Father expected his sons to behave in a certain way. I never did. Not to suggest I didn't try, when I was younger at least. Once I grew older, I knew how futile it would be. The only thing to do was to bear it and hope one day I could escape."

His fingers stroked the nape of my neck soothingly. "I'm sorry."

"Not long after Leander died, I was informed I would be attending Widdershins University, where I would study law. Upon graduation, I would join Father and Stanford in the family business."

"What happened?"

"I told him I wasn't going to do any of those things. Sounds simple, doesn't it? I suppose it was, in a way. I told him over and over, day after day, while he raged and threatened and ordered." I could remember standing in front of his desk with crystalline clarity: the fustiness of his tobacco, the portrait of great-grandfather glowering down at me from above the hearth, the way the light through the window played over the crystal decanters on the sideboard. And all the while, Father shouting and banging his fist on the desk, listing all of my faults loudly enough for the entire house to hear.

"Eventually, he just...gave up, I suppose," I said. "Mother sold some of her jewelry to pay for my education, since he refused to give me so much as a penny ever again. I went off to Miskatonic University, studied comparative philology, and found a job at the Ladysmith. After all this time, it shouldn't bother me...yet I sat down at the table tonight and I felt like I was ten years old and the family disappointment again. Well, I suppose I still am a disappointment, but—"

He cut off my words with a fierce kiss. "You're nothing of the sort," he whispered against my mouth. "To hell with them if they can't see how strong you are."

The words were only meant as a kindness, of course, but warmth curled in my chest nonetheless. "Shall we go to bed?" I asked. "I fear my bones won't thank me should we fall asleep on the floor."

Griffin gave me a searching look, but let me change the subject. "Of course, my dear. Anything you want."

I rose before Griffin the next morning and dressed quietly, not wishing to wake him. The sun had barely edged its way above the horizon, and I could just make out his face in the light of dawn, his hair tousled. He was beautiful, from the curve of his lips to the delicate wings of his eyelashes against his cheek. Perhaps I could climb back under the covers for just a little while...but no.

Time was surely running out; Blackbyrne would make his move soon. I might not know precisely when or where, but I knew we didn't have long to expose his plans and find some way to counter them. As pleasant as it would be to linger with Griffin, my time would be better served looking for a solution.

I shut the door quietly behind me and went into the study. The fire slumbered as coals; I stoked it and laid on more wood. At least Griffin would find a warm room when he rose and joined me. The pile of papers he'd been looking over last night still sat on the floor by his chair. Perhaps a fresh eye could uncover something new.

To that end, I pulled the chair closer to the fire, seated myself, and began to sort through the stack. Although there were loose papers, most were sorted into envelopes with labels such as "The Brotherhood," "Philip Rice," "Percival Endicott Whyborne—"

I read the words again, surprised. Why on earth would Griffin have information about me?

The envelope contained an assortment of notes, letters, and newspaper clippings. On top was a letter from Mr. Rice, recommending Griffin contact me to break the cipher. *"He has published monographs on various ciphers, where they intersect with his philological work,"* it read in part. *"He's a strange duck to be sure, but supposed to be brilliant. If his surname seems familiar, it's because he's the son of Niles Whyborne. You've probably traveled on some of his trains."*

In the margin, scrawled in Griffin's hand were the words: *Brotherhood member?*

Dear heavens, Griffin had suspected *I* was a member of the Brotherhood? It made a certain sort of sense, I suppose. I came from wealth, and I did have the sort of esoteric knowledge which might be of value to the Brotherhood. Obviously, he'd quickly ruled me out as a suspect, or else he wouldn't have shared his findings with me.

Unable to resist finding out what else had been said about me, I set aside the letter. Beneath was a page torn from a notebook, where Griffin had apparently written notes and questions to himself.

Seems to have had a falling-out with his father. About what?

Colleagues say he is brilliant but aloof. Secretaries and janitorial staff are fond of him. Women mention he has not made untoward advances, or let his hands rove, unlike most of the male staff.

Have not been able to confirm the existence of a lover, or indeed any friends outside the museum. Has reasons to be discreet? A Sodomite, perhaps?

My stomach clenched. The ugly word didn't seem to have anything to do with me, or with the man sprawled asleep in the next room. Certainly it had no connection to the way he'd held me last night after we'd retired, with such tenderness.

But he'd been the one to write it. He must feel differently. Perhaps he simply didn't know what else to call us.

There was another word after that one. *Blackmail?*

No prettier a word. Had he feared the Brotherhood might have been blackmailing me, or…

No. I wouldn't think it of him. I forced my eyes down to the next line and kept reading.

If not a part of the Brotherhood, then a valuable asset. Need to think how to recruit, if seems useful beyond the cipher. If a Sodomite, could be the simplest way.

My head was light, but the frantic beating of my heart seemed oddly far away. I read the damning words again, and then again, desperate for them to miraculously change into something else. But they didn't.

Perhaps another paper would shed light, or…or something. Anything. I set the note aside with a shaking hand. Beneath it was a newspaper clipping about Leander's death. It was a short article, but it gave the main details: we were childhood friends, we'd been in a boating accident on the Somerby Estate, and Leander had died while I lived.

Griffin had pretended not to know. He'd stood there by the bed, having secured my loyalty through sexual gratification, and acted as though he wasn't already familiar with every detail of the sordid story. Had he laughed inside, while he listened to my faltering account?

No, no, no, beat my heart. It couldn't be true. I had to be mistaken.

I'd seen his talent as an actor at the brothel. He had fooled others: hard men, men of the world. How much of a challenge had a lonely philologist, a virgin, proved?

Not much of one at all.

"Whyborne?"

I started badly. Griffin stood at the entrance to the bedroom where I'd let him…no, I couldn't think about it now. Where we'd *slept.* He had dressed for the day, handsome as always in his colorful vest and tie, such a contrast from the drab browns and grays I wore. How many times had I asked myself what a man like him could possibly want with someone like me?

Well. I had my answer now.

"Whyborne? What's wrong?" he asked, coming closer. Then he stopped abruptly, when he saw what I held. "Ival?"

Had I loved the pet name? I loathed it now. How simple I must have seemed to him. How naïve and pathetic.

I flung the papers into the fire with a sudden, convulsive movement. Griffin started forward, then stopped, his eyes wide with alarm.

I rose to my feet, clinging to whatever shred of dignity I yet maintained. "You could have been honest, Mr. Flaherty," I said. I don't know how I kept my voice from breaking. "But I can see how such a course might have been less entertaining for you."

His looked transformed into one of fear and worry. He was indeed an excellent actor. "I'm not sure what you read—"

"Enough," I snapped. There was something lodged in my chest, a black tumor crushing my heart and lungs as it swelled malignantly. "You knew about Leander, about my father, about *everything* before we met. Don't pretend otherwise."

"My dear, please, just let me explain."

"There is nothing to explain, Mr. Flaherty." My voice quavered, and I clamped down on the sign of weakness without mercy. "I suppose I should be grateful you decided I was an *asset* rather than a threat."

"Ival, *please,"* Griffin exclaimed, grabbing my arm.

I wanted to forgive him. Never to touch him again, never to hold him in the bed we'd shared, never to sit across the breakfast table with him…I was bleeding inside, the black malignancy shredding my organs.

He would let me. I could apologize right now, and everything would go back to what it had been. I would have the illusion of warmth. The illusion of love. And wasn't that better than nothing at all?

But could I do it, could I look at him, kiss him, speak with him, all the while knowing it was nothing but a sham on his part? His seduction had been calculated before we even met. It had nothing to do with *me* and never had.

In the end, even one such as I had some pride. "Don't touch me," I said, pulling my arm free.

He let go. I went downstairs to the hall and took my overcoat from the rack, flinging it around my shoulders.

"Don't worry," I said. Just a few more minutes, and I could give in to the burning behind my eyes. "I will not abandon the investigation. I'll let you know if I find anything useful, Mr. Flaherty. I'm afraid I must request you don't contact me, however."

"Whyborne—"

"Oh, and as for the blackmail, I suggest you don't try. My father may not care for me, but he cares for the family name and for his money, both of which he will protect ruthlessly. As for me, the only thing I have to take is my job."

I strode to the door. He made a small sound, like a wounded animal, and despite myself I glanced back over my shoulder. Shock was on his face, and grief, and something like resignation.

"You missed your calling in the theatre," I told him, before slamming the door behind me.

He did not try to follow.

I went to the museum, of course. Where else did I have to go?

I walked through the streets like an automaton. The world was a jumble of shapes and sounds, none of which fit together in a coherent pattern: not the newsboys, or the avenues I'd known since childhood, or the carriages and cabs. A driver yelled at me as I crossed the street without looking; the heat from the flank of his horse brushed against me, but it didn't seem real.

How could I have been such a fool? I'd spent my adult life in control of every urge, and yet I'd surrendered to Griffin with barely a fight. How could I have let him touch me, let alone believe I'd fallen in love with him?

The memory of his face, his smile, his voice, was like a live animal clawing madly for freedom inside my rib cage. How could I *not* have loved him?

Rockwell tried to speak to me when I walked past, but I was beyond caring. I would have struck him had he dared touch me. I kept my gaze carefully focused on the floor a few feet in front of me, as if deep in thought, and no one tried to engage me in conversation before I reached my office.

I threw the lock and stood there trembling, my forehead pressed against the solid oak. I couldn't do this. I couldn't.

But what other choice did I have?

"Back to work," I said aloud. Griffin might be a scoundrel and a cad, but the threat of the Brotherhood was no less for it.

I went to my desk and collapsed into the chair. Taking the *Arcanorum* from my breast pocket, I set it on the desk in front of me and stared down at the worn and cracked leather cover.

I could make him love me.

How, I didn't know, but there must be something. The book contained tantalizing hints of hypnotic suggestion, of exerting one's will over another, using certain signs and symbols. I could put them together into a coherent ritual. Griffin had used me without qualm; why should I not do the same to him?

I could have him back. I could have…

I could. But I'd still know, deep down, he hadn't chosen to be with me.

I shoved the book aside and propped my elbows on the table, pressing my fingers into my closed eyes. If only I'd never met him. If only there had been someone else who could have solved the cipher. I might have spent the rest of my life in happy ignorance.

Well, not happy. I hadn't been happy. I'd just existed, caught in some colorless limbo. How could I bear to return to that life?

Damn Griffin. Damn him to hell.

The locked door rattled, and for a horrible moment I imagined he might have followed me.

"Whyborne?" Christine called, pounding on the door with a heavy fist. "I know you're in there. You might as well open the door."

I sighed and let her in. She entered, smiling brightly, happier than I'd seen her in months. "Good news! I managed to book passage on a steamer leaving tomorrow!"

"That's…that's wonderful." First Griffin broke my heart, and now my best friend abandoned me. Which wasn't at all true, of course; I'd known she was leaving as soon as possible, and yet I couldn't suppress the emotion.

My thoughts must have shown on my face, because she stopped smiling and started frowning instead. "Is something wrong?"

"No. Everything is fine."

"Don't lie to me, Whyborne. I won't have it."

She'd only badger me until I gave in. I sat down and told her the whole, sorry tale. I stared at the blotter on my desk as I spoke, unable to meet her gaze as I detailed my complete and utter folly.

When I was done, she shifted uncomfortably in her chair. "Shall I go give him a good thrashing before I leave?" Was she joking? I hoped she was joking.

"I don't think it will be necessary," I said, dredging up a false smile.

"I'm no good at this kind of thing, as you are no doubt aware, but...have you considered at least hearing him out? Yes, his notes were rather cold-blooded, but if he made them as preparation for the case, he didn't know you then. After all, he thought *you* might be part of the Brotherhood."

"And then, what—he met me and changed his mind? Was so overcome by my charms he decided to pursue me for some reason other than an asset in his fight against the Brotherhood? Don't be absurd."

Christine let out a sigh. "I'm sorry, my friend," she said, and patted my shoulder awkwardly. "You're worth a hundred of him. There are other men in the world, believe me."

I didn't wish to point out the problem was me, not the existence of other men. I only said, "Thank you, Christine."

"Any time." She gave my shoulder a hearty squeeze and let go. "Well, there's work to be done. I'm going down to the docks to make sure they load my equipment correctly. I'll stop by tomorrow before I depart."

I nodded mutely. She closed the door behind her, leaving me utterly alone.

CHAPTER 25

SO I WORKED.

It was work or sit in my office and mope. Moping wouldn't stop Blackbyrne, more's the pity, which left only the first alternative. I collected the *Arcanorum* and all my notes, and went to face the library.

I immersed myself in the task, combing through the ghastly text printed on the crumbling pages of the *Al Azif* and the *Unaussprechlichen Kulten*. Now that I comprehended even a portion of the truth lurking behind the ravings of the mad prophet and von Junzt's weighty text alike, I shuddered at certain passages. The world was hideously fragile, everyday life nothing more than a thin film laid over infinite depths of chaos and terror.

But it was still *my* life, and I'd be damned if I let Blackbyrne tear it away without a fight.

Around five o'clock, Quinn found me still scribbling notes and crosschecking between the piles of books, which had grown steadily throughout the day. "Will you remain here after closing?" he asked.

I could stop for the day, but what would be the point? To go home to my barren little apartment, with nothing to divert my thoughts from Griffin?

"Yes," I said. "I'll return the books to their places before I leave."

He departed. I waited a bit, until the distant sounds of the library staff gathering their things for the day dwindled to nothing, then scooped up the books. I wasn't supposed to remove the valuable tomes from the library, but I couldn't quite bring myself to sit here amidst the shadows and half-heard sounds, especially not with the basement entrance open. Although we'd been assured the tunnel was now unusable thanks to the collapse, I couldn't help but imagine what might crawl up out of the depths.

As I walked toward the library entrance, memory sank unexpected hooks into my chest. Griffin had defended me to Bradley here, even when he had no idea I was listening. Coming to check on his asset after the theft of the night before I could understand, but why not cultivate Bradley in case he could prove useful as well? Why risk bad blood for my sake?

Unless I did mean something to him, after all.

But the things he'd written about using our shared inclinations to secure my cooperation were clear. And if I had a hard time reconciling them with the tender lover I'd found in him, it only served to illustrate just how deep a game he had played.

I'd been standing still, lost in my confused thoughts, for several minutes. Tightening my grip on the books, I hurried out of the library and made for my office, where I locked the door behind me. I would not hope. There was no chance of reconciliation with Griffin. None.

Damn him.

With a shake of my head, I reopened the books to various marked pages and took out my notes. Putting all thoughts of Griffin aside for the moment, I bent over the pages and was soon lost in the work.

I must have fallen asleep in the wee hours of the morning, because I woke to a frantic pounding on my office door. I lifted my head groggily, my mind a tumult of confusion. My neck ached abominably from sleeping in such a position, and my cheek had been pressed against the open pages of the *Arcanorum*. At least I hadn't drooled on the text.

"Whyborne? Whyborne, are you in there?" Christine called, but her voice held an unfamiliar note of fear, which had me on my feet almost before I was entirely awake.

"One moment," I said, stumbling to the door. God, my mouth tasted horrible. I longed for some dentifrice, a comb, and a cup of coffee. A glance at the clock revealed it was almost eight.

Her face was pale, and her mouth set in a grim line of worry. "What happened?" I asked. "Oh good Lord—did the steamer catch fire and destroy your equipment?"

"What? No!" She glanced at my desk, then at me. "You slept here?"

"I had work to do."

"You won't have seen the paper, then. It's all over the front page. Griffin's been arrested for the murder of Madam Rosa."

I hurried through the streets to the police station. In my haste, I'd forgotten my overcoat, and the wind bit through my suit with icy teeth.

The newspaper article had been disturbingly short on details, saying only Griffin Flaherty, lately of Chicago, was suspected of murdering one Rosa Waite, the "proprietress" of a saloon on the evening of December 12. He'd been taken into custody shortly after I'd left his house. What would have happened if I had still been there? Would I be sitting in a cell beside him?

The police were being paid off, as they had been in the matter of Philip's death. If the Brotherhood were aware of Griffin's involvement, surely they knew of mine. Did they have some plan to dispose of me as well, or did they hope Griffin's arrest would keep me quiet?

If the latter, they would soon learn their mistake. Griffin might have used me cruelly, but I couldn't leave him in jail. I would go down and give my statement: we had jointly found the madam's body. If it didn't work, I would invoke my father's name.

And if *that* didn't work, I would involve Father. I didn't know what he might ask in exchange for his aid, but I would give it to free Griffin. Even if it meant leaving the museum for whatever horrible job Father wished me to take.

I spotted the police station with relief; the wind had me chilled to the bone. Hurrying inside, I paused and looked around, wondering to whom I might speak.

The same officer sat at the desk as on my only other visit. He frowned uncertainly as I approached. "Dr. Whyborne, isn't it? How can I help you, sir?"

Well he might frown. I must look like a madman, with my hair uncombed, my suit creased from sleeping in it, my face pink from the cold, and no overcoat in sight. My case would have been better served if I'd gone home and tidied up first, but I couldn't leave Griffin sitting alone in a jail cell even for the hour it would have taken.

Devil take me. I still loved the man, despite everything.

"I understand Mr. Flaherty is under arrest," I said. "I would like to speak with him, if I may."

The officer's frown only grew, although now it was one of confusion. "I'm sorry, Dr. Whyborne, but Mr. Flaherty isn't here any more. Mr. Somerby came by earlier, paid his bail, and left with him. I was under the impression you had asked Mr. Somerby to come, sir, or at least that's what he said to the suspect when Flaherty was brought out."

"Addison Somerby?" I asked stupidly, although there weren't any other Somerbys in Widdershins.

"Yes, sir. Perhaps they missed you?"

"I…yes. Thank you."

I wandered back outside to shiver on the sidewalk, my thoughts whirling about like flakes of snow. Why on earth would Addison bail out Griffin? Addison had seen us both at the gala, and no doubt had deduced we were friends, but a newspaper article wouldn't send him rushing down here to help a man who was a virtual stranger to him. And why lie to Griffin by claiming I had sent him?

Unless it was the only way Addison could get Griffin to come with him.

Which still begged the question: why? The only people in Widdershins who had any particular interest in Griffin were myself and his employer, Mr. Rice. And the Brotherhood, of course.

The Brotherhood.

No. No, it was impossible. Uncle Addy would never do such a thing. Not my own godfather, Leander's father, who had welcomed me into his home with such warmth. I would go to him at once, and find Griffin with him, safe and sound.

Unless I was right, in which case I'd be delivering myself into the hands of the Brotherhood along with Griffin.

Father would know. He and Addison were best friends, had been since their university days. He would tell me my suspicions were foolish.

Tucking my hands under my armpits for warmth, I hurried in the direction of the nearest cab.

I didn't bother with the knocker this time, only flung open the door to Whyborne House and walked inside. Mr. Fenton scurried out of the front parlor, his face a study in outrage. "Master Percival! I wasn't informed you'd be coming by today."

"I must speak with Father immediately," I said, ignoring his affront. I'd grown up in this house, and even if I would never inherit so much as a matchstick, I still had the right to visit whenever I damned well pleased. "Where is he?"

"Mr. Whyborne is out," Fenton said, glancing at the front door, as if hoping I'd take the hint and leave as well.

Damn it. Of course he was. Why should anything ever be easy? "I'll wait."

"It may be some time. If you'll leave your card—"

"Then I'll speak to Mother." She wouldn't likely know anything useful in this case, but I was at my wit's end. Brushing past Fenton, I hurried up the familiar stair.

Mother sat beneath one of the large windows of her room, reading as always. When I entered, a look of surprise and happiness transformed her face. "Percival! What an unexpected pleasure!"

"Mother." I settled on the edge of the divan on which she rested. "I'm very sorry, but my visit isn't precisely social. I must speak with Father, but it seems he's out."

A dark cloud seemed to pass over her face, dimming her smile. "Yes. He came to see me before he and your brother left. He was acting a bit…odd."

Probably some business deal or other. "Do you know when he'll be back? I have a question about Uncle Addy."

She peered up at me quizzically. "Addison? I think Niles and Stanford intended to meet him somewhere. Niles was very vague, but he said they wouldn't return until tomorrow morning, and not to worry. Percival? Is something wrong? You're white as a ghost."

My hands had gone numb, and a cold sweat coated my skin, but I managed to stammer, "N-No, Mother. Nothing's wrong. I'm sorry, but I have to be on my way."

"Percival?" she called after me. I mumbled something incoherent and hurried to the stair. I had to get out, get away, into the free air where I could breathe again.

Once back on the street, I stopped and leaned against a lamppost, dizzy and sick. Griffin had been right to suspect me. The Whybornes were in it up to our necks. Only I, the rebellious son, hadn't been invited to join the society encompassing Widdershins's wealthy families.

It made perfect sense in retrospect. If Addison was a member of the Brotherhood, then his best friend would be as well. And why would Stanford leave his family behind in New York, this close to Christmas? Of course the favored son was in on it.

My own father and brother were in the cult. From what they had told Mother, the ritual would take place tonight.

And I had no idea where it might be or how to stop it.

Bereft of any other purpose, I walked to Griffin's house to check on Saul. The big marmalade tom ran up as soon as I stepped onto the walk, meowing piteously. I picked him up in my arms and carried him onto the porch.

The front door had been left unlocked when the police took Griffin. I let myself in, went to the kitchen, and found something for Saul to eat. That done, I wandered out into the hall.

Griffin's overcoat hung on the hook near the door. They'd taken him without letting him properly dress for the weather. I took it from its place, and the smell of his skin rose from the fabric to greet me.

Was he cold right now? Had they fed him? Was he even still alive?

I buried my face in the cloth, hugging it to me. Why hadn't I stayed to listen to his side of things? Why had I let pride rule my actions; why had I been so desperate to protect myself from one more embarrassment?

I knew the answer, of course. To remain and have him mock me, no different than Bradley or Stanford, would have broken me. So I had taken the coward's path, and now I'd never know for certain if he would have or not. Once again, I had been too weak, and the man I loved would pay the price.

"I'm sorry," I whispered into his coat. "Oh, Griffin, I'm sorry."

Addison—the Brotherhood—had taken him alive. Maybe they meant to kill him discreetly. Or maybe they meant to use him as a sacrifice of sorts. After all, the newly-raised dead needed fresh human flesh. Perhaps they meant to let whomever—whatever—they called forth tonight feed on him as revenge for his attempts to foil their plot.

I pulled on the heavy overcoat, even though it was too short. Saul wanted back out; I let him into the yard, closed the door behind us, and went to the street.

I walked blindly; there was nowhere left to go. We had lost the fight. Nothing remained but to wait for whatever horror Blackbyrne had in store for the world.

If I had known about Father's involvement, could I have talked him out of it? Could I have revealed what I believed Blackbyrne had planned for the world? Would he have listened if I had?

Of course not. He never listened to me. Why would this have been any different?

It shouldn't have hurt, really, finding out Father and Stanford were members in the Brotherhood. But it did. Addison's betrayal stung more, though, because I'd always believed him to be a better man.

I'd been a blind fool.

I found myself on Cemetery Road, the steep slope of Kings Hill stretching before me. A few flakes of snow drifted down lazily from the leaden clouds. The dark mass of the Draakenwood crouched on the horizon like a hunting animal.

Blackbyrne had been in the forest, the day Griffin and I went to the burying ground. Would the ritual tonight take place there? Should I go into it and search? What would I do if I encountered Blackbyrne there a second time?

The sound of clopping hooves came from behind me. Lost in my thoughts, I'd wandered into the road and was forced to step quickly to the sidewalk to make way for a funeral procession. A black horse pulled a dark catafalque; inside was a tiny coffin, too small to belong to any but a child. I removed my hat and watched the parents who followed behind the coffin on foot. The stoic father in his dark suit reminded me of Addison, who had never put off mourning for Leander.

Addison, who had allied himself with a cult capable of returning the dead to life.

Oh God. It was Leander they meant to resurrect tonight.

I entered Bradley's office without knocking. He sat behind his desk as before, this time scribbling notes onto a pad of paper.

"Really, Percy, can't you knock?" he said, as if he hadn't burst into my office uninvited a hundred times.

"What did Addison Somerby want the day he came to see you?"

Bradley raised his brows, apparently taken aback. "Why do you wish to know?"

There was no time left for niceties. "Just tell me."

"He asked to see one of the original maps of Widdershins. The one Theron Blackbyrne drew up himself."

"Show it to me."

Bradley drew himself up, puffing out his chest. "Now, see here, Percy, I have work to do. I don't know what you're about—"

"Bradley." I loomed over his desk, using my height to my advantage. A bit to my surprise, he shrank back. "A man's life is in the balance. Do as I ask, and it won't be yours."

Bradley blinked, started to say something, then visibly stopped himself. Pulling a key from his pocket, he said, "Um, yes. Come this way."

He led me to the rare map room, unlocked one of the cases, and left rather hastily. Possibly to report me to the director, but what did it matter?

Removing the map from its case, I spread it on a table. The old paper crumbled at the edges, but the ink was still clear enough to make out details. Blackbyrne's master plan for Widdershins. What was it Bradley had said, the day I came to ask about Blackbyrne? "*... it was all the rage to try to trace some kind of hidden message in the very streets of the town...*"

The old map was simple and bore little resemblance to the modern tangle of streets, which made things far easier. A quick trip to Miss Parkhurst's desk, and I returned with a pencil and onionskin paper, which I laid over the map.

I traced the streets: a circle around Kings Hill, a wing-like curve along the waterfront, the line of a talon. When I was finished, I had the phoenix-and ouroboros symbol of the Brotherhood, inscribed upon the very streets of the city.

And at the point where the serpent and the phoenix came together, the Cranch River briefly became a lake, with an island in the center.

My hands shook as I took away the onionskin. What was now Somerby Estate had a label on it, written in miniscule. Leaning forward, I squinted at the slanted letters. The old writing was badly faded but still readable.

Blackbyrne Manor.

Of course. The ritual would take place on the island in the lake. Leander had been right, all those years ago; cultists were performing terrible rites there. And now he would live again, resurrected in the very place he had died.

Ouroboros. The serpent ate its tail.

CHAPTER 26

I FOUND CHRISTINE in her office, scribbling out a last few instructions to the rest of the staff before her departure. "There you are!" she said, when I knocked on her door. "I was worried I wouldn't have the chance to see you again before I left. How is Griffin?"

Griffin. I'd avoided thinking about him while looking at the map, but now it all came rushing back. Was he alive? In pain? Afraid? "The Brotherhood has him."

All the color leeched from her face. "Oh. Oh dear."

"I need your help. I have a plan, but it will mean missing your steamer this afternoon."

Christine hesitated. "My equipment—"

"Wire ahead and have someone waiting to claim it when the steamer docks."

She stood up, shoving her chair back. Clasping her hands behind her, she paced to the other side of the room, deliberately putting space between us. "It isn't as simple as you're making out. If I miss the steamer, the first thing everyone will say is a woman can't be trusted to run an excavation. My colleagues from other museums are already muttering about the delay caused by the gala. It doesn't matter to them if the director ordered me to stay; they're saying the real reason is my feminine side couldn't resist the lure of a fancy party. Proof I don't have the dedication of a man. If I'm not in Egypt at the earliest possible moment, my professional reputation could be ruined."

"I know." I crossed the room to stand in front of her. "It's not fair, and I'm sorry. But we're out of time. Griffin is going to *die*, and the world might very well follow." I put one hand to her shoulder. "Please, Christine. I can't do this without you."

She hesitated, and I did not blame her. I was asking a great deal of her, and I couldn't honestly say the chances of success were high, even with her help. Very possibly my hasty plan would end with the two of us dead alongside Griffin.

Her piercing eyes regarded me for a long time. I met her gaze and let her see whatever she might, because I was asking too much to hide anything in return.

A resigned sigh escaped her lips. Looking away, she awkwardly patted me on the arm. "Very well. Tell me this plan of yours."

For the first time in over a decade, I knocked on the doors of Somerby Estate.

It had not changed much from my memory. The gravel of the stately drive was still immaculately groomed, and the thick hedges perfectly trimmed. The Draakenwood formed a dark line on the horizon, while nearer at hand the Cranch glittered in the sun. The lake itself couldn't be seen from the front of the house, which seemed a small mercy.

The door swung open, revealing a butler in starched livery. What had happened to the man who'd held the position in my youth? Had he retired due to old age, or was there a more sinister reason behind the change?

The butler's brow arched almost imperceptibly. "May I help you, sir?"

I firmed my spine and hoped my expression revealed nothing. "I'm here to see Mr. Somerby."

"Mr. Somerby is not in at the moment."

"Yes, he is," I said. "Tell him Percival Whyborne is here. I know what he's doing, and I want to help."

Addison received me in his study. The curtains were drawn over all the windows, and the only light came from the gas lamps and the cheerful fire burning on the hearth. A portrait of Leander hung over the fireplace. A photo of the two of us as boys hung framed on another wall; I averted my eyes quickly.

Addison rose to greet me, his expression guarded. "Percival. How can I help you?"

I couldn't think of Griffin, or of the way my heart pounded in my throat, or my knees wanted to buckle. "Uncle Addy." Was I projecting the right amount of hurt, or did I sound overly dramatic? "Why didn't you tell me?"

Guardedness gave way to uncertainty. "Tell you…?"

"It was all to bring Leander back." I swallowed against the thickness in my throat. "Don't you know saving him was my first thought as well, when I learned it was possible?"

A tremulous smile broke over his wrinkled lips. Had it been Leander's death which had aged him, or simply the natural passing of years? "It was?"

"Of course it was. Leander was my best friend." I gestured to Addison's black clothing. "I might not wear mourning, but I think of him daily. As soon as I read the grimoire, as soon as I realized the power it held, my mind flew to him." All true, and please let it be enough salt to make the lies go down easily. "If I'd known saving Leander was the goal, I would never have never opposed you. Surely you don't believe I'd choose the museum's reputation over him?"

His joyful smile filled my gut with self-loathing. "My dear boy," he said, rising to his feet and taking my hands. "Forgive me. It wasn't my decision. I suggested to your father…but he was adamant you not be involved. When I saw you'd been hurt at the gala, I knew we'd made a terrible mistake."

At least Addison hadn't wanted me dead, then. It shouldn't have made a difference, given the horrors he was willing to unleash on us all, but it did.

"I'm glad to have you here now," he went on. "Very glad. Let us—"

A soft knock on the door cut him off. Addison seemed surprised; he let go of my hands. "Come in?"

I sensed him like a cold wind at my back. "Oh," Addison said. "Mr. Blackbyrne, this is—"

"Dr. Whyborne and I have already met, although we've not been formally introduced."

This was it. Fooling Addison was one thing; tricking Blackbyrne another altogether. Perhaps the years I'd spent schooling my face not to betray embarrassment, or shame, or desire had not been for nothing after all. Keeping my expression as bland as possible, I turned and met his gaze.

His eyes were black and glittering, his smile crocodile-cold. None of which diminished his beauty, and I couldn't suppress the stirrings of warmth in my groin when he held out his hand. "Theron Blackbyrne," he said.

I shook his hand. His fingers curled around mine, the points of his sharpened nails scraping lightly against my skin, sending a delicious shiver up my arm. "Percival Endicott Whyborne," I replied, and thank God my voice didn't tremble with either lust or fear.

"I suspected my assessment of you was correct," Blackbyrne said; he still hadn't let go of my hand. "When I heard the decision had been made not to recruit such an asset, I wondered at its wisdom."

Asset. Apparently, I was doomed never to be anything more. "I'm glad to be here," I said.

He finally let go of my hand; I tucked it into my pocket to keep from wiping it on my trousers. "I have something you might want to see," he said. I wished he would stop smiling.

I nodded, a bit stiffly. "Excuse us, Addison," he said, and led the way out of the room.

I followed, wondering what he had in store. I didn't believe for an instant that he trusted me with such ease. But, like Griffin, he saw me as a tool he couldn't bring himself to discard, as long as there was a chance to get some use from it.

At least, I hoped he considered me too useful to discard. If not, he could very well be taking me to a nasty death.

My trepidation grew when he let us into a servants' hall. I'd never been in this part of the house before. "Has the estate changed much, since you lived here?" I asked. It was a stupid question, but I didn't want my silence to give the impression of fear.

Blackbyrne glanced over his shoulder, one brow raised. "You know about that? Somerby said it had been mostly forgotten, except for an odious little man at the museum who busies himself with the petty doings of a single, young country and thinks himself wise."

His contempt for Bradley made me even more uneasy, not because I disagreed with the sentiment, but because I didn't want to have anything in common with him.

"However," Blackbyrne added, turning back to the fore, "my old home is long gone. Burned upon my death, I'm told, by small-minded fools."

"Oh." I hadn't known. Would my ignorance decrease his opinion of my potential usefulness?

We went into the kitchen; there were no servants to be seen. The door on the other side of the room opened onto a stair leading into the basement. With another reptile grin, Blackbyrne gestured for me to precede him.

Nothing good ever happened in basements.

The smell of rot swept up from below. I wanted to run, but flight wasn't an option, not without Griffin.

I started down the creaking stair. "It's unfortunate," Blackbyrne said from behind me, and those were *not* words I wanted to hear in these circumstances. "There was no real way to hide these things from the servants."

My stomach turned over, but I clung to the blank expression which had gotten me through much in my life. "New ones can always be hired."

An awful thing to say, but any other response would result in my death here and now. Blackbyrne was a step or two above me; the sensation of his nails lightly resting against my shoulder made my skin crawl. Why did he keep touching me?

I half-suspected what I would see when I stepped out into the basement. For once, I wasn't remotely glad to be right. Griffin was on his knees with his head bowed, bound securely in thick ropes. Remembering his fear of underground places, my heart contracted: couldn't they have kept him somewhere else?

Maybe they knew, or at least suspected. Perhaps this was just one more careless cruelty.

Three Guardians lurked in various corners: two of them were the animal-human hybrids, while the other was somehow even more horrific. It was only human, but stomach-churningly *unfinished.*

Griffin lifted his head at our approach, and his eyes widened to see me. Despair flashed across his face, followed by surprise as he realized I was unbound.

"I thought you might want to see your friend," Blackbyrne said.

My hands itched to strike him. Instead, I shoved them into my pockets and conjured up my best imitation of Father's most lofty sneer. "Mr. Flaherty is no friend of mine."

Griffin stared at me in confusion. "Whyborne?"

My heart pounded; it seemed Blackbyrne must surely hear. "You picked the wrong man to betray," I told Griffin. "What do you think now of your *asset?*"

"No! I love—" Then he caught himself. His shoulders slumped wearily, and he looked away. "Never mind. It hardly matters now."

I couldn't breathe. There was no reason for him to say such a thing, not now, when he had nothing to gain from it.

"Ah." Blackbyrne's voice was low and soft in my ear. His breath caressed my cheek; it stank like something long dead. "I suspected there was something more behind your sudden desire to work with us. A lover scorned is a frightful enemy indeed."

"Are we done here?" I asked, striving to sound bored.

"Indeed." He turned back to the stair. "Come, Dr. Whyborne. We have many preparations to make yet for tonight."

"Please," I said, "call me Percy."

Out of the corner of my eye, I saw Griffin's head lift a fraction of an inch. I didn't dare look at him, though. I could only hope my signal had been received.

Blackbyrne smiled. "And you must call me Theron. I think we are going to work together very closely indeed."

He started up the stair. I followed, but at the moment, I would almost rather have stayed in the basement with the Guardians.

Father's shock upon seeing me with Blackbyrne verged on the comical. We found him in the study, sipping brandy with seven or eight other men, most of whom I recognized. The majority formed the elite of Widdershins, although some hailed from Boston and Kingsport. No wonder the police had refused to investigate Philip Rice's death.

Blackbyrne made a show of introducing me around. "I'm surprised to see you here, Percival," Father said. Stanford didn't speak, only glared at me sullenly, as if my appearance had taken something from him.

"Leander was my friend. He died at my side." Because I was too weak to hold onto his hand. "Don't you think I would do anything to change that?"

Father looked uncertain, but gave me a grudging nod. "Well. Good. Loyalty is everything." As if he'd ever shown the slightest hint of loyalty to me. "Glad to have you with us, son."

I nodded politely. Blackbyrne's long-nailed hand closed on my elbow. "Percy and I have some things to discuss," he said silkily, and drew me away. "What do you think?" he asked, when we were alone in the hall.

I'd not forgotten what he said at the Ladysmith. "Small-minded fools. They see money as an end in itself, not as a steppingstone to real power. Even those with higher ambitions only dare imagine themselves senators, or presidents."

Blackbyrne let out a delighted laugh at my audacity. "And I've had none but them to speak with since my resurrection," he said, his hand slipping from my elbow to settle rather familiarly at my waist. Dear God, please don't let him be taking me to a bedroom.

Thankfully, he merely led me to the library. "This is the ritual we will perform tonight, when the stars are right," he said.

The stolen scroll lay on a table. He lifted it, forcing me to stand with my shoulder pressed against his in order to read it.

I'd already seen most of it, of course, but now I could read it in full. *All being done, the gate closes; Yog-Sothoth closes; the Beyond-One closes. All not being done, the demons of the night will come through; Those Outside will enter in, and they will not hear you. Give to them a man; send him through the gate; they will accept the sacrifice; they will close the door. All being done, the container will be yours to command, and lo shall it make the rivers into deserts, and the desert into ocean, and lift up the land or cast it down as you say.*

The container. Leander. Did Addison really know what Blackbyrne had planned for his son? Or did he believe that Leander would be the one in control?

Blackbyrne carefully laid the papyrus back on the table. "You have the *Liber Arcanorum*, do you not?"

It wasn't really a question. "Yes. I've studied it as thoroughly as possible, given the brief time it's been in my possession."

"It was mine once, you know. Left behind in the care of the Brotherhood, along with instructions on how to bring me back." For a moment, a flash of hatred and anger distorted his features into something demonic, before smoothing out again. "Instructions they were…tardy…in following."

Perhaps if I kept him talking, he would say something useful. "How did it come into Philip Rice's hands?"

"The fools chose to recruit him instead of you, when they finally decided to restore me," Blackbyrne said with a sneer. "He had some small sorcerous skill—a dabbler only, not like you and me, but enough to follow the instructions I had laid out. After my return, he assisted with the creation of the Guardians—I believe he was the one who obtained the materials from the museum."

"But his nerve failed," I guessed.

"He was weak." Blackbyrne's dark eyes burned with contempt. "He mailed the book to his father, believing that would somehow act as insurance. But I had plumbed its depths long ago."

Had Philip known what he was getting into, when he returned Blackbyrne to life? Or had the Guardians—or Blackbyrne's own monstrous nature—proved more horrible than he'd imagined?

"But enough of these matters," Blackbyrne said, waving a negligent hand. "There are far more interesting things I wish to discuss with you."

He began to speak, then, about the arcane arts, the *Al Azif* and the *Arcanorum*, about his travels in Europe and the things he had seen and learned there. Conjecture, and theory, and the painstaking pursuit of knowledge.

I found myself drawn into conversation. And, God help me, I enjoyed it.

I'd conversed with my professors at university, of course, and somewhat with my fellow students. And of course there was Christine, but her interests and mine overlapped only in the matter of hieroglyphics.

Blackbyrne, though, was truly brilliant. When I spoke of the advances in philology and the hidden relationships between languages, he listened avidly, drinking in every word. Asking questions, making suggestions…

In any other circumstances, I would have hoped to call him a friend. And when he stepped up and let his fingers trail along the side of my face, my heart beat a bit too hard, and I wasn't as revolted as I should have been.

"What was Leander to you?" he murmured, studying me with those penetrating eyes.

"You already know." My voice sounded thick and a little breathy.

"Hmm. And you wished to uncover the secrets of the island, and he came with you."

I couldn't look away from him. "Our interests coincided in more ways than one."

He was too close, his lips only a hairs-breadth away. "He'll be a boy still. Caught in the moment of his death. Fresh and ripe."

The sour taste of bile coated the back of my throat. "In some ways, but he'll also be…more," I said carefully, and truly I was treading a tightrope over a bottomless pit. Except if I fell, I'd take Griffin with me.

"The Container. The Immortal Vessel. You know what it means, don't you?"

"I know Yog-Sothoth will open the gate, and something will come through and merge with him."

"It will. And trapped in a human shell, it will be at our command." His tongue flicked out, touching my lips. A tiny whimper escaped me. "Bound by the words we will speak, in the husk of your young lover. Shall we share him?"

I wanted to crawl out of my own skin to get away. "That seems only fair. And I suspect you know how to make things far more…interesting."

He drew back and gave me a look full of erotic promise. "Indeed. I would offer you a preview now, but alas, one must abstain before undertaking such a ritual. After, though…"

"I am filled with anticipation." Of a dreadful sort.

"As am I. It's been a *very* long time since I was able to indulge."

I shuddered to imagine what his idea of indulging might include. If the Immortal Vessel were truly indestructible, there would be no need to hold back in any fashion. Not to suggest he would anyway; how many bodies might be buried in various locations around the grounds of his old estate, a testimony to his appetites? Or had he simply recycled them into Guardians when he was done?

"Return to the others, then. I'll see you later."

I took his hand and lifted it to my lips, brushing them lightly against the knuckles. His flesh had an oddly rubbery texture, and the odor of the grave clung to it. A soft sigh of pleasure escaped him, and for a horrible moment I thought I'd gone too far, and he would pull me to him.

He didn't. I released his hand and went to the door, shutting it carefully behind me. I managed to make it to the next hall before collapsing against the wall, all the strength gone from my legs. I wanted to scrub my skin until it blistered; I wanted to drag the very thought of Blackbyrne from my head and dissolve it in bleach.

The sound of distant footsteps echoed from some other room. I hurriedly climbed to my feet; if anyone came along and found me in such a state, everything I'd managed so far would be for naught. I had to compose myself, for Griffin's sake as well as mine.

Taking a deep breath, I forced my spine straight. I had confronted Blackbyrne successfully. Now, I just had to do the same with my father.

CHAPTER 27

CONVERSATION DIED WHEN I walked into the study, and I assumed they'd been speaking about me. "He hasn't even been initiated," someone muttered, confirming it.

"We can initiate him later. There are more important things to do tonight," Father said, shooting a quelling gaze at the speaker. Straightening his jacket, he came to me. His eyes did a thorough once-over, and my gut twisted in on itself. "You might have dressed better, Percival."

I was a little boy again, being called to task for failing in some way, great or small. "Forgive my enthusiasm, Father. Once I realized, I could only think of coming here immediately." Which was even the truth.

He made a *tsk*ing sound in his throat, but let the matter drop. "It's all for your mother, you know."

"Er…no, I'm afraid I don't." What could Mother possibly have to do with this?

Instead of answering immediately, Father walked to the doors leading onto the wide veranda. I followed out of old habit. The wind numbed my ears, but colder still was the sight of the lake below. The huge lawn ran right down to the shore, the gray waters stretching off into the distance. The island formed a low smudge amidst the whitecaps whipped up by the fierce wind.

This was where it had all gone wrong. If I had only managed to hold onto Leander, he would still be alive. Addison wouldn't have gone mad with grief and resurrected Blackbyrne. I would not be standing here today, trying to trick a group of men willing to sacrifice the world for their own power.

Although, if Addison hadn't joined the Brotherhood and held rituals on the island, there would have been no reason for us to be out on the lake in the first place. Was that one of the reasons he'd had such difficulty accepting the tragedy? Did he feel responsible for his son's death?

Father went to the balustrade and rested his hands on the cold, white marble. "Your mother," he said, as if she had no name of her own, "was a beautiful, energetic girl when we married. No doubt it is difficult for you to believe now, but she loved to dance, to walk in the garden, to take the carriage out and visit with her friends.

"When she first became ill, I took her to all of the best doctors in America. When their cures failed, we went to Europe. All of them said the same: there was nothing to be done. I could only stand by helplessly while she wasted into a shadow of the vivacious woman I'd wed."

Although he seldom showed any emotion other than disappointment or anger, there was a misty look in his eyes now. Had he actually loved Mother once? Did he still?

I wouldn't feel any sympathy for him. I couldn't afford it, not here, not now, perhaps not ever. But to watch the woman he loved succumb to a force which cared nothing for his fortune, a force he couldn't threaten or bribe, must have been devastating.

"I thought Addison was mad, when he said he'd finally found what he'd been looking for all these years," Father went on, his gaze fixed on the heaving waters of the lake. "We both joined the Brotherhood in college, of course, just like our fathers did. I'd hoped you would, as well, but you did insist on going to Miskatonic instead. I hope you see how great a mistake you made."

"Yes, Father," I said, because right now I didn't dare answer otherwise. And yet, for the first time in years, those words didn't leave the taste of bitterness on my tongue.

He went on as if I hadn't spoken, or he had taken my acquiescence for granted. "When Addison said he knew how to return Blackbyrne to life, I believed his grief had unhinged him. He wasn't sure the instructions would work for anyone else, you see, or else I suppose he would have brought Leander back immediately."

"And Blackbyrne's methods?" I asked, not quite able to resist. I had to know if Father truly approved of the horrors he'd helped create, even if indirectly.

"Aren't ones I would have chosen. But everything has a cost. Addison wants his son back. I want my wife back. By tomorrow morning, we'll both have our wish."

"You think there's a way to heal Mother?" I asked.

"Of course," he said impatiently. "Those from the Outside have the secrets of immortality, Percival! With their aid, a man can triumph over age, illness, even death. Just look at Blackbyrne!"

An image of Mother healthy and whole bloomed in my imagination. Was it possible? What would it be like to see her dance and sing?

The figure in my mind's eye warped and darkened. Perhaps Father was right, but at what cost? Would she go forth in the night and kill as it seemed Blackbyrne had killed? Would Miss Emily's flesh feed some horrible new hunger? When she kissed me on the cheek, would her breath stink like the gaseous exhalation of a rotting corpse?

She wouldn't allow it. Father had blinded himself, assuming Mother would comply simply because he willed it. He saw her as a brilliant jewel, beautiful and graceful, but she'd always been a scholar at heart. She'd ask questions. And when she learned the truth, she'd refuse, because the woman who had raised me would never let anyone else die in order for her to live.

Hard to believe I could actually feel sorry for Father. Even if I failed tonight, even if the gateway to the Outside was flung wide and the fragile shell of reality broken for good, he would still lose. Indeed, he had already lost. He just didn't know it.

Nor could I tell him without risking everything. "Perhaps we can take her to the park, once the weather is warm," I said.

Father nodded, lost in some idyllic vision of our family which would never exist outside of his head. "She'll like the park. You'll see, Percival. Now that I have both my sons at my side, there's nothing we can't do."

I wanted to ask him if he'd known about the trap in the foul basement of the house Griffin and I had investigated, or if he'd known but never imagined I would be caught in it. If he'd invited me to dinner because he knew I'd been injured at the gala, and wished see me in good health with his own eyes. Or if I had been right all along, and he didn't really care at all.

I couldn't. "Yes, Father," I said a second time, and stood shivering at his side while he gazed out over the lake.

Returning to the island that night was like falling back through a crack in time. The shadowy boathouse, the frigid darkness, the lap of black water against the shore, all recreated the night Leander had drowned with painful clarity. At least there was no storm.

And of course, Leander and I hadn't been accompanied by a coterie of madmen including my own father, or Guardians shuffling behind, dragging Griffin roughly along by his bound wrists.

The robes the Brotherhood wore lent a sense of unreality to the scene. The deep hoods masked the faces of the men around me, with only the occasional glimpse of torchlight sparkling in their avid, hungry eyes. The offer of robes of my own had been an unexpected reprieve, as it meant I didn't have to worry quite as much about one of my companions noticing some oddity of expression.

We climbed into the boats; I rode with Addison and Blackbyrne, while a brutish thug rowed us across. I suspected the rough men Addison hired for the evening would never leave the estate alive. Blackbyrne needed to eat, after all.

Two robed figures awaited us on the small wooden dock, their hands folded and tucked into their voluminous sleeves, their faces shadowed by their hoods. They looked rather like monks, except they served no god dreamed of by human minds.

"Are the preparations complete?" Addison asked, as the hired man tied the boat up.

"Yes, sir," one of them said. The other just nodded.

We climbed out of the boat and onto the dock. The wind had died to a gentle breeze. The torches jumped and flickered, the shadows writhing as though something alive hid inside them. More torchlight showed through the tangle of trees. Blackbyrne led the way to the center of the small island.

There was nothing to do but follow. My throat constricted and the light dinner I'd eaten a few hours ago was in imminent danger of reappearing. Had I survived that awful night in my boyhood just to die here tonight? My plan was madness. It couldn't possibly work. How could I even think there was more than the smallest chance of success?

But even a small chance of success was better than none at all.

The path emerged from the tangled trees, and we stepped into a clearing illuminated by a ring of torches reeking of sulfur and tar. The wild light revealed a rough circle of standing stones, most of them taller than a man. Had Blackbyrne erected them when he had been master of these grounds? They seemed far more weathered than could be accounted for by a mere two centuries of exposure.

At the northern end of the circle sprawled a great stone altar, its surface dark with what could only be blood. Monstrous representations of Guardians were carved onto its sides. Tallow candles stood at either end of the altar, and from my reading in the *Arcanorum* I feared they had been rendered from human fat. In the center rested a copper bowl inscribed with blasphemous symbols, an urn beside it.

My heart gave an unpleasant jolt. No need to ask what—who—the urn held, his body already lovingly transformed into the perfect salts needed for a successful resurrection.

Blackbyrne walked straight to the altar, an excited bounce in his step. Addison followed more slowly, but the glimpse I caught of his face revealed an almost beatific smile. I moved to his side, under the pretense of helping him over the uneven ground, and escorted him to stand only a few feet from the urn.

The rest of the Brotherhood filed into the circle behind us, leaving an aisle leading to the altar stone. The Guardians loped through the space, and none of their masters seemed able to even look at them, flinching away when they drew too near.

In their midst, they dragged a bound, stumbling figure. My blood boiled at the sight of Griffin's pale face, shadowed eyes, and unkempt hair. He had no coat, his shivers visible even from a distance. Thank whatever fiend had devised this ritual for the hooded robe, or else my face would surely have betrayed me. My hands curled into fists within the wide sleeves, aching to strike the Guardians, to tear away Griffin's bonds.

But I could only stand and watch while they hauled him past me, before forcing him to his knees to the left of the altar. As for Griffin, he didn't look at me, if he even knew which of the robed figures was mine. His expression was one of defeat and exhaustion, a man broken by the hopelessness of his situation. Had he understood my signal? Or did he truly think himself utterly alone amongst his enemies?

Blackbyrne placed a wooden case on the altar, lifting out the papyrus scroll. "Welcome, my brothers," he proclaimed, turning to face his small audience. "Welcome to our hour, the hour which has been prepared and heralded for thousands of years, from the days of the pharaohs. I built Widdershins for this very moment; I escaped death for a purpose we will finally fulfill. Tonight, gentleman, we shall reshape the world to our liking, and all mankind will tremble at the sound of our names."

Addison's eyes fixed on the urn. I knew he couldn't see anything beyond Leander's return, just as Father no doubt saw only his vision of our family, transformed into the wife and children he'd dreamed we would be. Did the rest of them have similar weaknesses, longings which led them to ignore Blackbyrne's grandiose declarations? Or did they relish the idea of enslaving the bulk of mankind to their will? How many even believed it was possible?

"Tonight, we shall defeat death for all time," Blackbyrne went on. "And what better recipient of the gifts of Those from the Outside, than the child of one of our own, lost to the waters of this very lake."

His glittering eyes touched mine, and he gave me a secretive smile. We were in on the joke together, he and I. Despite all Blackbyrne's occult power, the men gathered here probably viewed us as much the same. Outsiders, devoted to the arts of the mind rather than the more manly pursuits of athletics and business. No doubt Blackbyrne's Puritan father had looked upon his fascination with words and books with as much suspicion as mine.

I had longed to make Bradley crawl, to force Griffin to love me, to compel Father to acknowledge I was just as good as—no, better than—Stanford. Did Blackbyrne see those dark longings, when he looked at me? Did he know we weren't nearly as different as I might wish?

Blackbyrne turned his gaze to the heavens. I automatically did the same, as did the rest of the gathering. The stars above us winked evilly, Aldebaran like a red eye low in the western sky.

"The stars are in alignment," he said, as if he'd personally organized the matter. "Let us begin the ritual."

"At last," Addison whispered, tears gathering in his eyes.

"Pour the contents of the urn into the bowl," Blackbyrne ordered. Addison hastened to obey with shaking hands. I half-hoped he would drop the urn, or spill the contents on the ground, but the fine, bluish-gray dust streamed unerringly into the wide copper bowl.

When he was done, Blackbyrne began to chant the spell of resurrection I recognized from the *Arcanorum*, calling upon Metraton and Almousin and Nyarlathotep. As he chanted, he threw various substances into the copper bowl. Smoke billowed out, obscuring the altar and carrying with it the tang of fresh-mown grass, the sweetness of vanilla, underlain by a faint musk as of a lover's skin. I involuntarily took a deep breath, and for a moment, I was transported back to Griffin's bed, awash in the afterglow of pleasure, all urgency gone and replaced by tenderness.

Then the scent curdled, notes of sour milk and burnt hair dispelling the vision. Blackbyrne's chant grew in volume and power, and all of the hair on my arms crackled. The smoke turned noxious, green-black in color and reeking of the grave, pouring forth from the bowl like the vent of a volcano. Was there something moving in there? Was there…?

Blackbyrne flung out his arms, back arching, his mouth gaping as he screamed out the words in Aklo. *"I call upon thee, Yog-Sothoth, let him ascend!"*

There *was* something moving in the smoke.

"You who are All-in-One and One-in-All, the God Behind the Veil, who open the gate and are the gate, Yog-Sothoth, let Those from Outside see and rejoice, let this container be filled!"

A titanic crack of lightning split the sky apart, striking the altar only feet from us. I hurled myself back on reflex, but the hem of my robe tangled around my legs, and I fell heavily to the ground.

Blackbyrne laughed, a high, wild cackle which turned my blood to ice. Some of the other men moaned, still dazed from the lightning strike. I blinked rapidly, and as my sight cleared, I saw the smoke had vanished without trace. The after-image of the lightning strike still obscured my vision, painted against the stars and the trees beyond. I moved my head, but the image stayed put.

There was nothing wrong with my eyes. A great, green-black *tear* hung in the air, as if the fabric of reality itself had been ripped open.

On the altar in front of the tear, something pale and white stirred. A head lifted, then an arm, and very slowly, the figure rose to its feet. I beheld the face I'd seen almost every night in the photograph beside my lonely bed.

The ritual had worked. Leander lived again.

CHAPTER 28

LEANDER WAS ALIVE, as if there had been no stormy night on the lake, as if I'd never let go of his hand: my sin absolved, my mistake erased. The phoenix flew away from the eternal circle of the ouroboros, freed at last from the cycle of life and death.

He looked so young. In my mind, he'd remained my elder, but death had stopped time for him, and he was still a youth. His golden hair fell fetchingly over his forehead, and his naked skin was pure and unblemished. His clear blue eyes blinked owlishly, peering out at the gathering in confusion.

"What's happening?" he asked, in the voice which had told me a thousand dreams during the summer of our youth.

Addison remained on his knees, his hands pressed to his face, weeping openly. "It's true! It's a miracle!"

"Father? Is that you?" Behind Leander, the crack in the world grew wider. Nacreous lights flashed from whatever lay on the other side, and tendrils of mottled energy reached out to slither along his arms and legs, like the questing fingers of something groping in the dark.

I didn't have long.

I stepped up to Leander. I was the taller of us, now. "Who are you?" he asked. "Why can't I move?"

My heart contracted at the sound of his voice, and tears burned my eyes, forcing me to blink rapidly. How many years had I longed for this moment? I would have given anything to get him back.

But I wouldn't give *everything*.

"I'm sorry, Leander," I said. "I'm sorry I wasn't strong enough then. And I'm sorry I'm not weak enough now."

Blackbyrne wasn't the only one who had read the *Arcanorum*, after all. Drawing a deep breath, I said: "Take back what has been given, Yog-Sothoth; let him descend."

Leander staggered, his eyes going wide in uncomprehending fear, but it hadn't been enough. My throat tried to close around the words, but this moment, before he had fed, before he was solidly a part of the world again, was my only chance. "Take back what has been given, Yog-Sothoth; let him descend!"

Blackbyrne let out a cry of rage. God, I had no time, only moments before he reached me, but I couldn't force myself to speak, not again.

There came the thunder of a rifle, and a bullet hit the altar, forcing Blackbyrne to take cover behind one of the standing stones. "Damn it, Whyborne, hurry!" Christine shouted.

But I couldn't. Staring into Leander's wide, frightened eyes, I couldn't move, couldn't speak.

"Whyborne!" Griffin called from somewhere behind me. "Hold on—I'm coming!"

At the sound of his voice, the constriction around my throat eased. Drawing all of my breath into my lungs, I shouted: *"Take back what has been given, Yog-Sothoth; let him descend!"*

Leander screamed. His flawless body arched, hands reaching out to me. Then he crumbled into fine, bluish-gray dust and blew away on the wind.

Addison howled and lunged forward, grasping frantically at the fine dust which was all that remained of Leander Somerby. I stared at Addison in a daze, even as he clutched at his chest with one hand, then slumped slowly against the altar. The life drained from his eyes, but the look he turned on me was one of such uncomprehending anguish as to haunt me for the rest of my life.

Which probably wasn't going to be very long. Another member of the Brotherhood let out a shriek of incoherent rage. I turned, but not fast enough: he'd pulled a pistol from within his robes and leveled it at my face.

The rifle fired a second time. The man jerked, his expression one of surprise and horror, before he fell down dead.

Christine stood behind him, dressed in the concealing robes of the Brotherhood, her hood flung back and her rifle in her hands. "You were one of the 'men' who met us at the docks!" I exclaimed.

"It seemed too good an opportunity to pass up," she said, snapping a shell into the chamber just as one of the Guardians rushed her. Her shot took it through the heart, and it crumbled into dust.

Like Leander.

I couldn't think about him now. All was chaos: men in robes fleeing from gunshots, wailing Guardians, and what sounded like a muffled howl coming from the still-open gateway.

Why was it still open? *"Give to them a man; send him through the gate; they will accept the sacrifice; they will close the door."* I had sent Leander back into death; according to the papyrus, the gate should be closed.

Griffin was free; either he'd worked his bonds loose, or Christine had freed him while the ritual distracted everyone else. At the moment, he held off a pair of Guardians with a stout branch. Pulling the revolver from the hand of the man Christine had shot, I shouted, "Griffin!" and tossed the weapon as close to him as I dared.

Only after I threw it did it occur to me the gun might go off when it hit the ground. Fortunately, it didn't. Griffin dove for it, rolled, and came up firing.

Christine slapped another shell into the rifle, tried to rack it into the chamber, then swore as the shell jammed. The Guardians were beyond all control, savaging their erstwhile masters as readily as us. They keened and howled in time to the horrific sounds coming from the gateway, and the hair on the back of my neck rose.

One of the creatures, a parody of the human form with the misshapen head and taloned feet of a vulture, came at me. The stench of death soaked the useless, greasy feathers covering its overlong arms, and its beak split open to reveal blunt, human teeth inside. I flung up my arm in a feeble effort to protect myself.

The report of a gun sounded almost in my ear. The Guardian let out a shriek, which ended as it crumbled into dust. I turned, expecting Griffin. But it was my father who stood there, a smoking revolver in his hand.

"Devil take you, Percival!" he shouted, his face flushed crimson with rage. "What are you doing? Don't you care anything for your mother?"

The words shouldn't have hurt. "Blackbyrne was going to destroy the world, you fool!" I shouted back. "Or at least, he meant to remake it in his image, by putting some abomination in Leander's body. The world would have burned. What good does it do to heal Mother only to have her die screaming in the dark along with the rest of us?"

I didn't expect him to believe me. His lips pressed together, and he calmly shot another Guardian. "Why didn't you tell me beforehand? Don't you trust me?"

"Why should I? You never trusted me."

A Guardian emerged from behind one of the dolmens, snarling through a mouth of ill-fitting fangs. "Shoot it, Fath—"

A long-nailed hand closed around the back of my neck and wrenched me to the side.

I struck the edge of the stone altar, cracking my right elbow, the pain spangling my vision with pinpricks of light. Blackbyrne stood over me, his visage so twisted by rage it no longer seemed human.

"You *dare* to defy me," he snarled. Seizing the front of my robes, he yanked me to him, his putrid breath washing over my face.

"You were right," I said, even as my mind raced. There had to be something I could do against him, against his power. "We are alike. As alike as the reversed reflection of a mirror."

Out of the corner of my eye, I saw Christine swing her jammed rifle at his head. Somehow, Blackbyrne knew she was there. He flung me from him and turned, catching the rifle in his hand. With a savage growl, he ripped it free from her grasp, then cracked the barrel hard across her temple. She fell to the ground and lay there moaning.

"Idiots," Blackbyrne spat. I'd struggled to my feet while he was occupied with Christine, but it did me no good. The rifle caught me only a glancing blow, but it was enough to send me sprawling against the dolmen at my back. Agony jolted through my abused elbow as I slid to the ground.

"Do you know what you've done?" Blackbyrne demanded as he loomed over me. "The gateway is still open! Those from Outside have already been summoned! One will come through, but thanks to you, there is no vessel for me to force it into."

He had to be lying. "I sent Leander back! The gateway will close." Except it hadn't.

Blackbyrne's mouth twisted into an incredulous sneer. "Fool. You merely returned him to the dust from which he was raised. The portal is open, and there is no container to receive what is clawing its way out even now."

Fear rose up to choke me. "Without a human host, you won't be able to make it do your bidding."

"That's right." He bared his teeth at me like a maddened animal. "Which means it will do as it wishes, rampaging across the earth as a force of nature, killing everything in its path. You've doomed all of humanity."

His expression twisted into something like a grin as he saw the horror blooming across my face. "So be it," he said, raising the rifle high to bash my head in against the stone. "Let the world burn."

Burn.

My first spell—the stupid trick of summoning flame, the one written in the *Arcanorum* only as a childish fancy—burst from my lips.

The powder in the jammed shell ignited, and with a tremendous bang, the rifle exploded in Blackbyrne's hands. I flung my arm up instinctively, even as I rolled to one side. Something hot and wet hit the back of my hand, reeking of blood and scorched meat.

Blinking against the dazzling after-image, I sat up slowly. Blackbyrne lay unmoving on the ground near the altar, the alien light from the gateway playing over his still figure.

The gateway, which would let through something humanity had no hope against. I'd failed. Despite all of my knowledge, I'd failed to *understand*.

The world was doomed, and at my hand.

~ * ~

Silence descended over the ring of stones. The Brotherhood and Guardians were either dead or fled into the dark. Only Christine, Griffin, and—to my unutterable surprise—Father remained. Above the altar, the gateway continued to grow in size and strength, as if something from Outside forced gigantic hands through a rip in reality itself, slowly tearing it wider. The howling grew louder, and an icy wind blew out, reeking of lightning and slime.

"Give to them a man; send him through the gate; they will accept the sacrifice; they will close the door."

I understood now what the words meant. A sacrifice was required. One life, in trade for all the lives in the world.

"Whyborne."

I turned at the sound of Griffin's voice. Grime and Guardian dust coated his skin, and his hair was stiff with gore, where a gash across his scalp bled freely. I wanted nothing more than to take him in my arms, to hold him tight and never let go.

"Are you all right?" I asked.

"I'll live. Assuming we can close the gateway." He nodded at it as Father and Christine approached. "You're our magic expert. How do we end this?"

His misplaced confidence in me nearly broke my heart. I gave Christine a plaintive glance; she caught Father's sleeve, holding him back to give us a few moments of whatever privacy could be had.

A few last moments, and, God, I wanted more time. A fortnight hadn't been enough. A lifetime wouldn't have been enough.

I took his hands in mine, heedless of our small audience. His brows quirked together sharply, but he twined his strong fingers with mine. "Whyborne?"

"I just wanted to say I'm glad to have known you," I said quietly. The howls of the thing dragging itself through the portal hid my words from anyone but him. "Despite everything."

He looked even more worried. Gripping my hands harder, he said, "I didn't mean for you to see those notes—"

"Hush. It doesn't matter now." I drew in a breath through the constriction in my throat and ignored the burning behind my eyelids. "The gateway is like a door which only opens in one direction. If you push hard enough instead of pulling, you'll break it. The analogy isn't perfect, but…I believe if a living body passes through from this side, the energies will be disrupted, and the gateway will collapse. Only…the Outside…well, it isn't a place hospitable to earthly life."

Griffin closed his eyes and took a quick sip of breath. He bowed his head a moment, as if in prayer, before his shoulders took on their usual, determined set.

I stepped closer to him, letting go of his hands and putting my arms around him. Leaning my forehead against his, I whispered, "I love you, Griffin Flaherty."

With all the strength I possessed, I shoved him to one side. Taken utterly by surprise, he stumbled and fell heavily against Father, who caught him.

Then I turned and ran straight for the gateway.

"Ival!" Griffin screamed, raw and broken, and if I'd ever doubted he loved me, I doubted it no longer.

I ran as fast as I could, arms and legs pumping, my heart pounding in my chest, every beat measuring the seconds before the last. The gateway loomed ahead of me, widened almost to a circle, its alien energies snaking out into the world.

Would it hurt when I died?

I was almost at the altar. I gathered myself, preparing to leap. This was it; I was going to cease to exist, and please let Griffin be all right, and Mother, and everyone else I'd ever loved—

Something dark and heavy cannoned into me, knocking me to the ground.

The impact struck the breath from my lungs and sent splinters of agony through my elbow. For a moment I could only flail helplessly, gasping until my lungs unfroze and drew a breath. Gathering my legs under me, I surged up and threw off my attacker.

It was Blackbyrne. His hands and face were mangled from shrapnel and burns, but he was still fiendishly strong as he grappled with me anew. His lips drew back from his teeth in an insane snarl, and his single remaining eye glowed with rage. Behind him, something like an enormous pseudopod slipped gelatinously through the portal and quested blindly in the air.

"No!" Blackbyrne growled. "If I must die again, then the world itself will die with me!"

"Whyborne!" Griffin shouted. "Get down!"

I went instantly limp, as if my nerves were wired to his. A shot rang out; blood arced from Blackbyrne's shoulder, and the impact spun him to the side and toward the gateway.

His outstretched hands touched the groping pseudopod. Like the feeding reflex of any mindless animal, it wrapped around him—and yanked him back through the gateway toward whatever passed for its mouth.

The colors of the portal heaved through a nauseous spectrum, before it abruptly shrank inwards, imploding on itself. The howl of some terrible thing vibrated in my bones, accompanied by Blackbyrne's final scream as the monsters he'd sought to command devoured him body, mind, and soul.

Then, with a soft pop like the opening of a champagne bottle, the gateway vanished. The wound in the universe had closed.

I blinked slowly, not entirely certain of the evidence of my own eyes. I'd expected to die. Instead, I sat on the grass, alive, while the gray light of dawn crept over the horizon.

The thud of sturdy boots against the ground broke me out of my confusion. Griffin fell to his knees and pulled me tight against him, his face pressed into my hair, tears hot against my scalp. A moment later, Christine was there was well, her arms around Griffin and me. "Damn it, Whyborne," she muttered thickly. "I'm not crying, do you hear?"

I couldn't reply, my throat too tight or my heart too big, and simply clung to them both.

After a few minutes, Father loudly cleared his throat. Christine let go of me, and Griffin drew away—but his hand still rested on my back, as if he couldn't bear not to touch me, to prove to himself I was real and alive.

Father loomed over me, but his expression was one of chagrin. He held out his hand; after a moment's surprise, I took it, and he hauled me to me feet.

"Good work, son," he said stiffly. He nodded at the space the gateway had occupied. "I think you're right. Your mother would never have approved."

"Stanford—"

"I told him to take one of the boats and leave, as soon as the trouble started."

I nodded, more relieved at his escape than I would have expected. Christine retrieved the papyrus from the altar; it at least had taken no damage. Together, the four of us limped to the dock. The sun was rising, and the first rays touched the gray waters, turning them to gold.

"Well, Whyborne," Christine said, "I think retrieving the scroll will be quite enough to salvage both our reputations, don't you?"

CHAPTER 29

"**WE MUST ALL** pull together," Dr. Hart said, when I shoved the door open and walked into the all-department meeting with Christine at my back.

Every eye turned to us, and Dr. Hart fell silent. Indeed, the entire museum staff might have been struck dumb at the sight of us. We had come directly to the museum from Somerby Estate: filthy, bloody, and exhausted.

I walked very deliberately down the long aisle, conscious of every gaze glued to me. Bradley's mouth worked comically as we passed, but even he didn't seem to know what to say.

"Dr. Hart," I announced, "we have successfully retrieved the stolen scroll."

Christine set it down on the table in front of the director. Dr. Hart stared at it, then at us, then back at it. "I am taking the rest of the day off," I told him. "I'll be in tomorrow to answer any questions."

"And I'm bound for the docks," Christine said, "where I intend to book passage as quickly as I may. I will see you all on my return from the field."

Griffin and Father awaited us on the sidewalk in front of the museum. They had not exchanged a single word on the way here, and I doubted that had changed while Christine and I were inside. Griffin's clothing was in a state, covered with blood and grime, and people gave him a wide berth as they passed by.

"Was the director suitably impressed?" he asked as we approached.

"I believe so," Christine said. "At least, I've never before seen him at a loss for words." She turned to me, hand extended. "And with that, I'm away. Do send me word, Whyborne, as to what story you decide to use so our accounts will match up."

I shook her hand warmly. "Of course. Thank you, Christine. For everything."

She shook hands with Griffin as well. "Goodbye, Griffin. Do try not to require rescuing before I return."

"I shall do my best."

"See that you do. Gentlemen." With a brief nod, she strode off, having not so much glanced at my father. Given some of the things he had been party to, I supposed it was just as well.

As for Father, he looked rather nonplussed; he was not used to being so soundly ignored. After a moment, though, he simply shook his head and turned to me. "We should return home and make certain Stanford is all right."

"Give my regards to Mother."

"Percival—"

"No." Gathering my courage, I met his startled gaze. "People are dead, Father, and I don't just mean your friends who perished last night. Philip Rice, Madam Rosa, the innocents Blackbyrne set upon, Addison's servants…I'm sure there are more I don't know about. Dear lord, Griffin was kidnapped with the intent to feed him to whatever horror Blackbyrne conjured up."

"I'll see that the police drop the charges," he said, with a quick glance at Griffin.

"Do so."

We stared at one another in silence for several moments. No doubt he expected me to give in, to say I understood why he'd gone along with the rest of the Brotherhood and Blackbyrne's plan. And truly, a part of me did understand, all too well.

His nerve broke first. "Yes, well," he said, tugging up the collar of his coat, as if he'd taken a sudden chill. "I'll send a check by the museum this afternoon, shall I?"

As an apology for almost destroying the world, it wasn't much. But perhaps it was the best I could expect from him. "I'm sure the museum will be most grateful for your donation. Tell Mother I'll see her on Christmas."

He nodded gruffly, then touched his hat to Griffin, before hastening to the nearest cab.

We were alone together for the first time since I'd left him in anger, intending to never return. I read uncertainty in Griffin's eyes when he glanced at me. "Will you walk with me?"

"Of course." I fell in beside him, clasping my hands behind my back to restrain the urge to touch him. "Are you well? Do you need to see a doctor?" What might the Brotherhood have done to him during his long hours of captivity?

"I'm fine. A few bruises and cuts, nothing more. How…how are you faring?"

"Well enough." I looked down at the slushy sidewalk. "Blackbyrne admitted to arranging Philip's murder, by the way. I'm not sure how much you'll be able to tell his father, but he should know the man chiefly responsible is dead. Again."

"Thank you." His eyes were worried, though. "Are you certain you're all right? I know it couldn't have been easy for you to…"

"Kill Leander," I said.

He shook his head. "That wasn't Leander, not really."

"Of course it was. A twisted version of him, just as Blackbyrne was a twisted version of whatever man he had been. But still him."

My voice trembled, and I pressed my lips together. Griffin put his hand to my shoulder, squeezing gently. "I'm sorry. You had no choice."

"I did, though. If this had happened a month ago, before I met you, before I'd seen and done the things I have…I might have chosen differently."

"I don't believe that."

I tilted my head back. Trees lined the road near Griffin's house, their black branches stark against the dazzling blue sky. "I spent over a decade mourning Leander. I felt guilty for living when he died, so I *didn't* live, not really. I clung to the past and to pain, and never took a risk or a chance. I locked myself in prison and pretended I didn't have a key."

We'd reached Griffin's gate. I stopped and rested my hand lightly on the iron bars. "Then I met an impertinent detective who refused to let me remain in my comfortable cell."

"Whyborne, I—"

"Let me finish. It-it was hard, putting Leander to rest last night. I almost didn't have the strength of will, even knowing the cost of letting him remain. When I heard you call out to me, though…well. I realized I couldn't sacrifice you, a-and Christine, or even myself, to a memory. No matter how fond a memory it might be." I turned to him. "To answer your question: I'm fine. Or I will be, in time."

His lips parted slightly, as if I had surprised him. Pushing the gate open, he asked, "Will you come inside?"

I followed him to the house. It was icy cold, the fires long gone out, so I kept on my coat as he led the way to the study on the second floor. He went to the hearth and set about laying a fire, his back to me. "When I saw you in the basement…"

I winced. "You didn't get my hint, then? It was the only way I could think to let you know I hadn't really joined them."

He crumpled up a sheet of newspaper to use as kindling, stuffing it among the fresh logs. "On the contrary, I thought it quite clever of you. But I didn't need it. I would never have believed you'd gone over to their side. No, my astonishment stemmed from the fact you came at all."

"I don't understand." Surely he didn't believe I would have simply left him there to rot?

He struck a match, silhouetted by the warm light. "My parents…they're good people, but when I was caught with the neighbor's son, they didn't understand. Instead of standing with me, they sided with the ones calling for me to leave the only home I knew.

"Afterward, I found a new home with the Pinkertons. But when Glenn died and I was injured, no one believed what had really happened. Even those I'd counted as friends said I was mad. They abandoned me to the asylum. And I began to wonder if they were right."

He rose to his feet and stood gazing down at the flames. "What if I was mentally aberrant in some fashion? What if my desire for other men and my imagined monsters were all part of the same sickness?"

It hurt to hear him speak so. I rested my hands on his shoulders, but he didn't turn to face me. "Griffin—"

"Hear me out, while I still have the courage. Once I knew I hadn't imagined the things I saw in Chicago, it made me angry, because no one had believed me. No one had stood up for me when I truly needed them. I swore I would never rely on anyone but myself. I couldn't—couldn't bear to be let down again.

"Then you walked into that basement, and I realized how wrong I'd been. You'd risked everything to come for me, and…and…I knew…"

He stopped, taking a deep breath, and his shoulders shook with a suppressed sob.

"Of course I came for you," I said. "Just as I know you would have for me."

"I'm so sorry," he said thickly. "About the notes. I'm sorry I ever considered using you, even for an instant. I was lonely. I thought we could at least pass a pleasant time together. As for not telling you immediately that I knew about certain things, about Leander…a good detective never lets on how much he knows, because it's more informative to hear it fresh from a witness, or a suspect. But you were neither of those things, and it was a poor way to treat a friend. I never intended to hurt you. I can only beg your forgiveness and-and hope you will give it."

He allowed me to turn him to face me. The tracks of tears still gleamed on his cheeks, but he didn't try to hide his expression of mingled hope and fear and regret.

I pulled him into my arms and kissed him: hard and desperate and deep. He returned the kiss, his arms wrapping around my waist and holding me tightly to him.

When it ended, I leaned my forehead against his. "You may take that as your answer," I said breathlessly.

His lips stole another kiss from mine. "I love you, Ival," he whispered. "When I saw you running toward that portal…God, I've never been so frightened in my life."

My pulse fluttered in my throat. "When I thought…when I thought I was going to die…the only thing I could feel, besides fear, was regret we hadn't had enough time."

We stood together silently, wrapped in each other's embrace. I laid my cheek against his hair: it was stiff with blood from his scalp wound, and both of us were covered in grime, but I didn't care. Nothing mattered except him, alive and warm in my arms. For the first time in my life, I felt truly at peace.

After a time, he drew back a little. "The night you went to your parents' house for dinner, you had originally intended to return to your apartment, do you remember?"

I couldn't imagine where the non sequitur was leading. "Er, yes?"

One of his hands stroked my back, but he kept his gaze fixed on my tie instead of meeting my eyes. "I was sitting here alone, missing you, and it occurred to me I have a spare room I'm using only for storage. It wouldn't seem at all odd if I were to take in a boarder."

I drew back in surprise. "Oh?"

"Yes." He still didn't quite meet my gaze, as if half-afraid of rejection. "I'm very particular, though. This boarder will be tall, handsome, and speak precisely thirteen languages. But read more. He must be willing to put up with a roommate prone to nightmares, occasional fits of brooding, and a fondness for chess. Must love cats, keeping odd hours, and sword canes. Do you…do you know anyone who might fit the description?"

I caught his chin gently, tilting his head back so he had to look at me. "You know," I said, bending to kiss him, "I rather think I do."

The adventures of Whyborne, Griffin, and Christine continue in Threshold, *Whyborne & Griffin No. 2.*

About The Author

Jordan L. Hawk grew up in the wilds of North Carolina, where her bootlegging granny raised her on stories of haints and mountain magic. After using a silver knife in the light of a full moon to summon her true love, she turned her talents to spinning tales. She weaves together couples who need to fall in love, then throws in some evil sorcerers and undead just to make sure they want it bad enough. In Jordan's world, love might conquer all, but it just as easily could end up in the grave.

For bonus material, updates, and more stories, please visit her on the web at http://www.jordanlhawk.com.

Made in the USA
Columbia, SC
26 March 2018